Pandora's Box

Pandora's Box

ALLISON HOBBS

A
S̸Bi
PUBLICATION

A STREBOR BOOKS INTERNATIONAL LLC PUBLICATION
DISTRIBUTED BY SIMON & SCHUSTER, INC.

Published by

SBI

Strebor Books International LLC
P.O. Box 1370
Bowie, MD 20718

ISBN 0-7394-4208-2

Distributed by Simon & Schuster, Inc.
1230 Avenue of the Americas
New York, NY 10020
1-800-223-2336

Cover design: Kris Tobiassen
Cover photo: © Don Cudney/Index Stock

Manufactured and Printed in the United States

In Loving Memory
of My Mother, Lois S. Hobbs
and My Brother, Michael A. Hobbs

ACKNOWLEDGMENTS

I would like to extend my deepest gratitude to the following family members and friends whose love, support and encouragement along the way made the writing and publication of this book a truly joyous experience:

To my father, **Sterling J. Hobbs**, you set the example and taught me to dream big dreams. **Amir Fatir**—Little Brother, thanks for paving the way; I'm honored to walk in your literary footsteps. **Rhonda Hobbs**—Thanks for the publicity, praise and sisterly pride and for copying those early chapters for the teachers in the Chester-Upland School District.

Ronald James, Jr.—There is much appreciation for your love and faith in me. I thank you for sharing my most cherished dreams. **Harry Kindle**—Thanks for proudly spreading the word and passing out fliers in the hot, hot sun. **Jack Glover**—You were there when the idea was conceived. You provided the peace and gave me the space that I needed to write. I thank you.

Stephanie S. Fitchette—Thanks for your comments and advice from the very beginning and for literally dropping everything to edit the first edition of this book. **Karen Dempsey Hammond**—You are my sister in spirit. Thank you being such a bright light in my life. **Phyllis A. Nelson**—Our time together was powerful but brief. I thank you for touching my life with your beauty, your spirit, and your song. **Yvette Davis**—Love transcends time and space. **Cynthia Waters-Tines**—Thanks for the love and support during the most confusing and difficult time of my life. Your kindness has never been forgotten. **Karen Fitchette-Gordon**—You'll never know how privileged I felt to be taken under your "sophisticated" wing! **Patricia Lowery**—Thank you for helping me lug those heavy boxes and many thanks for your superior decorating and organizational skills.

Many thanks to: **Tiffany Colvin** of Sisters In Spirit Book Club for my first on-line review, **Lorraine Ballard Morrell** of Power 99 FM for my first radio interview, and **Michelle Chilton** for putting me on the front page of *The Philadelphia Tribune*.

I'd like to thank the following Philadelphia area African American Bookstore owners for their support: **Emlyn Q. DeGannes** of Mejah Books, **Betty Jean** of Liguorius Books, **Lecia Warner** of Basic Black Books, **Juanita Koukoui** of It's A Mystery To Me.

Zane—Thanks for everything!

And last but not least, much gratitude to:
Kyndal, Korky, Kameron, Keenan, CJ, & Kha'ri
I Love, Love, Love my **Hobbs/Johnson crew!**

Prologue

Victoria awakened from a fitful sleep clutching her chest and panting for breath. Overwhelmed by a feeling of impending doom, she was certain she was going to die. Easing her legs off the bed, she managed to stand.

Across the room a blur of white blinds and lavender print curtains beckoned her. She made feeble steps toward the window, convinced she'd be okay if she could just get some fresh air. But the feeling intensified. Her heart raced unreasonably, and then began to beat irregularly—slowing down, skipping beats. Oddly, she felt nothing that could be identified as pain, just sheer terror and a suspicion that death loomed.

The window was too far away; she'd never make it. With that realization Victoria retreated and collapsed onto the bed. As she reached for the phone to call for help, she suddenly changed her mind, and withdrew her hand. If she could endure the discomfort for a few moments more, perhaps the symptoms would go away, disappear like before.

Finally, the sensations began to subside. Victoria's emotions flickered from relief to embarrassment. She wasn't going to die after all; it was just an anxiety attack. The fourth in a week.

Victoria was a singer. An unknown singer. Her agent, Justice Martin, had insisted that she invest in her career by recording an expensive, high-quality demo. Long hours at the recording studio had affected Victoria's performance at her day job, a low paying clerical position that, nevertheless, had kept the bills paid. She suffered the first anxiety attack when she was terminated. There was nothing to worry about; she'd never miss the loss of income, Justice assured her. A record deal with a healthy advance was close at hand.

Then Victoria received the distressful news that the A&R director of her future label had been fired. The anxiety attacks became more frequent and more intense. Victoria was devastated, while Justice, upbeat and optimistic, appeared untroubled.

"I forgot to tell you about the incredibly short life span of A&R directors," he said with a chuckle. "They hop from label-to-label. No big deal. I've got something better in the works. I'll get back to you in a few days."

But he didn't get back to her in a few days, or a few weeks. In fact, he no longer answered or returned her calls. Victoria continued to speed-dial his number by rote.

One day, to her surprise, instead of getting Justice's answering machine, Victoria listened incredulously to the British-sounding voice of a woman: "Good Day. Justice Martin & Associates, may I help you?"

Astonished, Victoria stammered, "This is Victoria. May I speak to Justice?"

"Victoria?" The British voice asked, perplexed. "May I have your last name please? And may I ask what this call is in reference to?"

"I don't need a last name, and no you may not ask what this call is in reference to," Victoria exclaimed, fuming. The next sound Victoria heard was the disconnecting click. She stared at the phone in disbelief. In record time she rushed her son to the babysitter down the street, and hailed a cab.

With blazing eyes, Victoria burst into Justice Martin's smartly furnished City Line Avenue office. Framed photographs of Justice posed with noted entertainers and prominent public figures were on display everywhere. The numerous photographs that once impressed Victoria now annoyed her. They were crammed together on walls, tabletops, and atop Justice's sleek chrome and glass desk.

"Where's Justice?" Victoria demanded.

The startled receptionist, sputtered, "Mr. Martin's not here; he's upstairs in his flat. Shall I ring him?" Victoria rolled her eyes and headed for the elevator in the lobby. Tapping her foot impatiently, she rode to the 26th floor.

Tall, dark, and roguishly handsome Justice Martin stood barefoot outside his apartment, posed against the doorframe. He wore a black silk lounging jacket, left open undoubtedly to flaunt his tight abs and hairy chest, the drawstring of his black silk pajama bottoms were pulled tight. With long locked hair, pulled back and twisted into a roll, he was indeed, a striking figure, but Victoria sucked her teeth at the sight of him.

Apparently not wanting his well-heeled neighbors to be aroused by a scene, Justice ushered Victoria inside.

At first his tone was soft, placating. "Vic, calm down. Things are going to work out, but you have to be patient. Now, I have to be frank with you. Word travels fast in this business, and some of the companies that had expressed an interest have changed their minds. They don't want to get involved with an artist that the competition doesn't want."

Victoria could feel the room spinning; she wanted to vomit.

"To be honest," he said looking at his feet, "your material sounds a little dated...maybe we need to go back and cut something with, uh, a little hip hop flavor."

"Hip hop?" she screamed. "Another demo? Who's going to pay for another demo? I don't have a job, remember? Which means I don't have any more money." Victoria's voice went up several pitches.

As if in deep thought, Justice laced and unlaced long sinewy fingers and then tapped together fingertips that had been manicured and polished high-gloss clear.

"So how do you plan on paying off the six gees you owe the studio?"

Victoria looked at Justice like he was crazy. "What are you talking about? I paid..."

"Justice Martin & Associates is not a charitable organization," he announced, interrupting her. "You signed my contract; I get twenty percent of your earnings, plus my investment."

"I didn't earn anything Justice," Victoria blurted, uncomprehending. "And you didn't invest anything. I did! I spent ten thousand dollars on this project. How can you make a statement like that?" Victoria shook her head in disbelief, her eyes brimming with tears of anger and humiliation.

"Baby, time is money and I don't work for free. I thought that was understood. I couldn't predict that dude would lose his job and blow the deal. But I don't take risks. I have a track record. People respect me in this business. That's how I was able to get you studio time on speculation."

Victoria's mouth dropped open. "Speculation! Justice, I paid for studio time."

"No, baby," he sneered. "You paid for Justice's time; I took mine off the top."

"How could you do this to me? I used every penny of the money my grandmother left me because you promised I'd get it back tenfold."

Justice yawned dramatically, and then said, "Come on baby, I only charged you seven Gees. I had to give the producer his cut. I think my time and expertise are worth a lot more than that." He was thoughtful for a moment, then he added with a sneer, "I should have charged you twice that amount for having to listen to you sing those sad-ass songs."

The cruelty of his words doubled her over as if she'd been physically hit. Reflexively, her hands flew up, ready to attack, but his empty eyes halted her. Justice was not the type to restrain a hysterical woman. Victoria sensed he'd feel justified and take great delight in hitting back—leaving hard evidence such as a bloodied lip or a blackened eye.

Distraught, Victoria returned home. Her mind swirled with desperate thoughts. There had to be a way to repair the damage. She still had her precious demo, she'd go out, pound the pavements of New York and get her own damn deal.

But Victoria needed more than the single CD that was in her possession. Until the balance on the account was paid, the master tape belonged to the recording studio. She had no money, no product, nothing.

Visualizing Justice lying in a pool of blood became her favorite pastime; but when the bills began mounting, anxiety attacks distracted her from contemplating murder.

An eviction notice brought Victoria back to life, propelled her to take control. She would not allow her innocent son to end up in a shelter, or even worse, foster care. She had to pull herself together. There was no time to waste on job hunting, and waiting for a paycheck. She needed cash and she needed it now!

Chapter 1

Victoria Carlton gripped the telephone receiver, lifted it, and then quickly replaced it. She wasn't ready. How could she trust her voice to convey polish and sophistication when she was quivering with fear? She willed herself to relax, and tried again. She pushed the numbers, and this time, stayed on the line.

"I'm responding to your ad in today's paper," she announced, with a surprisingly steady voice.

"Done this kind of work before?" a gruff male voice asked.

"Yes," she lied.

"Where?"

She hesitated, then replied, "In California...uh, L.A."

"How old are ya?"

There was a longer hesitation, then another lie. "Twenty-five."

There was no response on the other end. She sensed that she'd given the wrong answer. She should have cut her age down even more—perhaps to eighteen or nineteen. Victoria knew she looked good—damn good for thirty-three, but her mouth would not form itself to say anything younger than twenty-five.

"Measurements?" The man finally asked.

"What?"

"What are your measurements?"

"Oh! 34-26-36," Victoria answered, squirming.

"Height?"

"Five-six." She thought that sounded better than her actual five-four.

"Are you black or white?"

Taken aback by the question, she answered with an edge, "I'm African American."

"Okay," he said unenthusiastically. "You can come in today for an interview."

"Today! What time?" she blurted in sudden fear.

"As soon as possible. We get a lot of calls. First come, first served. By the way," he added, "what name do you use?"

Victoria's mind went blank for a moment. She paced back and forth in her bedroom, wildly surveying her surroundings as if the answer lay hidden somewhere in the room. Then, zooming in on the bureau, she spotted a bottle of cologne: *Pleasures* by Estee Lauder.

"Um...Pleasure," Victoria said, with a question mark in her voice.

"Okay, Pleasure," the man said. "I'll see you in an hour."

❦

Victoria skidded around her apartment, trying to get herself together for the interview. She scanned the closet and chose a simple black knit dress that clung nicely. Now which shoes should she wear? Did she have any clean pantyhose—without runs? Random thoughts crowded her mind. Would she be asked detailed information about her previous employer? The time constraint prevented Victoria from getting her lies together, but when it occurred to her that she might be asked to give her date of birth, she stopped in her tracks and attempted to do the calculations.

❦

The 34 arrived much too quickly. Before Victoria had time to get her story straight, she was paying the fare and sliding into a seat. As the trolley made its rickety way down Baltimore Avenue, she gazed out the window. It passed the familiar sites along the route: the deli on the corner of 49th Street with the usual array of misfits loitering outside, the video store, and the Amoco gas station.

Oddly, there were no passengers standing at the designated waiting areas along the route, and so the trolley rumbled along without stopping— shortening the time that Victoria would reach her destination.

What would she say? What would be expected of her? How does one apply for such a job? Victoria needed more time to think, to rid herself of the queasy feeling.

The biting January cold, Victoria noticed, didn't deter the joggers who circled Clark Park. Or the pet owners who dutifully endured the weather while their dogs romped at play. She felt her heart sink when the trolley turned into the depot that led to an underground tunnel. It wouldn't be long now. Thirty-seventh Street flashed by. Would she have to give some sort of demonstration? She wondered, worried.

Someone boarded the trolley at 33rd Street. Victoria didn't bother to look up but was grateful that the trolley stood still for a while. The driver patiently waited for the passenger to pay the fare. The out-of-town students from Penn were notorious for holding up trolleys while they groped through their pockets, looking perplexed, as if needing to deposit the exact change was a thoroughly new concept. Their Ivy League status apparently should have exempted them from this senseless inconvenience.

Victoria looked up when the trolley finally lurched forward, causing the bespectacled student who was stooped by a backpack, to fall into his seat.

Another passenger boarded at 30th Street. A teenaged mother, burdened with a toddler, a folded stroller with diaper bag dangling from the handles, and a huge bag of disposable diapers. Neither the driver nor the Penn student moved to help as the young mother struggled onto the trolley. Weighed down by her own problems, Victoria had to quell the urge to assist the young girl. Expecting a lengthy delay, Victoria settled back into her seat; she began to practice a breathing technique that would help calm her.

As it was, the young mother was a skilled commuter, who paid the fare effortlessly without causing a delay. Victoria was amazed by the ease with which she maneuvered baby and bundles.

There were so many distractions; Victoria couldn't concentrate on the breathing exercises. Troubling images crowded her mind: the eviction notice that was stealthily slid under her apartment door, the words SHUT OFF NOTICE stamped across utility bills, bold threats from collection agencies over the phone and through the mail. These thoughts were wrenching reminders of the series of events that had led to her steep slide into debt and despair.

Victoria stood up at 19th Street. She emerged from the trolley on the intersection at 19th and Market Street and walked another block. The building she was looking for was sandwiched discreetly between a pizza shop and a bank. There were no identifying signs, just the numbers of the address glued to the door.

Taking a deep breath, Victoria opened the door. The chime of a door-bell announced her entrance. A gust of wind accompanied her inside a waiting room with three folding metal chairs and a chipped wooden coffee table that was cluttered with portions of *The Philadelphia Daily News*, old lottery tickets, a crumpled cigarette pack, and an ashtray filled with cigar and cigarette butts. In a corner stood a dust-covered silk plant. Pictures of girlie magazine-type models were plastered on the walls surrounding a huge sign that read:

WE ARE OPEN 24 HOURS...
$100.00 FLAT RATE FOR FULL-SERVICE MASSAGE...
NO TIPPING REQUIRED...
FOR YOUR PLEASURE, WE HAVE A SELECTION OF 25 GIRLS...

Within seconds, the inner door opened. Six scantily clad women stood on the other side of the door—five Caucasians and one light-complexioned young black woman. Five of the women about-faced and disappeared from view. A young woman-thin, white, with long chestnut brown hair and glossy pouting lips, remained at the door.

"We thought you were a customer," the woman said, explaining the speedy retreat of the others. "Can I help you?"

Victoria was embarrassed by the woman's attire. In the broad of day, she had on black stiletto heels, thigh high stockings with black lace gathered at the top, red satin panties and pink nipples peeked out of a red push up bra! Her breasts—too large to be real—were poked in Victoria's face, but determined not to stare at them, she focused on the woman's eyes.

"I called earlier and spoke to someone—a man. I didn't get his name, but he told me to come in for an interview."

"Rover!" The brunette turned around and yelled. "Did you tell someone to come in for a job?"

At the end of a long corridor, Victoria could see the shadowy figure of the person she presumed to be Rover.

"Yeah, tell 'er to come on back," the man shouted.

Murmurs of discontent were heard as Victoria passed a room where the women lounged. "Don't we have enough girls?" she overheard someone ask, irritated.

"I thought Gabrielle said only one black girl was allowed to work the morning shift—ME!" the light-skinned black woman complained.

"Looks like you may have some competition, Zoe!" one of the women taunted.

There was a bed in each of the three empty rooms Victoria passed. What was she getting herself into? Well, it was too late to think about that now. Her rent was three months past due, the eviction date loomed!

Foolishly she had chased a dream, she'd taken a risk and lost. There were no other options, she reminded herself; it was time for damage control.

Chapter 2

I t had not been a profitable day. Seven women milled about the smoke-filled room. The *Action News* theme song blared from the television, heralding the start of the second shift. No one was watching. The women were in different states of waiting, and all were waiting for the same thing. Sessions. Those who had worked the first shift but hadn't made any money, or enough to leave, wore tense, solemn expressions. They peered in mirrors and tended to make-up or hair in a futile attempt to ignore the threatening exuberance of the girls who had just come in. Their arrival had changed the climate of despair and hopelessness to one charged with expectancy.

Sydney, one of the newly arrived, settled in the room with quick and certain movements that suggested confidence that she'd leave with a full purse. With her back turned to the others, she purposefully pulled articles of lingerie from an oversized plastic satchel and studied each appraisingly. Finally, she turned and proudly displayed a flashy red sequined bustier that was bound to catch the eye. In a taunting tone she asked no one in particular, "Ya think I'll make money in this?" The others responded with sighs and groans.

Sydney was not pretty. Her eyes were set too close on a face too wide and her straggly brown hair wouldn't hold a curl. But she was young, thin, and white—the only requirements for the top moneymakers at Pandora's Box. Just the week before, Sydney had been meek and unsure of herself, but her quick popularity had gone to her head, producing an air of arrogance.

Though most of the girls felt a twinge of envy toward her, there was a certainty that Sydney's reign would be short-lived, that she'd be replaced by the next new face and would become as bitter and afraid as the rest of them.

Rover, the manager of Pandora's Box, stuck his head in the doorway. "Did Bethany get here yet?"

"No," replied Chelsea, a thirty-somethingish black woman whose striking good looks had no effect on her cash flow. Chelsea had worked the previous shift and hadn't made any money.

Rover glanced at his watch. "This is the second time Bethany's been late this week. I'm gonna have to give her a twenty-dollar fine. When she gets in, tell her to come back to the office to see me. She can't work until she pays her fine."

"Damn Rover, the girl just had a baby," Chelsea replied. "Why are you being so hard on her?"

"I don't make the rules, and I'm not changing them for Bethany. Instead of lying around with her bum boyfriend, she needs to get here on time so she can take care of that baby and her other kid. If I really wanted to be nasty, I'd send her home."

Chelsea shook her head.

"I hope Bethany don't come in, we got too many girls here now," complained Miquon, an overweight brown-skinned twenty-year-old with a limited clientele of men who snubbed the frequently sought-after slender women to indulge in private yearnings for the amply endowed. "Shit, seven women scufflin' for the same dollar is more than enough."

"Then maybe I should send you home, Miquon," Rover threatened. "You've been late a coupla times this week, too."

Miquon sucked her teeth and mumbled something about having baby-sitting problems.

Rover ambled back up the hallway to the dreary room that served as both his home and the office of Pandora's Box. The small room was filled with his possessions: a TV, two VCRs, dozens of videocassettes, a microwave oven, a miniature refrigerator, and a cot. A monitor on top of a battered metal desk allowed Rover to oversee the comings and goings in the lobby.

Rover worked two shifts a day. The first shift started at 10 a.m. and ended at 5 p.m. and the second shift ended at midnight. In his absence, Dominique, one of the older girls, collected the money for the third shift. After work each night, he frequented nearby adult peep shows or hung out at the all-night diner where his tips bought the attention of Amelia, a tired looking, washed-out waitress who wore a faded pink uniform bedecked with her own plastic nametag. Amelia laughed uproariously at Rover's stupid jokes, stomach-holding, side-splitting laughter, while wishing she were home with her feet up watching Nick At Nite, the Home Shopping Network, or anything on cable TV.

Around three in the morning, Rover would sometimes return to the massage parlor to check on Dominique and the others to make sure that no one was getting high, drinking, or pocketing money that belonged to the house.

"Who's Bethany?" Sydney asked as she pulled out and slowly unfolded yet another dazzling outfit. Pairs of worried eyes landed on the negligee that was blue and sheer with tassels.

Just as Chelsea began to describe Bethany, Rover yelled from the office: "Bethany's on the news; turn on channel six!"

"Oh my God! That's Bethany!" squealed Chelsea as she scrambled to turn up the volume. Bethany, who should have been there with them, was being led away in handcuffs from her Wharton Street apartment in South Philly.

In the midst of the excitement and confusion over Bethany's arrest, the doorbell rang. The seven women abandoned the TV immediately and rushed to the door dressed unashamedly in skimpy lingerie. Bethany was barely a distant thought.

As Chelsea swung open the door each woman struck a seductive pose.

A rather handsome young black man who drove a bus for SEPTA stood in the doorway wearing his work uniform. He looked delightfully surprised as he beheld the array of scantily clad, heavily made-up women. The young man literally licked his lips and rubbed his hands in lustful anticipation.

Sydney and three other young white women threw their heads high and abruptly turned away; most of the white working girls refused to service black men. A puzzled look crossed the bus driver's face.

Miquon rolled her eyes at the retreating figures. Then she turned to him and parted her lips in what she considered a sexy smile and stuck out her 38Ds. "You want a session, baby?" she cooed.

"Uh…how much is it?"

"A hundred dollars."

"A buck!" His eyes widened. "That's too steep for me."

"You get a whole hour. Come on," she cajoled.

"I don't know…"

"Maybe we can work something out." Miquon reached around Chelsea to open the glass door that led from the lobby to the session rooms.

The young man took a few hesitant steps forward, then stopped. "What am I gonna get for my money?"

"Whatever you want," Chelsea piped in, brushing her hand lightly across her crotch. The bus driver brightened perceptibly.

"Come on with me." Chelsea took his arm and proceeded to lead him up the hall.

"Hold up!" Miquon demanded. "You don't have to go with her. You can choose whoever you wanna see."

He peeked into the room where the others were lounging.

Miquon's eyes were wide with indignation. "Why you checkin' them out? They ain't interested in you. They sat the hell back down because they don't mess with no black men." She punctuated the statement with a hand on her beefy hip. "So, whassup? Who you wanna see?"

"Uh, I'll take her." He pointed past Miquon and Chelsea to Arianna, who had remained standing but hadn't bothered to assist in the sales pitch. Arianna's smug attitude and seeming contempt irked her co-workers but intrigued the customers.

"Follow me," Arianna said, leading the man up the hallway to one of the three smaller session rooms.

Inside each room was a hard narrow cot-like bed with plain white sheets and a folded towel placed at the bottom. A box of tissues and generic brands of toiletries sat atop a metal nightstand, along with a metal waste can and folding chair. There was a sign on the wall behind the bed, a wooden plaque that prohibited tipping. The other walls were decorated with cheap mirror panels.

After collecting the fee, Arianna informed her customer that he was entitled to a full body massage with his choice of powder, lotion, alcohol, or baby oil. Promising to be right back, she slipped out of the room and went to the office to record the session.

Arianna handed Rover the money and entered her name on the first line of the paper where sessions were logged.

"Good for you!" Rover said cheerfully. "Tiffany got the first session this morning and she ended up with six sessions out of nine." It was considered good luck to get the first session of the shift.

Arianna deliberately kept a straight face. Rover irritated her, but she was inwardly pleased.

When she returned, Arianna found her customer poised on the edge of the bed, naked. He leered at her and boldly stroked himself. Repelled by the sight, Arianna averted her gaze. "Do you want your massage with baby oil or lotion?"

"We can skip all that." He reached for her hand and attempted to guide it between his legs.

Arianna jerked her hand away. "You'll have to cover that up." Unable to conceal her disgust, Arianna's face creased into a scowl.

The young man recoiled when she removed the covering from the condom that she retrieved from her purse. "I don't want that thing on yet. Come on baby, let's play for a while."

She exhaled audibly. "As I said, you'll have to cover yourself before I do anything."

"Hey, I didn't come here to play no fuckin' games. I could have stayed home and took care of myself for free."

Sensing that she was about to lose her customer, Arianna began a seductive act of slowly untying the strings of her velvet bodice. The bus driver gaped as the bodice fell open, revealing perfectly shaped breasts. Arianna bent slightly and began peeling down a lace-topped thigh-high and then stepped out of a black velvet shoe. He continued to stare stupidly before his gaze shifted to the stiffening between his legs. He was panting by the time Arianna stripped out of the thong bikini.

Arianna stood naked before him. Still holding the condom, she challenged him. He looked at her helplessly.

Arianna was petite with an unidentifiable exotic look. She was black and most people thought she looked mixed with something. Asian, Hispanic— something. She had a tiny waist and a surprisingly big heart-shaped, protruding butt.

Arianna's dark almond-shaped eyes gleamed as she caught a glimpse of herself in the mirror. She shamelessly admired her image. This incited the customer to reach for her. From his seated position he pulled her down on the cot and attempted to cover her mouth with his. Arianna turned her head; she would never allow a trick to kiss her on the lips. Undaunted the man moved down to her breasts, lightly kissing and licking her nipples until she seemed to relax. He assumed that she'd been stirred by the foreplay and raised his head, expecting to see defeat in her eyes. Instead, he found eyes that mocked him as she quickly tried to get the condom in place.

"Hey, slow down baby. I have a whole hour, don't I? So what's the rush?"

Arianna recognized the determined look in his eyes. Getting him off would not be easy, the session could drag on endlessly. The man obviously had the impression that the money he spent entitled him to prolonged lovemaking: kissing, cuddling, caressing. He was the type who'd use every trick in the book to extend his stay. She'd be drenched in his sweat as he panted and snarled and fought to hold back an orgasm. He was also the type who'd become violently angry when she refused to comply with his fanciful desires. He'd demand his money back. Or insist upon seeing another girl.

"Does a blowjob come with that buck I just gave you?"

"That's extra," Arianna said dryly.

"That sign out there says full service and tipping is not allowed." His top lip curled. "So what kind of game are you trying to play? Seems like you trying to beat me."

Arianna spoke slowly and deliberately. "Full service includes a massage and intercourse with a condom. You said you didn't want a massage, so I assumed…"

"Don't assume, baby! I called before I came and the dude who answered the phone said I could get a blowjob."

"Oh! Then I guess *he's* going to give you one." Arianna had had about enough of this asshole. She hated cheap bastards who didn't want to tip. Sure, the crazy owner, Gabrielle, posted signs all over the place that prohibited tipping, but anyone with a modicum of decency should know that for extras, he has to tip. Arianna began to gather her discarded garments.

"What are you doing?" the bus driver demanded.

"I'm leaving. Do you want to see one of the other girls?"

"No." His face softened. "I want to be with you."

"Well you can't see me. You can either have your money back or see someone else. It's up to you."

"Aw, come on, why you gotta come off like that? I was just kiddin'."

"I don't have time to play games, and you've wasted enough of my time," she said, checking her watch.

"Wait a minute, gorgeous." He attempted to chuckle. "This is my first time here and I was just going by what dude told me on the phone. Let's start over. I don't want to see nobody else. I picked you because you the best-looking shorty in this joint. Your girlfriends out there should be ashamed to stand up next to you."

"And that being the case, you had a lot of nerve coming in here giving me such a hard time."

"I'm sorry. Look, I'm in your hands, you can do whatever you want." He delivered a gleaming smile but Arianna looked at him stone-faced.

"Put this on," she demanded again, handing him the condom. She walked across the room to dim the light. He'd be out of there in less than ten minutes and his pompous ass would only get a hand job. No stupid trick could match wits with her. The other girls obeyed the rules, foolishly giving the customers a massage, and a blowjob along with sex and all for the measly fifty dollars that was left after the house got its cut. Arianna prided herself on doing as little as possible for the same amount of money and always insisted on a generous tip.

When the customer realized that the release he sought would be manual, he pleaded to remove the condom.

"I will not touch you with my bare hands," Arianna said with unmasked disdain. "It's unsanitary. If you take it off, I'm going to have to wear a rubber glove." He opted for the thin, surgical rubber glove. Arianna poured baby oil into her palm and after only a few slippery strokes, he exploded. Remarkably, at that very moment she could hear the distant sound of the doorbell. There was no time to get back into her bodice and heels, so she wrapped a towel around herself, grabbed her things and brightly waved goodbye. Arianna rushed from the room and ran barefoot to join the others greeting the most recent caller.

❦

On her first evening at work, Victoria strode into the lounge where the women languished on mismatched furniture. Clutching an empty beaded purse that she prayed would be filled with money by the end of the shift, she smiled a greeting that no one bothered to return. Feeling conspicuous, Victoria looked around for a place to sit, but all the seats were taken.

Kelly was sprawled on a dilapidated sofa. Pink-tinted hair hung in her face as she absently scratched at a sinister-looking tattoo on her upper arm.

Chelsea, squeezed into a corner of the sofa, was bent over, polishing her toenails.

Miquon sat slouched in a faded flower print chair with one hand stuck in large bag of jalapeno potato chips, her jaw working overtime.

Before sitting on the loveseat that was patched up with duct tape, Arianna spread out a fluffy towel and placed a pricey tan Coach duffel bag on the cushion beside her. She opened *The City Paper* and folded it neatly to the Adult Entertainment section.

Sydney milled about, primping in preparation of the evening ahead. She piled her clothing and other personal items on top of a vacant folding chair, claiming it.

A television, elevated on orange crates, was positioned in the middle of the room. It was turned at an angle to accommodate everyone in the room, but hardly anyone was watching. While a few of the women passed the time passively, others fretted over what to wear, compulsively changing from one outfit to another.

"Is it okay if I sit here?" Victoria asked Arianna. Clad in a black teddy, taken from her sparse lingerie collection at home, Victoria felt exposed.

Arianna frowned and sighed before taking a portion of the newspaper and placing it on the scruffy, grayish colored carpet. She yanked up the heavy leather bag and dropped it on the newspaper. It landed with a thud, which made Victoria flinch.

Carefully avoiding Arianna's towel, Victoria sat down. She glanced nervously at the faces in the room, hoping for a welcoming look. But her eyes met defiant stares, and so she fixed her gaze on the blurry image on the television screen.

From snatches of conversations, Victoria concluded that someone who worked there, someone named Bethany, had been arrested after the suspicious death of her infant. Whether Bethany and her black boyfriend Fred were involved in the child's death was the central theme for the entire shift.

"I think Bethany and Fred were in there getting high and that poor baby's little lungs just couldn't take no more," suggested Miquon.

"That's ridiculous," Arianna said with a derisive laugh. "Bethany got high during her entire pregnancy and it should have been immune to any fumes in the air. If that were the case and it died from inhaling cocaine fumes, there wouldn't be any physical evidence, now would there? Something else happened," Arianna said. "And considering the lifestyle of those two low-lifes, I shudder to think what really took place."

"Wasn't Bethany breastfeeding?" asked Kelly, raking through her colorful hair. Her ears, nose, tongue, navel, and brow were pierced; her entire body was splashed with tattoos.

"Breastfeeding!" scoffed Arianna. "Well then, you have the answer. It starved to death!"

The women in the room exchanged astonished glances.

"Bethany pulled doubles and sometimes triples," Arianna explained. "She practically lived here. When was she ever home to feed it? She left it and that other child in the care of Fred—a strung-out crackhead. And why did she work all those hours? For drug money, that's why."

"That's not true," Chelsea said. "Bethany was working hard to get a bigger place for her family. Did you know that Bethany, Fred, and the two kids were living in a one-room studio apartment?"

"Oh!" Arianna dragged out the word. "So she should be commended because she emerged from a drug-induced haze and realized that she and her sordid little family were living in substandard conditions? Two adults and two children require more than a room. They should have been arrested a long time ago for subjecting those kids to that. I'm not going to join you in the notion that poor Bethany was the perfect mother when we all know about her warped view of motherhood."

"Why are you being so disrespectful?" Chelsea pursed her lips. "And I wish you'd stop referring to Bethany's baby as *it*!"

"Did you forget about her other kids, the two that were molested by her last boyfriend? Those two were put in foster care, and Bethany seems to have forgotten about them. Instead of trying to reclaim her children, she simply replaced them with two more. Now, at her rapid rate of procreation, you can't expect me to refer to her offspring by gender."

"But you should show some respect for Bethany's son."

"Well *he's* dead, so what difference does it make?"

Chelsea sighed in exasperation.

"I wonder why Bethany stopped talking about her other children?" Kelly inquired. "She used to buy them stuff and visit them in the foster home."

"I heard she signed them kids over, and they got adopted out to two different families," Miquon offered, her lips curled in disapproval.

"Bethany just surrendered her rights, and let them people legally adopt her kids. Now you know that's a damn shame."

"Really?" Kelly sat up straight, her eyes wide with curiosity.

"Oh Jesus!" Arianna's eyes rolled to the ceiling. "I don't feel like listening to another rehash of that old story." She swept up the Coach duffel bag that had been displayed by her feet on the floor, gathered the newspaper, stuffed it into the bag, then rummaged through the bag and pulled out a bottle of Evian, a current edition of *Elle* magazine, and a pen. She buried her head in the magazine and turned the pages sharply.

Snatching off the cap of the pen Arianna made huge check marks next to designer clothing and circled the location of the stores.

As Arianna got up to go to the bathroom, she turned down the corner of a page and left the open magazine where she had been sitting. In the tension-filled room, stolen glances were directed at the creased page with the image of a brand new white Lexus.

Among the women there was a solid belief in scarcity, a belief that there wasn't enough to go around. Most of the women had experienced the ups and downs of the business of prostitution—the good days when the heavens smiled on one particular person, and the bad days when nothing worked for the same seemingly blessed one. To end a shift without breaking luck was everyone's greatest fear. To leave Pandora's empty-handed after sitting for seven or more hours was the worst thing that could happen.

Arianna, it seemed, never experienced the ups and downs. Some believed that her insatiable desire for expensive, trendy objects, the latest, the newest-the best, caused her to take more than her share. The unspoken, shared sentiment was that Arianna's constant craving was at the expense of everyone else. And no one in the room could afford for Arianna to buy a new Lexus.

Victoria also saw the picture of the car. But unlike the others, she was not threatened. Richly clad with manicured nails and perfectly coifed hair, Arianna was the image of pampered self-indulgence. Though Victoria watched Arianna with a touch of envy, she felt optimistic that she too would reap financial rewards.

At the sound of the doorbell, the women sprang instinctively from their seats and raced to the door. Feeling self-conscious and awkward, Victoria hung behind. When the door was opened, a swarthy, rather handsome man of Greek or Italian descent stood smiling in the lobby. The group of women did a rapid retreat and collided with the lagging Victoria.

"What's wrong?" Victoria asked.

"He's her regular," Miquon responded, pointing to Kelly who had confidently remained standing in the doorway. "Damn foreigners love blondes," Miquon complained.

"She's not blonde," Victoria said.

"Yeah, well she used to be. He don't even care how weird she look with that pink hair and all those tattoos and earrings. I bet her cooch is pierced too!" Miquon shook her head. "Junkie bitch!"

By eleven that night, there were nine recorded sessions. Kelly and Arianna had four apiece, and a sulking Sydney had only one. The shift would end in another hour and those who hadn't made any money were quiet and sullen.

At eleven-fifteen the bell sounded. Arianna and Kelly shrieked with glee. They darted to the door ahead of the others, whose movements were slowed by their sagging spirits.

Victoria remained seated. It was pointless to continue running to the door. The customers were assholes, and never had she seen such greedy, ruthless women. She hated them all. It irritated her no end to have to listen to her co-workers' nonsensical conversations. Agitated and battered from being trampled over each time she scuffled to get to the lobby where unworthy men appraised the women, it occurred to Victoria that she should just get up and walk out the door.

The tastes of the men who paid for sex baffled Victoria. With Arianna's exotic beauty and the air of mystery that surrounded her, Victoria was not surprised that she was a favorite of the patrons. The customers' attraction for Kelly, however, was puzzling. The woman was covered with hideous ink images: a cobra curled around her upper arm, a black panther ran the length of her left leg. In addition to a spider web and cross bones, there was a human skull on Kelly's back.

Victoria thought her decision to work in a massage parlor would assure her of a truckload of cash instead of the empty purse she'd been holding for over six long hours. She turned her attention to the antics at the door. She didn't have a clear view but could tell that the man standing in the lobby was a young Caucasian. Despite the girls' most provocative poses, and Kelly's enthusiastic sales pitch, the man was indecisive.

"Come on, Manny." Chelsea's megawatt smile didn't persuade Manny.

He had already been with her; he wasn't interested. In fact, he'd been with all of them.

Manny gave Chelsea a half-smile while making a continuing roving gaze over the nearly naked bodies that quivered with expectation before him.

"What happened to that redhead that was here last week?" he asked.

"We told you she don't work here no more," Miquon blurted. "Damn!"

"We're not sure if she's coming back, so come on and try one of us?" Sydney tried a softer approach.

"I've seen all of you; I wanted to try the redhead," Manny whined.

Feeling exasperated, Arianna threw up her hands and abruptly left the lobby.

"You got any other new girls?"

"No! Now pick one of us!" Miquon poked out her lips.

Arianna joined Victoria in the lounge.

"You should go out there," Arianna suggested. "Manny only sees new girls."

Victoria was rooted to her seat, fearful of more rejection. "Yeah, but..." she stammered.

"It's up to you," Arianna said, unsmiling. "I couldn't care less." She gave Victoria her back and continued flipping through the pages of the magazine.

Victoria sat in stunned silence; Arianna had dismissed her! Astonishment progressed to indignation. Fueled by anger, Victoria jumped up. Swinging her hips, she strutted from the lounge and joined the others in the doorway.

Inspired by the sudden realization that her time had finally come, Victoria became coquettish. "Hi, my name is Pleasure," she said, liking the sound of her new name. Would you like to see me?" She turned around slowly, teasingly, providing Manny with a full view of her lean, toned body.

"I sure would!" Manny replied.

With her heart quaking, Victoria had entered the room where Manny waited. Friendly and talkative, Manny put her at ease. Seeming to expect Victoria to be flattered, he talked about his weakness for women of a darker persuasion for at least twenty minutes. Ordinarily, before Pandora's, she would have been insulted by this admission.

But in the surreal surrounding of the session room, practically anything was permissible.

Time passed quickly while Manny chattered incessantly. Not anxious to do the dirty deed, Victoria listened intently, as though the drivel that fell from his lips were pearls of wisdom. Her heart sank, when in mid-sentence, he swiftly stripped down to his briefs.

Trembling hands tore open the condom package. Victoria chewed her bottom lip as Manny came out of his briefs, then she gasped. Manny had the smallest, pinkest, most non-threatening penis she'd ever seen.

"It'll get hard if you play with my nipples," Manny stated, suddenly blunt.

"I beg your pardon?"

"Pinch them," he demanded as he climbed on the bed. Lying prone, he motioned Victoria to straddle him.

Without bothering to undress, she straddled him and began to apply light pressure to his pale nipples.

"Harder!"

Victoria twisted and turned the hard knots as if they were miniature doorknobs that refused to open.

"Show me your pussy, you cunt!" Manny snarled.

Victoria's eyes narrowed in disbelief. The little white twerp did not just call her a cunt! But it was okay, she told herself. They were only role-playing. Victoria instantly made the mental adjustments and pulled the flimsy material of her panties to the side, revealing her dark, bushy pubis.

Manny grunted in what Victoria assumed was ecstasy. She felt something brush against her butt. He had an erection. His not quite throbbing, more like shivering, little penis had managed to stand straight up; it fluttered against her backside. Propping up his head with a pillow, without warning, he pulled Victoria forward; his tongue, cold and clammy struck like a snake. Victoria tensed, her thoughts swirled: Was it safe to let him do that? Could she catch something? Before she could organize her thoughts, Manny moaned. Instinctively, Victoria pulled away. Bucking and thrusting into the air, he exploded.

Victoria bolted for the restroom to wash off. There had been no penetration, but his tongue had touched hers and she felt defiled.

❧

Victoria was able to pay her son's babysitter and buy a few groceries with the fifty dollars she earned from her debut at Pandora's Box.

Charmaine, a neighbor with a son Jordan's age, had agreed to keep him overnight. Victoria felt lucky to find someone who was tolerant of her odd hours and didn't press when she provided only vague information about her job.

"Leave me a telephone number in case of an emergency," Charmaine had requested.

"Oh! Well, it's hard to reach me. I'm going to get a pager, okay?"

Victoria earned one hundred and fifty dollars on the second night. She bought a pager, called a laundry service that picked up and returned six bags of laundry, bought more groceries, and treated Jordan to lunch at McDonald's.

Sleeping over at his friend Stevie's house was exciting. Luckily, Jordan was too young to understand or question the change in his routine.

Other than the few material comforts, there was no evidence that two immoral nights had passed. Perhaps there'd be posttraumatic episodes later. Though she did not have a puritanical concept of morality, Victoria never thought she'd compromise her values—values instilled by Nana. Now that she had, surprisingly, nothing had changed. Nothing perceptible, at least. She had assumed with ease a decadent role in a lifestyle that she thoroughly disapproved of, and was exhilarated by it.

The next day felt a lot like Christmas. Victoria had two customers. A refined man with a New England accent, who claimed to be a college professor, was her first customer. Victoria had no reason to doubt him. With the exception of having to dodge his wet kisses as he declared love and adoration, he was extremely polite and easy to please. As he prepared to leave, the professor embraced Victoria and slipped her an additional fifty dollars. He told her that he'd be back to see her the next week. When his lips sought hers, she acquiesced. The kiss made her flesh crawl, but if it ensured his business on a regular basis, she could endure the brief discomfort.

Her second customer, Ted, was an awkward sandy-colored black guy in his late twenties. His light brown hair was wiry and seemed to bend every which-a-way, hazel eyes squinted behind thick glasses and outdated, ill-fitting clothing gave Ted the appearance of someone who was unstable, apt to do most anything.

It turned out that Ted was quite nice, seemingly sane and another talker. His wife, he confided, had had her tubes tied after their second child was born. Their sex life had diminished after the operation. Despite the fact that their second child was two-and-a-half, Ted chose to believe that his wife's limp libido was related to the operation and was simply a temporary condition. One look at his boxy physique, and his spindly legs sticking out of dingy, boxer shorts and Victoria couldn't blame Ted's wife for pleading failed health or any other lame excuse that would keep him at a distance.

"You're pretty," Ted said.

"Thank you."

"I better watch out. You could be dangerous."

"What do you mean?" Victoria feigned wide-eyed innocence.

"You could make me fall in love."

Victoria suppressed a groan.

Ted handed her a twenty-dollar tip, and Victoria tried her best to look excited by the possibility of winning Ted's love.

Chapter 3

With ripping speed, Rover vacated the premises when the shift ended at midnight. The scent of the cologne he wore lingered long after he'd gone. His favorite waitress at the diner was leaving work early and needed a ride home. Perhaps she'd invite him in for coffee or just to talk. He hoped to get lucky and end up beside her in bed.

Dominique blew in five minutes later, clutching a Styrofoam cup of steaming coffee. She was bundled from head to toe in heavy winter regalia and didn't make much of a fashion statement. Incongruous with her professional appearance, her look was frumpy, homespun.

The midnight shift was rarely busy on weeknights, though on the weekends the customers came in droves. But it was only Tuesday and there was just a skeleton crew. Only Dominique and Reds were scheduled to work.

Reds had come to work a half-hour early and had quickly changed into a daring halter gown. A push-up bra elevated her sagging bust line, creating cleavage and the impression of an ample bosom. Though enticing, the long gown concealed flabby thighs, saddlebag hips, and a protruding gut. A shock of frizzy hair was brushed tame, styled and in place, and her make-up, heavily applied, was complete.

Reds came to work early to snag any customers who happened to call amid the pandemonium that occurred during the change of shift. At that time, the women who had just arrived were busy preparing for the night ahead. They changed from street clothes to work attire, applied make-up, fixed hair, and hardly any of the women were in any state worthy of exhibit at the front door. Therefore, customers who were unwilling to sit unattended in the cold, brightly lit lobby would grudgingly agree to a session with Reds.

High yellow with a wild mane of flaming hair, Reds had commanded top dollar in her day. But time and booze, the diabolic duo, had wreaked havoc on her figure, and though her face was still pretty, her fair skin was now beginning to crack. Reds had to constantly devise new ways to coax the clientele into a session with her.

"What's Sheena doing here?" Dominique asked, referring to a frail figure asleep on the sofa.

"Don't ask me. She was knocked out when I got here," Reds answered.

"Did Rover straighten up the rooms?" Dominique inquired.

"I don't know. I didn't check." Reds responded absently. She had gotten a whiff of Dominique's coffee and was debating ordering some from the all-night deli on Sansom Street, but remembering the two-dollar delivery charge, she changed her mind. Having sat without a customer for two days in a row, Reds didn't have a dollar to spare. She opted for a cigarette instead. Dominique carelessly hung her hat, coat, and scarf on a wobbly coat rack and marched up the hall to inspect the rooms. Eager for the excitement of Dominique's reaction if the rooms hadn't been cleaned, Reds trailed behind.

The two women peeked in the first session room and frowned. Rover had obviously thrown the room together haphazardly. Bits of tissues and other debris were scattered on the floor, evidence of slipshod vacuuming. Though both the ashtray and the waste can had been emptied, the ashtray hadn't been wiped clean and the waste can needed a fresh plastic liner. The bed, made hastily with crumpled linen, added to the unkempt appearance of the room.

"Did you hear about Bethany? She was trippin' so bad they had to put her away!" Dominique exclaimed to Reds as she smoothed out the sheet and rearranged the towel.

"Put away?" Reds asked. Feeling exhilarated by the possibility of new gossip, she retrieved a cigarette and lit up. "I thought Bethany and Fred got released after they took 'em in for questioning."

"Fred's out, but they put Bethany in a loony bin."

"For real? Who told you?"

"Gabrielle. But check this out…just before she snapped the fuck out, Bethany told the cops that the baby was alive when she got home from work. Well naturally they asked her where she worked…" Dominique scowled as she detected grimy smudges on the containers of massage essentials. "And that dumb ass told 'em she worked at Pandora's Box!" She wiped off the bottles of baby oil and lotion with tissues yanked from a cheap store-brand box. "The cops called to verify her employment."

"Why the hell would she tell them where she works?" Reds asked. "It's not as if this is a legal business with taxes and shit coming out of our pay. We damn sure don't need the IRS snooping around here. Bethany's so damn stupid." Reds paused, shaking her head. "Gabrielle must be pissed!"

"She's beyond pissed. I had to listen to that hoe rant and rave about being raided and being shut down."

Reds snickered at the irreverence. She knew Gabrielle would not take too kindly to being called a hoe.

"She bitched about everything—how she's not making money like she used to…. And guess which shift is to blame?"

"Midnight, of course," Reds chimed in, tightening her lips as she rolled her eyes.

"She wanted to know how many sessions we had last night. You should have heard how that bitch went off when I told her we only had two. She cussed me out, like I'm the one responsible; like I block the door and refuse to let the customers in."

Reds shook her head in disbelief.

"Now she's talking about putting some new black chick on our schedule. Said the girl has customers lined up at the door."

"Well, if she's such a moneymaker, why does Gabrielle want to change her shift?"

"How do I know? She's supposed to be real pretty with a lot of class, and Gabrielle emphasized the word class, like we ain't got none."

Reds thought for a moment as she studied her nails. At first she felt hurt, slighted by Gabrielle's words. Then irritation washed over her. "Gabrielle should realize that it don't matter who she puts on this shift. Classy or not, the fact is...customers don't come out late at night during the week. She should be grateful that we're willing to hold down the fort, none of the other girls would have the patience to sit through this shit." Reds looked down at the floor, and frowned at sprinkles of powder that Rover had failed to vacuum. "Everybody wants to work the midnight shift on the weekend. And that's the time we should be reaping the benefits of sitting in here all week. But nooo! We have to share the wealth with all them greedy bitches from the other shifts."

Reds started pacing. Dominique eyed her curiously. It wasn't like Reds to get so worked up.

"Gabrielle ain't got no kind of loyalty," Reds continued the tirade. "We been making money for her for four years! Now she wants us to work with some siddity new bitch who's gonna cut into the little bit of money that does come our way." Reds took one long, last puff before snuffing out the cigarette in the glass ashtray Dominique had just sprayed with disinfectant and wiped clean.

Without a word, Dominique emptied the ashes. Then, changing the subject, Dominique said, "I still can't understand why Bethany would draw attention to us like that. Do you think she deliberately tried to get us busted? Think about it...the night the baby died, Bethany left work broke and mad as hell."

"Naw, I don't think Bethany would deliberately try to get the place raided," Reds said, suddenly calm, as she followed Dominique to the second session room. "She needs Pandora's as much as we do. Believe me, Bethany will be back. As soon as she pulls herself together, she'll be back—trickin' like the rest of us. Where else she gonna go?"

Dominique didn't answer.

"Is Fred gonna take care of the baby's funeral?" Reds inquired.

"I doubt it. I don't know what's going to happen with the funeral. Gabrielle is going to let us know when she gets some more information."

A worried look crossed Reds' face. "We ain't been busted in years. I don't know... Bethany runnin' off at the mouth and all..." Reds shook her head. "I sure hope nothing happens."

"If the money was still as good as good as it usta be, I could stand a couple of raids," Dominique said playfully. The two veterans slapped hands and laughed heartily.

"Remember how we used to spend one-hundred dollar bills like they was ones?" Red said, grinning as she recalled more prosperous times.

"No, Reds," Dominique said with an edge to her voice. "You used to spend money like that. My black ass wasn't in demand, but I knew how to stretch a dollar—still do."

Dominique's meaning wasn't lost on Reds. Reds was painfully aware that now the tables had turned. Through no effort of her own, thirty-six years old Dominique still had a beautiful body. Blessed with good genes, she didn't work out and didn't know or care about the nutritional value of the food she ate. Tall, lean and muscular, Dominique was an imposing figure. Her short hair was permed bone straight and slicked back. She was dark with strong masculine features. Dominique made a living, albeit, a modest one, from a clientele that was exclusively masochistic, Caucasian men. Reds, on the other hand, could barely make ends meet.

At the sound of the doorbell Dominique and Reds both hurried down the hall. Dominique was still wearing her street clothes. It didn't matter; she'd change later. Rules were relaxed, broken on the midnight shift.

"Get up, Sheena. Someone's at the door," Dominique yelled to Sheena as she passed the lounge.

Sheena stirred, but didn't get up.

Without so much as a glance at Sheena, Reds threw open the door and to her dismay, it was Miquon pushing past her, with a beat up canvas workbag.

"What are you doing here?" Dominique asked, one hand on her hip. "You're not on the schedule."

"I know I'm not on the schedule, it's my day off. Gabrielle said I could come in to make some extra money."

"She didn't mention your name when I talked to her this morning."

The sight of Sheena stopped Miquon. She rolled her eyes dramatically before flopping down on dilapidated flowery chair.

"Yeah, well, I guess Gabrielle don't tell you everything!" Miquon exclaimed as she rifled through her workbag.

Dominique and Reds exchanged worried glances. Miquon would not be regarded as competition on the other two shifts, but after midnight there was no set standards, the most bizarre and outlandish could be queen of the night.

"Why didn't she just let you work your own shift?"

"Because she realized that this shift needed some flava!" Emphasizing her point, Miquon snapped her fingers and twisted her neck.

Miquon shot an angry glance at Sheena, who had begun to snore loudly. "I see Sheena's gittin' her nod on-as usual. I'm damn sure the customers get sick of coming here and seeing just the two of you. And every now and then y'all throw Sheena up in the mix. What a selection! That's why y'all be havin' so many walk-outs on this shift."

Reds felt a twinge.

"What walk-outs? You don't know nothin' about this shift," Dominique snapped.

"I know y'all be having just two or three customers written up on the sheet for the whole, entire night. Now that's crazy. So if they ain't walkin' out, then y'all must be pocketing the money!"

Reds lowered her eyes guiltily toward the floor. She didn't think that the money Dominique sometimes let her keep would ever be noticed; it wasn't that much, anyway.

But Reds couldn't speak for Dominique; she had no idea how much session money Dominique skimmed off the top.

"Look at her!" Miquon pointed to Sheena's prone body. "She's knocked out and she ain't waking up no time soon. Sheena just uses this place as a crash spot. The dope man won't let her hit the pipe when her money runs out, so she comes here. She ain't bringing in no money so I don't know why Gabrielle don't just get rid of her sorry ass."

"Gabrielle and Sheena go way back. Reds and me knew her back when she first came out, didn't we Reds?"

"Uh huh. When I met Sheena, she was only about fifteen or sixteen. She was 'bout as country as they come. Sheena's from Georgia, right?" she asked Dominique.

"No. Alabama."

"Oh yeah, that's right. Birmingham. Sheena was one of those big ol' corn-fed country girls," Reds reminisced, smiling. "I know it's hard to believe, but once upon a time, Sheena was built like a brick shithouse."

"Brick shithouse," Miquon mimicked. "I forget how old y'all asses are until you start talkin' like that."

"Anyway," Dominique interrupted, glaring at Miquon as she put on a black latex two-piece. "Gabrielle looks out for Sheena. She'll always have a home at Pandora's Box."

Reds recalled how, as a young girl, Sheena had been wild and fun loving. But Sheena had been smoking crack now for at least five years, and the drug had ravished her body, destroyed her soul. A vacant gaze had replaced the light that had once brightened

Sheena's eyes. Reds doubted if the bedraggled creature curled up on the sofa would ever find the strength to reclaim her life.

Most girls in the business offset the pressures with alcohol or drugs in some form or another. Reds was no exception; drunken binges masked her pain. But nothing that Reds was aware of—not even heroin—had the devastating effect of crack. Hit with waves of sudden and overwhelming sorrow-sorrow for herself as well as for Sheena, Reds grew listless.

"If Gabrielle wants to turn this place into a damn shelter, that's on her," Miquon exclaimed. "I'm here to get mine; I'm not worrying about Gabrielle, Sheena or nobody else."

In a flash, Miquon was out of her street clothes and naked, boldly revealing rolls of flab and stretch marks. Her discolored, ample derriere was riddled with unsightly dents from cellulite. Both Reds and Dominique turned their heads in disgust.

Miquon pulled a white lace teddy from her bag. Still perturbed by the exchange with Dominique, she grumbled to herself as she struggled to get into the too small outfit, The front of the teddy did not cover Miquon's protruding stomach as it was meant to. Instead, it gathered in the middle, exposing part of her pubis and revealed her hanging lower abdomen. When asked why she would wear such an unflattering outfit, Miquon responded, "Ain't no shame in my game, I wear whatever I want!"

As Miquon rubbed the ash from her body with gobs of Vaseline, the doorbell rang. Looking like an ill-tempered rhino with one ashy leg, Miquon stomped ahead of Dominique and Reds. No one attempted to awaken Sheena.

A chunky white guy wearing a green Eagles parka eyed the women suspiciously. His face was blotched and red from the cold.

"Have you been here before?" Miquon inquired.

"No," he said. His eyes quickly roamed over the three women before resting on one of the signs on the wall.

"What's your name, sweetheart?" Reds threw back her hair and puckered her lips.

"Uh, it's uh, Bob. Where are the other girls? That sign says I get a choice of twenty-five-where ya hiding the other twenty-two?" He snickered.

"We have twenty-five girls spread out on three different shifts," Dominique interjected. "Just the three of us tonight. So come on and try some hot chocolate. I'll warm you up," she said, soothingly.

Bob smiled indulgently, and then said, "No offense to you's, but are there any white girls working tonight?" He didn't want to hurt their feelings, but he wasn't into black chicks.

"She said it was just us three. Do you see any damn white girls," Miquon flared up.

A deeper shade of red covered Bob's face.

"We're all the same in the dark, baby," Dominique said playfully, defusing the situation. "Just close your eyes and pretend I'm a white girl."

Bob shifted uncomfortably. "No, I don't think so…"

"Come on, baby. Let me take care of you," Dominique cajoled. "We'll start with a massage, then we'll…" She rubbed her hands over the length of her body and stopped at her crotch, moving her fingers in a circular motion.

"What the hell," Bob said, blushing with resignation. "I'll stay."

"Who do you want to see?" Reds figured he wanted to see Dominique, but one could hope.

"Her," he said pointing to Dominique. Dominique offered a smile.

Reds shrugged her shoulders, and joined Miquon, who trudged back into the lounge, muttering, "I can see this shit is going to get on my nerves. Y'all bitches is too foul for me."

"You're getting on my nerves!" Reds snapped back. "Why do you have to be so loud and crude?"

"What do you expect me to do? I get tired of these racist motherfuckers axing for white girls all the time." Miquon slumped down on the sofa where Sheena was still sprawled out.

"Move over, Sheena," Miquon grumbled. "You takin' up the whole damn couch." She scooted over, using her butt to push Sheena out of the way. Sheena snored louder.

"You're crazy, Miquon! A trick can spend his money any way he wants. A good hoe should be able to convince him to choose her. That's what Dominique just did! You need to stop complaining and start taking lessons from the pros."

Miquon waved Reds away. "I didn't know I had to convince him by rubbing on my tits and playing with my coochie. Y'all too slimy for me. We don't roll like that on the second shift."

Reds pointed to Miquon's groin. "Look at the way your stuff is hanging out, you can't talk."

Surprised, Miquon attempted to cover her pubic area.

Not one to carry a grudge, Reds felt better after putting Miquon in her place.

"We heard there's a new black girl on the second shift…" The statement hung in the air. Miquon ignored Reds.

"What does she look like? Come on, Miquon. You know you want to tell me," Reds teased.

Miquon sucked her teeth, and then acquiesced. "She looks all right. Brown skin, nice shape. But, I don't like her."

"Why not?"

"She puts on airs."

"Sounds like another stuck-up Arianna," Reds cut in, and then leaned back in the chair with her arms folded, nodding sagely.

"No, she ain't that bad. Ain't nobody as conceited as Arianna. I wonder why all those uppity bitches wanna work here, anyway?"

Miquon waited for Reds to respond, and then she began tearing off the wrapper of a Snickers candy bar. Miquon sank her teeth into the gooey chocolate and closed her eyes blissfully.

"What's the new girl's name?"

"Her name is Pleasure," Miquon answered, perturbed. "Anything else?"

Reds shook her head no. Then for lack of anything better to do, Reds craned her neck to look at the front of a magazine that was lying on Miquon's workbag. Reds didn't recognize the pretty young black woman on the cover, who posed in a form fitting, cut to the crotch dress. The woman was someone in the entertainment business, but Reds wasn't sure if she was a singer, actress, or rapper. And not knowing was another reminder of the age disparity between herself and most of her young co-workers.

For the umpteenth time, Reds reprimanded herself for not holding on to some of the money that had come so easily when she was young. Five and six hundred dollars a day was the norm back then, on an exceptional day she made at least a grand. Now she pulled in fifty dollars a day—if she was lucky. That's what she had been reduced to and Reds despised herself for being so stupid.

She couldn't put up with the shit much longer. These new breeds of wild-ass young girls, with their don't-give-a-fuck heathen ways, were taking over the business, trying to push her aside. And the customers didn't treat her much better; they gave her disdainful glances that suggested it was time she was carted off to the glue factory.

Reds cut her eyes at Miquon, and marveled at the sight of her. Miquon had devoured one bar of chocolate and was champing down noisily on the second—this one, a Hershey with almonds. It didn't matter that she was crude and grossly overweight, Miquon believed that her youth alone gave her an edge over Reds and Dominique. Back when Reds had started out, someone like Miquon would not have been hired to work inside a massage parlor. She would have been forced to walk the streets. For reasons, unknown to Reds, Gabrielle did not discriminate; diversity prevailed at Pandora's. Gabrielle hired women of all sizes, colors, and shapes—something for everyone.

Chapter 4

Reds dozed off and was startled awake when the doorbell chime announced another patron. Without bothering to check hair or make-up, she hurried to the door. Dominique and Miquon were unavailable, both were engaged in a session—Dominique's third and Miquon's first. Reds feared that the two women would hear the doorbell, and greedily dart out of their current sessions to join Reds at the door.

There were only a few hours before the shift ended, and Reds still hadn't had a session. With spirits low, she managed a sexy stance and cheerful greeting when she opened the door to a grimy old black man in dated, ill-fitting clothing. Reds stifled a snicker; the wretched figure she saw huddled in the doorway would be an easy mark.

"Have you been here before?" she asked.

He looked her over, long and disapprovingly.

"Yeah, a long time ago," he replied, unsmiling. His shoulders were hunched from the cold, hands stuck deep down in his coat pockets. "Does Tina still work here?"

Panic washed over Reds. Even he, a cruddy old geezer, held her in low esteem. She simply couldn't go home broke again. Come on you dirty old motherfucker, she thought, it's the wee hours of the morning, and freezing cold. You know you're desperate and horny, so please stop wasting time!

"No, she's not here anymore." Reds didn't know who the hell he was talking about. "But why don't you come on in anyway. You can see me." She motioned for the man to come inside. He looked around warily and didn't move.

"What about Sheba? Does she still work here?"

Reds wondered if he was referring to Sheena? It was possible. Sheena had a clientele of weirdoes who stopped by occasionally. It was possible but Reds didn't dare inquire further.

"Nobody by that name works here."

"Where are the other girls?"

"I'm the only one here tonight," she said lamely. Her eyes bounced back and forth nervously from the old man to the closed session doors. Reds couldn't afford for Miquon or Dominique to pop out now and provide the old fool with options.

"Come on with me, honey. It's cold out there. You need some of this body heat to warm you up!" Desperation shone in her eyes as she attempted to tantalize the man. She moved her hands seductively over her slack, misshapen body, and threw in a half-hearted wiggle.

Reds tugged at the man's arm.

The old man stiffened. "I don't know...I wanted to see Tina or Sheba because they both know me, and uh, understand what I need."

"Tell me what you need; I'll take care of you." There was a higher pitch to her voice.

"Well it's in this here bag." The old man pulled a crumpled brown paper bag from the deep pocket of his tattered coat.

Reds braced herself. He probably had a double-headed dildo or something just as fucked up and weird. It didn't matter; she'd seen it all.

"Come on with me," Reds said firmly. She practically strong-armed the man as she guided him to the only available room and quickly shut the door. Instead of handing over the fee when Reds requested it, the old man nervously scanned the room, as if he expected something or someone to pop out of some hidden place. She blinked, irritated. It was becoming increasingly difficult for Reds to contain the rage that was building.

Stirrings were heard in the hall. Dominique or Miquon had finished her session. Reds shot a frantic glance toward the closed door, and then thoroughly angry, enraged eyes turned his way. How dare he continue to act up after she thought she had him tucked safely away from the feline predators who lurked outside the door? No one could blame her if she suddenly just lost it-just went off on the man.

"What's the matter?" she asked with forced control.

"Are you gonna wear those shoes?" he asked, looking contemptuously at her feet.

Ostrich feathers adorned the top of the pretty black satin pumps she wore.

"What's wrong with my shoes?"

"Tina and Sheeba always wore high heels. Those itty bitty heels won't work." His face was clouded with worry.

"They won't work!" What did he want her to do? Walk on his back with spike heels? Reds mentally scanned the items in her bag. There was a pair of thigh high boots with a short, narrow heel, and a pair of silver slippers, but no fucking high heels. She tried not to wear them anymore.

Her thighs, covered with unsightly spider veins, had begun to resemble a Rand McNally map, and recently, to her dismay, she'd discovered that the red, blue, and green broken veins were now traveling down to her lower legs. And as if that wasn't enough, her gait was unsteady when wearing high heels, causing her to place last in the race to the door.

The high heel thing was just another of the many frightening indications that she was getting too old to continue in this business.

In search of high heels, Reds dashed back to the lounge. She groped inside Sheena's workbag, a faded Tommy Hilfiger copy, and pulled out a pair of black and gold stilettos. BINGO! Perfect whore-wear!

"Now before I pay you my money," the old man cautioned when Reds returned, "I think I better explain what I want you to do." He shook the paper bag. "I got in this here bag a jar full of all kinds of insects…" With slow, deliberate movements, he drew the jar from the bag. As if he were about to display the Hope Diamond, he beamed with pride.

"Wait a minute! What do you have in there? Insects? You mean bugs and shit?" Surely, she misunderstood him. Reds stood frozen, waiting for some clarity. She wasn't ready to accept that the money she expected to receive had just sprouted wings.

"Now you get ready," he continued. "Cause I'm going to open the lid and let all of 'em out and I want you to step on 'em-squash 'em before they can get away."

Her mouth fell open in astonishment. "What the fuck is your problem? I'm not stepping on no fuckin' bugs, you crazy mothafucker." Reds pummeled the old man with one of Sheena's shoes. Escaping the sharp heel of the shoe, he ran out the door and almost collided with Miquon as he scampered down the hall.

"Damn, Reds, why'd you let that bum in here?" Miquon asked in a voice filled with wonder. "Times couldn't be that hard. I just know you wasn't in there trickin' with a vagrant. Didn't you recognize him? That's the man who be hangin' outside the Reading Terminal—begging. If he don't get no money, he gets mad and starts threatening to throw bugs on people." Miquon shuddered. "What's wrong with your nose? Couldn't you smell his funky ass? Mothafucka bumped all up on me—got me itchin'." Miquon scratched herself dramatically. "Now I gotta go get some alcohol and disinfect myself."

Reds stumbled back into the lounge and slumped in her seat. She should just quit, she told herself. Leave before things got any worse. How could she have even considered a session with a derelict? Thoughts of her glory days swirled in her head.

Her customers used to line up to see her, they wouldn't settle for anyone else. There had been Caribbean vacations paid for by her johns, front row seats at championship fights, the red Corvette, luxury apartments, the full-length ranch mink coat, and oh so much money, booze, and drugs.

Her accomplishments had been an example of what a working girl could achieve. But now her existence served as a warning to every girl in the life, that if she didn't get out before it was too late, she'd end up just like Reds.

Reds felt a lump forming in her throat, and tried to will it away before the warm tears that filled her eyes streamed down her face.

Chapter 5

The widely held myth that the rain brought tricks out in droves again proved true. On Thursday it rained, and no one was surprised that business was booming. The morning shift ended with eleven sessions on the books. The second shift had just begun and already there were seven sessions logged. Victoria had three of those.

"Where are you keeping your money?" Rover asked as Victoria handed over the house's portion of the fee.

"In my purse."

"Make sure you don't lay it down. These girls have sticky fingers," he warned.

She had made two hundred dollars, including tips, from the three sessions. It would appear that it was money earned easily if compared to the time and toil necessary to acquire the same amount in a more conventional way. But from the soul's perspective, it was the hardest money Victoria had ever earned, and to have it stolen was unthinkable.

The troubled look that crossed her face did not go unnoticed.

"You can be straight with me, Pleasure. You're new to the business... am I right?" Rover's tone was gentle, his expression, fatherly.

Victoria nodded, lids lowered.

"Believe it or not, I'm a nice guy," Rover began. "But I had to harden my heart toward most of the girls here. Being a nice guy has got me burned more times than I care to admit. Once upon a time, a hard luck story would get me right here…" With a balled fist, Rover thumped his chest. "Not anymore. This place is filled with nothing but cold, conniving women. Most of 'em don't start out that way, but that's how they always end up. Believe me, I know."

"I don't intend to work here longer than I have to Rover." Victoria paused, then feeling compelled to confess, she blurted, "My grandmother left me some money, and I did something incredibly stupid and…"

"That ain't my business." He held up a silencing finger. "Just straighten out your problems, and put all this behind you as soon as you can. You're a nice girl and I've seen what this business can do to nice girls." Rover paused. He shook his head sadly. "It destroys 'em."

Victoria thought Rover was laying it on a little heavy. She appreciated his concern, but did he honestly believe she was stupid enough to stick around long enough to be destroyed?

"There's something else I forgot to mention."

Victoria smiled tolerantly. "Yes."

"Fast money can be addictive."

Victoria looked at him quizzically.

"That's right. After the girls get used to having that high from quick cash, they lose patience for waiting around to be paid every two weeks. I've seen it happen. They go back to the work force and after about a month or so, they're right back here."

"You don't have to worry about me, Rover. Between the two of us, I'm not an inexperienced young girl. I lied about my age."

Victoria noticed that Rover didn't bat an eye. "I'm thirty-three," she confessed. "Coffee is my only vice; it's not likely that I'll develop a new addiction at this point. I'm going to be fine, Rover," she said, patting his arm. "Now where can I keep my money?"

"I can lock it up in the safe if you want," Rover offered.

"Okay."

"But it'll cost you. I charge $2.00 a night."

Victoria shrugged. "Sure. Okay."

"Oh! Another thing I forgot to mention. Gabrielle wants me to get twenty bucks from every girl who gets a session. We're taking up a collection toward the funeral for Bethany's baby. She works here. It's a damn shame that innocent baby had to suffer."

A chill went through Victoria. She didn't ask how the baby died. She didn't want to know, fearing that the unhallowed environment of Pandora's Box was somehow associated with the baby's death. Victoria made a mental note to call and check on Jordan as soon as the one pay phone was free.

"You can give me the money now or you can pay at the end of the shift."

Victoria handed Rover twenty-two dollars and put the rest of her money into an envelope to be placed inside the safe.

In addition to managing the massage parlor, Rover had turned the office into a mini-mart of sorts, selling everything from candy, condoms, and cigarettes to pantyhose and feminine hygiene spray. And from his vast video collection, the girls often rented movies to take home or to view in the lounge when business was slow.

"By the way, are they giving you a hard time?"

"Who?" Victoria asked, distracted. Her thoughts were on Jordan.

"The girls don't like it when a new girl comes in and makes all the money. So you watch yourself because they've been known to pull some real dirty tricks—the stories I could tell you."

"I'm all right. They don't seem particularly friendly, but I can handle it."

"Okay, just watch your back and make sure you don't get too comfortable here."

When Victoria reentered the crowded lounge, she sat in the only available seat, next to a ginger-colored woman who appeared to be in her late twenties. She couldn't recall having seen the woman before. In fact, there were quite a few new faces among the nine women who moved about in the lounge. Some were from different shifts and others worked weekends only. The weekend at Pandora's Box began on Thursday.

"You're doing pretty good tonight, aren't you?" the ginger-colored woman asked Victoria.

Victoria nodded. "I hope it keeps up."

Wearing a leopard body stocking with leopard designs on clawed, sculptured nails, she looked like the stereotypical whore. She batted false eyelashes, a heart-shaped mole was drawn on her left cheek and a big blonde wig with cascading curls sat atop her head. At first glance she appeared hard, coarse, but upon closer inspection, Victoria was surprised to find beneath the layers of make-up, a child-like face with soft features, a little girl, dressing up as a lady of the night.

"You're new, aren't you?" the woman asked Victoria.

"Does it show?"

"I overheard some of the girls talking about you. They say you stay in the room with your customers for almost an hour."

"What's wrong with that? They're paying for the time."

"We don't roll like that around here; we try to get 'em out in a half hour or less. Let me give you some advice," the woman said in a loud voice that invited everyone in the room to listen. "These customers will wear you out if you let them. You have to get them out of there as soon as possible. Otherwise we'll lose a lot of business."

Eavesdropping, Miquon chimed in, "Girl, you can't be tyin' up the rooms on the weekend. A lot of money comes through on the weekend, and we all wanna make some dough. These tricks will walk right out if we tell them they have to wait for a room." Miquon screwed up her lips and twisted her neck to punctuate her statement.

Muffled laughter and murmurs filled the room. The other women in the lounge were eager to gang up on Victoria now that the conversation had turned into an open forum.

Victoria's face flushed. She didn't like being publicly chastised. "How was I supposed to know that?"

The woman in the leopard body stocking replied, "No offense, but we all assumed you knew what you were doing, but it's obvious you don't. You can get burned out real fast around here. I'm trying to help you out while you still have that new girl thang going on." Her full lips, outlined in black and painted a dark mahogany, parted in a smile. "By the way, my name is Jonee. You're Pleasure, right?"

Victoria wanted to sulk, but gave in. "Yeah, my name is Pleasure."

"I like that. Who gave you your name?"

"Didn't somebody named Pleasure usta work here before?" Miquon interrupted. "Don't y'all remember her? Real skinny, looked like she was on drugs."

Victoria decided that she detested Miquon. "Nobody gave me the name," she said, then turned away from Miquon and directed her response to Jonee only. "When I called, Rover asked for my work name. I didn't have one, so I took the name from a bottle of cologne," Victoria confessed, laughing. "And when I came in for an interview, he asked again. I knew I had chosen the right name when I noticed the word *Pleasure* in the title of a video lying on his desk."

"That figures. He's such a pervert," Jonee whispered. "It was probably one of his fag boy movies."

"Rover's gay?" Victoria asked, whispering also.

Miquon hovered, waiting for an opportunity to get back into the conversation, but the whispering excluded her. Clutching a few dollars and some change, Miquon stomped out of the room, headed for Rover's commissary.

"I don't know if he's actually gay," Jonee said as she brushed a fallen blonde tress from her face. "All men are fucked up one way or another—especially in the sex department. Rover's always looking at porn flicks with preoperative transvestites. His face is glued to the screen while he's watching those chicks-with-dicks movies."

"You're kidding."

Jonee shook her head. "I'm not kidding. That's how he gets his freak on." Jonee paused. "Honey, those dudes look better than most women. They have big tits...plump, round asses...and the tiniest waistlines you'll ever see. And then...bam...they be sportin' these big, rock-hard dicks! That shit's amazing. You never saw one of those videos?" Jonee asked incredulously.

"Can't say I have," Victoria said, chuckling.

"Ask Rover, he'll be happy to show you one of his freak shows." Jonee's shrill laugh seemed a bit much.

"But truthfully," she continued. "I don't know whether or not he's gay. I know he's fascinated with the subject, and that makes you wonder." Jonee looked at her watch. "Damn, I wish some more money would come through. What happened to the rush we had earlier? Everything's slowed the hell down." She leaned in. "And that's another thing you need to be aware of...this is the most unpredictable business in the world. You can't count on shit around here."

Many girls arrived at work dressed down in jeans or sweats and without make-up. They looked plain and often, downright unattractive but within minutes could morph into utterly glamorous beings. Jonee on the other hand, had walked through the door in full costume: make-up, wig, cleavage showing, skin-tight clothing. Victoria wondered how Jonee was regarded out in public as she shamelessly flaunted her profession. Despite Jonee's wit and good sense, Victoria knew she'd never feel that certain kinship one feels for a person of like mind. Jonee was cut from a different cloth.

An hour elapsed and the women continued their vigil. During that tense time, the women changed outfits, touched up hair, nails and make-up. They stumbled among one another in an awkward dance of dressing and undressing. Boots, high-heels, stockings, garter belts, curling irons, make-up, hand mirrors, and toiletries were strewn about.

A musky aroma, a mixture of cigarette smoke, cheap body spray, and sex permeated the air at Pandora's. It clung to everything—hair, clothing— and the upholstery of the furniture. Contained inside her workbag, the assaulting odor went home with Victoria and unfortunately was released inside her bedroom—her sanctuary—when she unpacked the bag, trans- porting thoughts and images that were best kept in Pandora's Box.

Thankfully, the bell announced the arrival of the next caller. There was a stampede to the door. Not wanting to appear greedy or desperate, Victoria deliberately lagged behind.

Jonee led the pack and gave the familiar spiel: "Have you been here before? It costs one hundred dollars for an hour and you get a full-service body massage."

There were so many women in front of her, Victoria could hardly see the customer. She stood on her toes and was able to discern that he had very white, pasty skin against dark clothing. He was wearing a black hat. Unwilling to be concealed completely, Victoria maneuvered herself into view. To her utter amazement, an Amish man stood in the lobby. Rain dotted his wire-rimmed glasses and his face. He didn't have on a coat, and his wrinkled black suit was damp.

Victoria had recently rented the old video, *Witness*, and lately there had been shocking reports about child abuse, drug addiction, and even murder among the Amish. Although she had learned that they were far from perfect, it was hard to fathom an Amish trick! How on earth had he arrived, she wondered. By horse and buggy? And what nerve! The man had walked in, as bold as you please, into a den of iniquity, and stood there stroking his beard, appraising the girls and enjoying the deliciously difficult task of making a selection.

Victoria's less than eager demeanor set her apart from her coworkers.

"How about her?" The Amish man pointed a crooked finger at Victoria. She recoiled and was about to decline. But remembering her money woes, she accompanied the unusual guest up the hall to an empty room.

He told her his name was Ezekiel.

"My name is Pleasure." Victoria managed an impression of a smile. She couldn't help feeling offended by his shabby, strange appearance and was further offended by the body odor he emitted as he disrobed. Taking Jonee's advice, she was rid of the Amish man in less than twenty minutes.

By the end of the shift Victoria had earned seven hundred dollars.

Victoria had taken the trolley to work, but afraid of being robbed of her hard earned money, she took a cab home. She could afford it now.

Tossing in her workbag, Victoria slid into the back seat of the cab. As the cab rolled along Market Street, she rested her head on the back of the seat and closed her eyes. The sound of the ticking meter lulled her into a peaceful state. She couldn't recall having ever ridden in a cab without anxiously leaning forward, monitoring the running meter, or at least wanting to.

Chapter 6

Over coffee the next morning, after picking up a too-talkative Jordan from the babysitter, Victoria scanned the real estate section of the newspaper. She had to find another apartment. At first the thought gave her a queasy feeling. But recently those feelings had been replaced with stirrings of excitement. She perused the rental listings. From the many options, she selected the sections of the city that were familiar: Southwest Philly, West Philly, and University City. She was looking for something in the affordable range of five to six hundred a month. A devilish smile crossed her face as she realized that if she continued making money like she did last night, she could afford to live practically anywhere she wanted.

Her current apartment had severe plumbing problems. Water from the leaky pipes of the apartment above her seeped through the ceiling tiles in her kitchen. A couple of tiles were missing, having collapsed from the weight of the water, exposing rusty pipes and rotted wood. Buckets, pots, and rubber wastebaskets were placed strategically on the worn linoleum kitchen floor to catch the brownish drops of water. After placing a trillion calls, someone from the License and Inspection Bureau had finally come to investigate. The investigator seemed appropriately appalled but the situation was never remedied.

The pending eviction was a good thing, Victoria decided. Paying back the rent she owed while continuing to live in squalor was obscene.

An ad for a luxury apartment in Mount Airy caught her eye. The ad boasted that every apartment overlooked Fairmount Park, that each unit had a washer and dryer. There was a pool, a tennis court, a health club, and a twenty-four hour doorman on the premises. Victoria thought wistfully that she could get accustomed to living like that.

That thought brought back sad memories of a time when, young and naïve, she had had the briefest of flings with an NBA rookie. He lived in a condominium in an affluent, gated community in Mount Airy. In his world, a world Victoria had yearned to enter but could only glimpse, everything was shiny, bright, and brand new. From the dozens of pairs of Nike sneakers to his BMW, there were no signs of wear on any of his possessions.

The morning after their tryst, the rookie pulled up in front of her shabby row house. Victoria was greeted by the sights and sounds of her urban neighborhood, and was embarrassed. An expression of disgust crossed the rookie's face as he hastily pulled the car from the curb, and screeched away. He was off to give false hope to another poor soul who thought she could escape a fretful urban existence by riding his coattails.

A few years later Victoria had seen his smiling dark face in an *Ebony* magazine, posing on his wedding day. Five other tall, black, and equally wealthy NBA players flanked him. His Caucasian bride had a pale, Scandinavian look—as did all five bridesmaids. There was not one visible black female face in the photograph. Not mother, sister, aunt, nor cousin.

No knight in shining armor would ever rescue a black woman.

Victoria had vowed to never again attempt to take a shortcut to a fresh air, tree-lined environment. She'd wait until her own ship came in.

But it hadn't. It was supposed to come in with a cargo of gold and platinum records, Grammy awards, and her image on the cover of dozens of magazines. She was supposed to have all those trappings of a successful music career, along with a healthy bank account and portfolio as well. Victoria thought of Justice Martin and was surprised that her rage was finally beginning to dissipate. She hadn't forgiven him, she doubted if she ever could, but at least she was able to get through a day without fanta-sizing about putting a bullet through his head.

She spread out on the kitchen table the money that it had taken only three days to earn. Minus the twenty-five dollars a day she paid the babysitter, carfare and other miscellaneous expenses, Victoria counted nine hundred and twenty dollars. The sight and smell of all those large bills made her heart race. She'd been making do with so little for so long. But no more. The weekend had just begun and she couldn't wait to get back to work.

At 13th Street the trolley came to a halt. Victoria bounded the stairs that led to the corner of 13th and Market. She felt irritated and personally offended as she breezed through the entrance of the former John Wanamaker's department store. Wanamaker's, a landmark, a part of local retail history, a part of her life, had changed overnight and had become Lord and Taylor. This violation, Victoria felt, had stolen the grace and elegance that the great stone building had possessed.

She strode into the store ready to do battle with the uppity Lord and Taylor staff. Once, when she had shopped at the City Line Avenue store, she had not been treated well. The sales clerks, or associates as they now were called, had looked past Victoria, eager to assist the Caucasian clientele, but Victoria had made a fuss, and insisted that it was her turn. She had never returned because it was draining to have to wield a sword while shopping.

But on this day, armed with nine hundred tax-free dollars, and the where-with-all to make much more, she defied any of the so-called associates to try to snub her.

Victoria stepped onto the escalator and rode to the Intimate Apparel department on the third floor. She needed something new for work. She passed the girdles and other painfully confining body armor that was cleverly advertised as body shapers. Feeling irrationally annoyed that any woman would buy that crap instead of exercising, Victoria sucked her teeth and whisked by. She approached rows of delicate pastel items, and paused to touch an incredibly soft peach tunic. The label inside read 100% raw silk. It cost one hundred and fifty dollars, which was much,

much more than she intended to pay. She surveyed other dainty little stringed things but soon realized that the articles that attracted her were more suitable for a romantic evening at home than her seedy work place.

Amid the racks of tasteful apparel she discovered a fanciful line of lingerie, glitzy and glamorous and a tad bit sleazy. Perfect!

Victoria chose a shimmering pale green two-piece bra and panty set with a sixty-dollar price tag. Glittery fringes fell down the front of the thong back panties. Identical fringes decorated the bottom of the push-up bra. As she sorted through the rack she noticed that the outfits became bolder and sassier. She wanted everything she saw, but limited herself to buying only two selections. A seventy-nine dollar dramatic Asian red camisole with red ostrich feather and matching G-string caught her eye. Standing before a mirror, she held the outfit up in front of her. She liked what she saw. The thought of posing at the door in either of the provocative outfits gave her an adrenaline rush.

"Cash or charge?" The sales person looked like a mannequin.

Victoria replied, "Cash," and then pulled out a wad of money. The wad, too thick to fit inside her wallet, was held together by a rubber band. She peeled off seven twenty-dollar bills, which the sales person regarded with a sigh and a frown. Victoria put the money on the counter.

"Do you have a problem with cash?" Victoria challenged.

"Oh no, not at all." The woman gave a nervous laugh and carefully folded and wrapped the purchases in tissue paper and placed the items in a bag. She rang up the sale, snatched the money from the counter and slid Victoria her change—a five-dollar bill, which Victoria placed in her old leather wallet. Victoria hadn't realized just how worn her wallet was until she noticed an ever so slight scowl form on the sales woman's face.

All eyes turned suspiciously on the Lord and Taylor bag when Victoria arrived at work.

"What did you buy, Pleasure?" asked a naked Sydney.

Victoria didn't think she'd ever get used to the immodesty of her white co-workers. They traipsed about completely nude and struck up conversations as if they were fully clad. Well, call her repressed, but Victoria found it as uncomfortable to view their nudity today as she had back in the locker room in junior high school. There she and her black classmates made the startling discovery that white girls had no problems with nudity. While the black girls hid behind towels, and jumped back into their clothing as quickly as possible, the white girls proudly paraded around naked. Laughing, talking, blow-drying their hair, all completely naked.

Sydney threw back her carelessly tousled hair and waited for Victoria to indulge her curiosity.

"I bought something to work in." Victoria averted her gaze. She wondered why Sydney and the others were so impressed with her purchases. Surely they could shop wherever they pleased. Victoria couldn't get over how cheap and tacky her co-workers seemed to be. One would think with the amount of money made at Pandora's Box, her co-workers would dress a hell of a lot better, that they'd have expensive jewelry, or better cars or luxury apartments. But as far as she could tell, aside from Arianna and a few others, that was not the case. Most of the girls wore cheap clothes, rode public transportation and lived in fifty-dollar a night transient hotels. She wondered if they were all on drugs.

Victoria went into a vacant room to change and swished back into the lounge. She looked and felt great in the pale green-fringed set.

"Where'd you buy that?" Arianna asked in a snippy tone.

"Didn't you notice my bag, everyone else did." Victoria matched her snippiness.

"I know you bought it at Lord and Taylor. Which one? City Line Avenue or King of Prussia?"

Victoria softened. "Neither. I went to the 13th and Market store."

"That figures. It's so tacky there. As far as I'm concerned the store has the name but none of the class."

Weary of dealing with a succession of combative personalities, Victoria had no response to Arianna's remark. Provoking hatred seemed to be Arianna's goal in life.

Chapter 7

S aturday morning. Victoria awakened feeling groggy with a foul taste in her mouth from a night of drinking with the girls. She needed coffee before she could even consider picking up Jordan, whose energy level was bound to be full force. Most of the time she was able to subdue him with TV and videos; he had a collection of beloved Disney cartoons, and he'd watched *Spiderman*, *Shrek*, and *Monsters, Inc.* over and over. But he was a rambunctious boy; he needed open space, fresh air, and some sunshine. If she could get rid of the grogginess, she'd take him out today.

Victoria stumbled around the kitchen; it was an obstacle course. She attempted to navigate, but stumbled into the assortment of receptacles scattered throughout the kitchen. She checked the buckets, and was surprised they were empty. Craning, she looked up at the exposed pipes in the ceiling. No leaks today! She gathered the unsightly containers and put them away. Every now and then she was able to enjoy her coffee without the annoying drip, drip, drip.

On the previous night one of Victoria's new co-workers, Lauren, a sweet-faced blonde, had smuggled in a six-pack of beer and a bottle of chilled Asti. Victoria had turned down the beer but eagerly accepted the sweet sparkling wine. After work she had gone out to unwind and drank even more. Now she was hung over.

Victoria had been surprised when Lauren invited her, along with Chelsea and Sydney, to one of the vacant session rooms to share in a celebration of her boyfriend's pending return from India.

Lauren and Victoria started the celebration without the other two. Chelsea hadn't changed from her street clothes and Sydney was in the office tending to some business with Rover.

"I don't really know you," Lauren said, hopping up on the bed and looking intently at Victoria, who sat across from her in the chair. She offered Victoria a plastic cup, "but you seem nice, not rowdy like some…" her voice trailed off. She nodded her head toward the closed door, indicating Miquon, Victoria presumed.

"What did you say you're celebrating?" Victoria asked, taking a sip.

Lauren lit a cigarette before answering. "I was engaged to this guy from India," Lauren spoke in a whisper.

It was hard to picture pale Lauren with a dark-skinned person.

"His family is very wealthy. We were living together…we had a beautiful apartment on Delaware Avenue, by the river. The view was fabulous. At night you could see the fucking lights on the Ben Franklin Bridge. It was awesome. Raj…my fiancé, was so good to me, Pleasure. He gave me everything."

Victoria shifted uncomfortably and took another big swallow of Asti. She hadn't gotten used to her own alias.

"He gave me this." Lauren caressed a hollow gold heart that hung from a delicate gold chain. "The heart and the chain are both 18K," Lauren said reverently.

"It's beautiful," Victoria, responded, nodding for Lauren to go on with the story.

"And this is nothing compared to the jewelry locked in my safe deposit box. I've got a strand of pearls, a diamond and emerald choker, a two-carat diamond ring, all kinds of stuff that would just freak you out!"

Feeling a pleasant buzz from the Asti, Victoria decided that she liked Lauren. Lauren had a girlish exuberance that was endearing, non-threatening.

"I never wear my jewelry; it's too expensive. Where would I wear it anyway?" As an afterthought she added, "Oh! I also have a full-length mink. I'll wear it to work one day to show you. It looks so cool when I wear it with my jeans."

Victoria gave Lauren a kind smile. The necklace really was beautiful and looked incredibly expensive and Victoria didn't doubt that the girl had more and better goods locked away. But there was a sadness about Lauren that no amount of baubles and beads could take away.

"Raj is coming back, and we're going to get married." Lauren had a dreamy look in her eyes. In the dimly lit room she seemed to have an ethereal glow and reminded Victoria of the pictures of white baby angels she had seen as a child in Nana's enormous, frayed Bible.

"His parents thought that separating us would kill the relationship. But we love each other more than ever. They even went so far as to pick out a bride for Raj, told him they'd disinherit him if he married me. He had to obey his parents. That's their custom." She sadly shrugged her shoulders.

"So what happened to his bride? Did he burn her? That's their custom too!" Victoria couldn't resist throwing that in. She giggled wickedly, and then chastised herself. Dowry deaths and bride burning in India was a serious issue for the women in that country, an age-old custom that was finally getting some international exposure. In her normal state, Victoria would never joke about such a thing. She blamed her morbid humor on the sparkling wine.

"What?" Lauren twisted her face into a grimace. She apparently hadn't heard about bride burning in India.

"Just kidding. Go on."

"I don't know what happened. He just called and said he was coming home." Lauren hesitated a moment before continuing in a flat tone. "My life fell apart when Raj left, but now he's coming back." She brightened. "He sent me the most beautiful silk robe..." The smile left her face. "But I made the mistake of bringing it here and someone lifted it from my bag. We're surrounded by thieves, you know," she confided.

Victoria nodded. "So how'd you meet this guy, Raj?" Victoria struggled to look serious, but she wanted to burst out laughing when she imagined Raj as a snake charmer, sitting cross-legged in a white turban, blowing a flute or whatever they blew. The Asti was making her silly.

"I met him here."

"Here! He was a customer?"

"Yep. And when we met, it was like we already knew each other. He didn't want the normal kind of session; he just wanted to talk." Lauren snapped open a beer, threw back her head, her long pale hair swept the towel on the bed; she guzzled down an enormous amount. She dabbed at the corner of her mouth, looking rather proud of the feat. Then her expression turned serious. "Look, I'm a white girl from Northeast Philly. Where I come from, white girls date white guys, only. Before meeting Raj, you couldn't have told me that I'd get involved with someone from—of all places, New Delhi. Sounds like a weird place from a geography book, right? I mean who actually knows anyone from there?"

Lauren took another swig, this one, modest. And Victoria poured more wine in the plastic cup.

"Raj changed my life. He took me out of the business and treated me like a little princess." The word *little* made Victoria pause. On the chubby side, Lauren could be described as voluptuous. She was cute. But *little* she was not.

There were three soft knocks at the door. Lauren cracked the door to make sure Rover wasn't on the other side. It was Sydney.

"Damn. What happened to the Asti?" Sydney asked, holding up the nearly empty bottle.

Victoria smiled sheepishly.

"What took you so long?" Lauren asked, cutting her eyes at the bottle of Asti. She cocked her head, surprised that Victoria had drunk so much. "Here, Sydney, have a beer," Lauren said soothingly.

"I don't like warm beer."

"Oh, stop complaining, it's still cold. I was telling Pleasure about Raj and how his family tried to break us up."

"Tried? Why the hell do you think he went back to India—to open a 7-11?" Sydney said maliciously.

"You're not funny." Lauren frowned.

Victoria thought the 7-11 joke was hilarious, but managed to keep a straight face. Sydney didn't deserve even a faint smile from her. Sydney was one of the white girls who rudely twirled on her heels, retreating to the lounge whenever a black customer appeared at the door.

Victoria observed the two girls. They were both at least ten years younger than she and yet she was being included in their silly conversation. It had been sort of okay listening to Lauren's sorrowful love story, but putting up with the bickering between the two of them was wearing her patience thin. Victoria politely excused herself and rejoined the others-the rowdy crowd in the lounge.

After work that night, with five hundred dollars added to her bankroll, and needing to unwind, Victoria had agreed to go out for drinks with Chelsea and Jonee. Business had been good for the three of them. They took a cab to a bar on South Street and sat at the bar talking shop, drinking, and eating greasy appetizers until last call.

Desperate men, out to score and unable to comprehend the women's lack of interest, had at first smiled flirtatiously, then growing bolder, sent drinks with a wink and asked to join them. But the last thing any of the weary women wanted was to be in the company of a lonely, horny man.

❦

As soon as Victoria finished her coffee, water gushed from the ceiling. Instead of getting the buckets and pans, she ran for the tall trash container, and pulled out the filled plastic bag, and positioned it under the leak. In a matter of seconds, there was a major rusty puddle on the kitchen floor. Victoria's slippers were soaked.

It was definitely time to start apartment hunting. Victoria opened the newspaper and searched for the real estate section, but somehow, ended up with the automobiles for sale section in her hands. She scanned the section and made red circles around the blocks of print that listed car prices that she could afford. She had twelve hundred dollars to play with.

Actually, the urge for a car was not sudden. It had been in the back of her mind. Who would watch Jordan when she moved out of the neighborhood? She liked her current babysitter and rationalized that she would need a car to transport Jordan back and forth.

Suddenly, it occurred to her that she had mentally swerved all around the subject of getting on with her life. She was making plans for a car, an apartment, as if she'd come up with an appropriate way to maintain herself and her son.

She knew with certainty that she'd never have a singing career. There was no strength left to pursue that far-fetched dream. But she was resisting the idea of going out and seeking a "real" job. The thought of clerical work made her want to cry. But what else was she trained to do? She could go to college, she thought optimistically. Then, her negative mind asked: To be what? The answer was as elusive as her long-lost dream and the thought of the energy needed to pick herself up and begin again, made her very, very tired.

The twelve hundred dollars that was tucked safely away in her bureau drawer along with the big recording studio bill, and a myriad of smaller bills, provided little solace. Victoria needed more. Much more. And she knew where to get it. The place that was supposed to be a temporary means of income was becoming a bizarre safe haven. It kept her hidden from inquiring friends who left anxious messages on her answering machine. *What's going on Victoria? Are you okay? You never return my calls. Did you sign that record deal yet?*

Pandora's Box, undetected by the mainstream, was an underworld. And like a magnet, it pulled in the misfits of society, the disillusioned, and the emotionally impaired.

It was a place where money flowed freely through the hands of wounded souls. It was where she belonged, at least for now.

Still hung over, but guilt ridden, Victoria decided to take Jordan out.

"I don't wanna go to no mooseum; I wanna go to Discovery Zone. Please, Mommy?"

"The Please Touch Museum is just for kids. You'll have fun," she cajoled. Then, feeling the need to be stern like her Nana, she changed her tone. "Look, we don't have to go anywhere. We can just stay home if you don't want to go."

"Okay," Jordan pouted. "Can we go to DZ next time?"

"DZ?"

"Yeah, Discovery Zone." Jordan's laughter was filled with pride. He knew something his mother didn't know.

"As soon as we get a car. We can't get to Discovery Zone on public transportation."

Jordan looked at his mother quizzically.

"Trolleys, buses, the subway-that's considered public transportation because it's available to the public," Victoria explained.

"Are we the public?" he asked with a fearful look.

"Well...yes," Victoria stammered. She wanted to be a responsible parent despite her secret life and despite the fact that she hadn't had enough sleep and her head was pounding. It was, therefore, darn considerate of her, she felt, to take her son anywhere. No one could blame her for being unwilling to provide a lengthy explanation. "Jordan, let's start getting ready, okay? I'll explain what public means later," she said testily.

"Mommy, can Stevie go with us?"

"No, Jordan. This is quality time for me and you." She was in no mood to put up with another child.

"Is Stevie the public?" Jordan asked, looking suspicious.

"No, Jordan...I mean... Stop asking me so many questions." Victoria hoped she wasn't damaging Jordan's psyche by her refusal to answer his numerous questions.

❦

Victoria held her son's hand as they exited the trolley on 22nd Street. The museum was a couple of blocks away. Pandora's Box was also nearby. Victoria wondered if she looked like a normal mother out with her child. Or did she exhibit telltale signs of her decadent behavior?

They arrived at the museum and Jordan loved it. Victoria couldn't pull him away from an old-fashioned trolley car exhibit. He and a group of newfound friends tirelessly boarded the immobile trolley, pretending to be passengers. The children took turns being the driver. Jordan beamed when it was his own turn and Victoria smiled back at her son. She patiently helped him dress in an authentic SEPTA uniform that included a cap, requisite attire to drive the trolley car.

Jordan scampered from one activity to the next with Victoria trailing, snapping pictures. Impatiently he'd pose while his mother fooled around with the orange light on the disposable camera.

Exhausted from trying to keep up with her exuberant son, Victoria took a break. She sat down on a child-sized chair and breathed a satisfying sigh. Her son was having a cultural experience while simultaneously busy at play. She felt like a good mother.

The other parents came in pairs, she noticed. Most were white. They wore pleasantly patient expressions, and their responses to their children's questions were lengthy and in depth. She promised herself that she would start having more patience with Jordan.

Victoria wondered how the happy couples would respond if they knew her secret. Then she gave a wry laugh. The husbands all looked like customers at the massage parlor. She imagined all those seemingly wholesome fathers flocking to Pandora's after depositing their unsuspecting families back in suburbia.

Victoria glanced at her watch. It was 2:30. Time to go if she planned on getting a nap before work.

"Jordan, come on honey," she called. "Let's get ready. We have to go."

"Aw, Mom," he whined. "I didn't even get to play store yet." Jordan pointed to a table where a slew of kids were lining up, pretending to purchase miniature canned goods, boxes of cereal, waxed vegetables and fruit. A little girl was tallying up the order on a toy cash register.

"Honey," Victoria cupped her son's face. "It's getting late; Mommy has to go to work later. We can come back another time."

"Are you going to go to work all night long again, Mommy?" he asked loudly.

Victoria felt a tinge of embarrassment and guilt. She looked around to see if anyone had heard. "You know I work at night, Jordan. That's why you sleepover at Stevie's."

"I don't want to stay all night at Stevie's house no more."

"Why, Jordan?" There was panic in Victoria's eyes.

"Because he only wants to watch *The Cartoon Network* and I want to watch *Toon Disney*."

Victoria relaxed. With all the child abuse and molestation stories in the news, she was terrified of what Jordan might say. She reminded herself to talk to Jordan again, to reinforce what she'd already told him about inappropriate touching.

Chapter 8

"Gabrielle left a message for you. You can't work tonight. You have to leave," Rover announced in his dry, gravelly voice. A slight smile betrayed the pleasure he derived from delivering the message.

There was a trail of white shoe prints from the hall to the middle of the floor where Miquon stood—half in, half out of her snow-dusted coat. Stunned for a few seconds, she didn't move, one arm poised, mid-air. Then she sighed and put her arm back into the dangling sleeve.

"What? What are you accusing me of now?" Miquon demanded.

"You know the rules. If you don't work the slow days, you can't come running in here on the weekend."

"I was here all week," she protested.

"Not according to my records. What happened to you on Monday?"

Miquon looked bewildered, squinted in thought, then said, "Oh yeah! Monday...I called out because my babysitter got sick. I told you that, Rover."

"That's not my problem; you know the rules," he said, firmly.

"Well why the fuck ain't you say something last night? Why you wait 'til now? I can't believe I wasted my time coming out in this snow and shit. This is fucked up!"

Miquon scanned the room, looking for support.

And though there was great interest in the outcome of her predicament, no one met her gaze. There was the typical frenetic activity of preparing for the long night ahead. The floor was strewn with articles of clothing; lingerie draped the arms of chairs.

"It's not my decision. Take it up with Gabrielle," Rover said.

"How can I? That bitch ain't ever here!"

A collective gasp filled the room. Victoria had never met or spoken a word to this all-powerful Gabrielle, but even she knew that Miquon had crossed the line.

"Yeah, I'll let Gabrielle know how you feel," Rover replied.

Hurling a string of curses, Miquon blew out the door.

No one felt sympathetic. There was one less girl. The chatter resumed. The general consensus was that Miquon would probably be fired because Gabrielle didn't tolerate disrespect.

Victoria cut her eyes at Jonee. Jonee winked at her, indicating that she too, was glad to be rid of the loud, abrasive girl who was usually behind the constant bickering, the infighting that occurred daily.

Saturday night was a mob scene; twelve women had shown up to work. The lounge was in total disarray, with the women stepping over each other trying to get ready in the confined space of the lounge. Some had to dress in the restroom, while others readied themselves in the three vacant session rooms.

The doorbell rang in the midst of the chaos. Jonee, wearing turquoise contact lenses and honey blonde hair piled high, led the pack of women in the frantic rush to the door. Without hesitation, the client, a pudgy Caucasian with flecks of gray at his temples and mustache, chose Jonee.

The white girls, indignant as the black girls when it came to race disloyalty, grumbled to themselves.

Inside the room, the client handed Jonee two hundred dollar bills and winked. Her lips spread into a wide grin. The hundred dollar tip was extremely generous.

There was a pounding on the door.

"Who is it?" Jonee demanded, annoyed.

"Do you see my Lancôme bag in there?" It was Sydney.

"No, I don't. Now would you please leave me alone!"

Jonee could hear Sydney complaining about her bag to Rover and within seconds there was another knock at the door.

"I don't believe this shit," she complained to her client. "What now?" she yelled to the closed door.

The response was from Rover. "Sorry for the inconvenience, but I have to let Sydney look for her bag."

"I'll be right back," Jonee promised her client. He had begun to disrobe and looked perplexed. Jonee waved her hand, indicating that he should continue. She stepped outside the door, closing it behind her, careful not to let the client see Sydney, who stood beside Rover. She didn't want the trick to change his mind and choose Sydney.

"Rover, can't this wait until after my session?"

"No it can't because all my money is in that bag," Sydney shot back. "I know I left it in there when I ran to the door, and it better still be in there."

"It's not my fault that you can't keep up with your shit. My customer is waiting, Rover. Can I get back to my session?"

"I'm sorry Jonee. She claims she had a lot of money in her make-up bag. You know I'm not supposed to let the girls get dressed in the session rooms, but it was so crowded tonight, I had to. I could get in a lot of trouble if this gets back to Gabrielle."

Inside the room with Jonee and the client, whose nakedness was covered by a towel, Sydney fluttered Maybelline lashes and greeted the man with a breathy, "Hi." She peeked under the pillows and patted around the bed. The client's eyes bounced off her jiggling breasts. When Sydney bent down to look under the bed, her butt, adorned with a temporary tattoo— a pair of lips, was aimed at the client's face. He was mesmerized.

"Look, your shit's not in here, so would you hurry up and leave?" Jonee spoke through clenched teeth.

"I thought it was in here," Sydney replied, sending the client a look of distress. "I don't know where it could be."

Gripping the towel that barely covered his wide frame, the man assisted Sydney in the search for her bag. And though it wasn't likely that her bag would be found beneath his clothing, he grabbed a handful of his things and one-by-one, shook each article of clothing.

"Uh, I think I've changed my mind," he stammered. "Can I see her?" He nudged his head toward Sydney.

"You can't change girls in the middle of the session." Jonee was livid.

"But we didn't start, I..." the customer stammered.

Sydney cut in. "He can see any girl he chooses and you know it, Jonee." There was a policy at Pandora's that allowed a customer the option to switch girls if he did so before the session started. Jonee left the room in defeat. Humiliated, she reentered the lounge.

The white girls regarded Jonee with smirks. The black girls shook their heads sympathetically.

Remarkably, Saturday night was not the big money night Victoria had expected. After waiting five torturous hours, she finally got a customer, a weasel of a man, who without warning, went into character as soon as the session began. He pretended to be a naughty student.

Aside from being extremely short, he seemed normal. Victoria was stunned when his voice tone abruptly changed to whiny and childlike. She was taken completely off guard when he began whimpering and pleading for her forgiveness. His homework, he said, had not been completed. The little man cowered ridiculously, as if he expected Victoria to start slapping him around at any moment.

Her mind screamed, *Oh my God, he's crazy!* But she remained calm, and responded in a no-nonsense tone.

At first her improvised dialogue sounded awkward, but within a few minutes she assumed the role of a stern schoolmistress with surprising ease. It was a weird session and some dark part of her actually enjoyed it! Her customer left, promising to study harder.

Victoria rejoined the girls in the lounge, feeling elated to have earned fifty dollars so easily. She disclosed the nature of the encounter to Jonee, who frowned with disapproval.

"I hope you charged him extra."

"For what? I didn't really do anything but pretend to be his teacher."

"Yeah, and that's extra. That's considered S&M."

"S&M! I wasn't in there with whips and chains... And there was no sex involved. We just talked, role-played.

"So what. That cheap bastard got over. He got a dominance session for the price of a regular one. You better wise up, girl. Don't be letting these tricks trick you. Why do you think they're called tricks?"

Victoria was sorry she confided in Jonee. The woman was obviously still fuming over the incident with Sydney.

"Here's an example," Jonee continued to Victoria's deep regret. "It can be slow as hell in here and you haven't had a session all night. Then all of a sudden, one of your regulars shows up. You break out in the biggest grin 'cause you're about to get paid. But when you need him the most, what does that mothafucka do? He'll act just like he don't know your ass, and pick somebody else."

Victoria gazed at Jonee but didn't know what to say, so she shook her head in sympathy at the injustice of it all.

Following a lengthy silence, Jonee said, "You can't trust a trick. That's why I treat 'em all like dirt! You can't believe a word they tell you. And I've heard it all: 'You're the prettiest girl here. How did someone as nice as you...? I think I'm falling in love.' Girl, don't believe their bullshit."

Victoria chuckled. In the short time she'd been in the business, she'd already heard those lines, and had been flattered by them.

"To tell you the truth," Jonee said, "I think most tricks hate us."

"Hate us! I suppose they express that hatred by giving us their money."

"They don't *give* us a damn thing! They pay for a service they think should be free. They hate having to pay, which makes them hate us. Girl, tricks ain't shit!"

Chapter 9

Reds arrived early for the midnight shift and plopped down in a seat near Victoria. She tried to strike up a conversation but was discouraged by Victoria's monosyllabic responses. Victoria wore the familiar expression of a girl who'd had a bad night. And it served her right, thought Reds. It was about time the uppity bitch had a taste of reality and experienced the sting of going home empty-handed. For Reds, going home broke was not unusual.

"I'm gonna ask Rover if we can stay for the next shift."

Victoria looked at Jonee and smiled sadly. "I don't want to. I'm tired of sitting in here. I just want to go home."

"Our luck should change at midnight."

"Why?"

"Because it's technically a new day."

"You have an answer for everything," Victoria replied.

"C'mon, girl. Don't give up."

"Okay," Victoria said with a deep sigh. "Ask Rover if I can stay."

"I think I should change my hair." Jonee pulled a long braided wig out of her bag.

With Jonee distracted, Reds sidled up to Victoria.

"What happened, didn't you break luck?" Reds asked Victoria, her voice filled with phony concern.

"Yeah, but I only had one customer."

"Only one?" Reds said sarcastically. "When you learn how to work it, one can be more than enough."

Exhausted from having sat around watching others make money, Victoria couldn't come up with a snappy retort.

"Don't pay her any attention," Jonee said when Reds walked away. "She's jealous because you're a moneymaker, and…"

"A what?"

"A moneymaker. A girl the customers like."

"Oh," Victoria said with a smile. The compliment lifted her a little, but with only fifty dollars in her purse, she didn't feel much like a moneymaker.

"Reds used to be a moneymaker too," Jonee whispered. "Now she can't make a dime and she's jealous of everybody, especially new girls. If she stopped counting everybody else's money and started worrying about her own, maybe she could make enough dough to buy some new gear." Jonee now spoke in a voice loud enough for Reds to overhear. "Tricks get tired of seeing her tired ass wearin' the same old funky shit everyday."

"She can hear you, Jonee," Victoria cautioned.

"Who cares?" Jonee's voice grew louder. "Old ass bitch always fuckin' with people 'cause she's so miserable. She needs to give it up and retire."

Victoria glanced at Reds and gave a nervous chuckle.

"How come some folks just don't know when to quit?" Jonee asked with a malicious grin.

"I'm not in this conversation, Jonee. Stop being so mean," Victoria admonished, still chuckling.

Reds was sorry she had opened her mouth. She had perceived Victoria as being too soft to retaliate verbally, but she hadn't expected Jonee to butt in. Reds knew better than to confront Jonee, whose razor sharp tongue could rip her to shreds. She began fussing with her hair and pretended not to hear the words that cut to the core.

Dominique arrived fifteen minutes before the midnight shift began.

"Those two are working on our shift tonight," Reds informed Dominique. "Did Gabrielle call?"

"Not that I know of. Rover gave 'em permission."

"I am so sick of his bullshit," Dominique raved as she slipped on a spandex bodysuit. "He needs to stop trying to run my shift."

"You ought to take it up with Rover," Reds suggested.

The doorbell rang and Dominique took the first customer of the night. She tossed Victoria and Jonee a triumphant look as she ushered the man to a session room.

Victoria got the next customer.

Reds and Jonee sat alone in the lounge, ignoring each other. Reds feared that Jonee would get the next customer and she'd be left to wait alone, unwanted.

It was so unfair! Reds sank dejectedly into her seat. She peered into a mirror and began vigorously applying mascara to her lashes, thrusting the wand in and out of the pink and green tube. A fleck of mascara popped out and landed on the skin near her eye. Reds wet her little finger with her tongue and dabbed at the spot, careful of the delicate skin where tiny crow's feet clustered.

Dominique suddenly appeared in the lounge, barefoot and naked beneath a frayed towel. Reds looked up, curious and grateful for the distraction.

"He wants a double," Dominique whispered to Reds.

Reds brightened.

"He wanted to see me get it on with a white girl, but I don't have any white girls working tonight, so I had to convince him to see another black girl. He asked me to get her." Dominique nodded to Jonee, and the bright look left Reds' face. "But I told him he'd be wasting his money because these new girls are nothing but amateurs. I said, 'Look, if you want the real thing, you better stick with the pros.'"

"How much is he tipping?" Reds asked sadly, knowing she'd be burdened with the brunt of the work.

"He's gonna tip you a hundred," Dominique said without mentioning what she was being tipped.

Reds followed Dominique down the hall to the room. She was certain that Dominique had worked out a deal that would pay her a lot more than a lousy one hundred dollars. Still, it was good money and an excellent way to start the night.

Inside the room, Dominique let the towel fall to the floor. The beefy white man was sitting on the bed snorting cocaine that was lined up on the bottom of a tissue box. He passed the box to Dominique and turned his attention to Reds.

"My name's Bob, baby girl. What do they call you?" Reds was taken aback by his thick southern accent.

"How you doin'? My name's Reds."

With furrowed brows and serious tone, the man asked, "Is that hair of yours red all over?"

It was a tired line, but Reds nodded seductively.

Bob reached for Reds and grabbing the bottom of her camisole, he jerked her toward him. "Come on out of them clothes and let me see that peach fuzz."

Annoyed by the rough treatment, Reds pulled away. But when she noticed a scowl forming on Bob's face, she shrewdly lowered the camisole's thin strap and attempted to tantalize him by slowly undressing. Normally, Reds would have dimmed the light to conceal her bodily flaws, but Bob was so coked up and disgusting, she didn't bother. Now naked, she joined him on the bed. She hoped to seduce him into forgetting his expressed desire to see two women in action.

Reds ran her fingers through her thinning reddish-brown pubic hairs. Thanks to L'Oreal, the hair on her head was a bright red. She stroked Bob's flaccid penis, determined to will it back to life.

"Don't worry about him baby girl. His lazy ass done went to sleep." Bob lightly flicked his penis. "Yeah, that little fella's plum tuckered out."

"I've been know to raise the dead," Reds said in a voice that sounded sexier than she felt. From the little plastic pouch he was holding, she used a single long fingernail to retrieve a small amount of cocaine. She smoothed it over his sagging phallus and made little flicks with the tip of her tongue, teasing around the head, and then licking the length of his shaft. But it remained limp. Undaunted, she curled her tongue around the cool, soft flesh and drew it into her mouth. Reds was old school. During her prime, working girls only used condoms to prevent pregnancy. That was before herpes and HIV and anything else a dose of penicillin couldn't cure, and she'd done a little bit of everything you could possibly do sexually and, miraculously, had never contracted anything. But times had changed. She knew she should be more careful, and in most cases she was. But tonight she was willing to risk it. Bob looked healthy enough. She had to get him hot, horny and hard so that he'd forget about the two-girl thing. She wanted to make him come quickly so that she could collect her money and get the hell out of there.

Reds covered Bob's private with her mouth. Her head bobbed up and down vigorously, her long, wiry red hair brushed against his thighs, tickling them. Trying to appeal to his auditory senses, Reds alternated between moaning and making loud, slurping sounds.

Dominique and Bob exchanged a look of amusement. He pointed a finger at Reds as she diligently worked on him.

Finally, Bob patted Reds on the head. "Okay, all right, Carrot Top. You get an E for effort. But like I said, that ol' boy is dead to the world."

Bob and Dominique snickered in cahoots when Reds came up for air. Then Bob's expression turned cold and serious.

"I'm paying good money to have some fun. So come on Peach Fuzz, let's get this party started."

At that moment, Dominique, who was standing beside the cot, threw one long leg on the bed, tapping it with her pointed toe. Reds knew what was expected of her. Reluctantly, she caressed Dominique's foot.

"Kiss it!" Dominique demanded, she tapped her toe impatiently.

Dominique fancied herself a dominatrix and had a clientele of adoring masochists who returned repeatedly for the mental anguish and physical pain she loved to deliver.

Since Dominique had so graciously shared the session with Reds, Reds would have to show her gratitude by assuming a submissive role.

It wasn't as if Reds didn't know what was in store for her when she accepted the session, but that didn't stop her from hoping that the three of them would engage in a regular menage-à-trois.

Reds hadn't snorted in a week. Not by choice, but due to lack of funds.

She had relied solely on liquor to get her through each day. But clearly she needed some extra help to get through this ordeal.

"I need a hit, Dominique?" She formed the words as a question.

Dominique handed Reds the rolled up bill and the tissue box. Two lines quickly disappeared. Then Dominique sprinkled cocaine over her toes.

Bob's eyes lit up. "Now that's kinky! Get over there, Peach Fuzz!" he said excitedly. "Lap it up, girl. Come on!" With a glazed look he settled back, his head propped up with a pillow, ready to direct the show if necessary.

Chapter 10

The handsome young black guy wearing a Rocawear jacket, matching knitted cap, and Timberland boots chose Victoria. His equally handsome and well-dressed buddy picked Jonee. The pair resembled urban-wear models, or rappers. Or, as Victoria strongly suspected, drug dealers.

Jonee had been right; their luck had changed. The young guy was Victoria's fourth customer and it was only 3:30 a.m.

She wondered why two handsome young men would come out in the middle of the night, in the freezing cold, to pay for sex?

The young man introduced himself as Kareem.

"My name is Pleasure," she said with a sincere smile. "How are you, Kareem?" The money in her purse had changed Victoria's mood from somber to gay.

"I'm doin' all right," Kareem said looking her up and down and nodding with approval as he dug into the pocket of his baggy jeans.

"Two Benjamins should cover it, right?" Kareem grinned confidently as he handed Victoria two hundred dollar bills.

"What's the extra hundred for?" Victoria instantly wanted to take back the words that Jonee would certainly frown upon.

"For your pleasure, Pleasure," he said with a wink, which made Victoria blush.

She couldn't get over how long and dark his lashes were. Damn, he was fine! Not at all like the sad-looking patrons she was accustomed to. His good looks influenced her to behave demurely. Speaking softly, Victoria excused herself and took the money to Dominique.

Today's youth were a mystery. The crude street jargon and the thuggish behavior were disgusting. Victoria viewed them as angry, disrespectful hellions, and she made it a point to steer clear of them, avoiding places where they gathered, such as the corner deli in her neighborhood where 40-ounce bottles of malt liquor were the most frequently purchased items. That lack of respect was apparent in the way they dressed and in their music. Profanity had become acceptable speech in rap music—and the way women were referred to as bitches and hoes was unconscionable. To think that her music was deemed unacceptable, dated, non-commercial, while record companies rolled out the red carpet for hoodlums whose music boasted of criminal activities: selling drugs, robberies, killing sprees... Oh, but let me not go there, she reminded herself. The music industry's lack of good taste was of no concern to her.

Who was she to pass judgment? she asked herself. It wasn't as if she had room to talk, working in a bordello and all. So Victoria allowed her thoughts to return to the handsome young guy who was waiting for her. He seemed different. Maybe he wasn't a drug dealer. For all she knew, he could be a professional athlete, or... the hell with stereotyping, he could be a medical or law student, a congressman, or senator, a teacher, a preacher or any damn thing he wanted to be. Why, she chastised herself, did she label him a drug dealer?

Victoria avoided the eyes of a surly Reds when she went to the lounge. She gave the money to Dominique and rushed back to her cute customer.

Kareem had stripped down to his wide-striped boxers. He looked relaxed, as if he were lounging on his own bed. His jacket hung from a hook on the back of the door, his cap dangled from the doorknob. Seeing his cap made Victoria take notice of his hair. It was well groomed, cut close with neat, tiny waves trained to stay in place. The rest of his clothing was folded neatly on the chair. Though she couldn't see the label, Victoria supposed that his jeans sported the Rocawear label also.

Ready to take charge, Victoria said, "So tell me, Kareem, what brings you out in the middle of this cold, wintry night?" Her demure demeanor was gone. She was feeling playful. Flirtatious. Happy!

"I came out and in this treacherous weather," Kareem said with a teasing grin, "to meet the woman of my dreams."

Unprepared for his quick come back, Victoria cast her gaze downward; she felt her face flush.

She recovered and though it was difficult, she looked Kareem in the eye, determined to hold her own.

"Well, I'm glad you did because seeing you has made my night. Look at you! You're so cute..." She paused, enjoying watching him squirm. "With those pretty eyes...and mmm, I love your lips."

It was Kareem's turn to blush. Victoria watched as he involuntarily lowered those long lashes and self-consciously moistened his lips. She had disarmed him!

Her eyes ran the length of his body. His chest and arms were developed. Boldly, she placed a hand on his shoulder and turned him around. Not bad, she thought, blaming Evander Holyfield's beautiful back for her appreciation of a man's posterior view.

"Would you like a massage?" she asked, reaching for the baby oil. She wanted to touch his hard, young body. His taut, smooth chocolate skin looked edible.

"Nah, that's okay. I just want to look at you." Kareem gently pulled Victoria onto the bed.

"Hey, I like that," he said, indicating the red crushed velvet teddy she wore. "Red is definitely your color." Kareem touched the fabric lightly and ignited a spark. Victoria flinched. Without a word, he drew her into his arms, inhaled her. "You smell good too," he whispered into her neck. His lips moved up to her face. Victoria stiffened as she recalled one of the top rules of the working girls' code of conduct: never kiss a trick.

But throwing caution to the wind, Victoria offered her lips and clung to him. Her hands, with a will of their own, traveled Kareem's wide, muscular back-caressing, kneading, massaging, and all the while soothing her own aching heart.

The sexual encounter was intense, yet tender. And when it was over, instead of jumping up and darting out the door, Victoria nuzzled next to Kareem. Like lovers, with their bodies entwined, they lay together in the dark. She listened to his even breathing, feeling his chest rise and fall. And for this intimacy, shared with a stranger, Victoria would be eternally grateful.

There were three thumps on the door.

Kareem stirred. Victoria jumped.

"Time's up," Dominique said gruffly.

Victoria felt embarrassed. As if she'd done something wrong.

Feeling unsure of what had transpired between them, she smiled weakly at Kareem. She hoped she hadn't made a complete fool of herself.

Victoria noticed that Kareem no longer had the self-assured look he had earlier. There was no way to exit gracefully, so she grabbed a towel and wrapped it around her naked body and began gathering her belongings.

"Thank you, Kareem. I hope you'll come again." Her normal closing spiel sounded awkward and inappropriate.

"Yeah, I'm definitely coming back to see you again." Kareem nodded his head as he spoke, as if to reassure her.

Victoria detected tension when she returned to the lounge. Dominique and Reds mumbled under their breath, and Jonee wore a stony expression that suggested she too, was in a foul mood.

"What's up, girl?" Victoria asked Jonee, playfully speaking in street vernacular, but enunciating clearly.

"We got some mad hoes up in here tonight," Jonee announced.

"Angry at me?"

"Yeah, and I don't blame them. You can't be in there for a whole hour, with the room on lock-down. You wouldn't believe how many customers walked out because all the rooms were tied up."

"Was I supposed to kick my customer out to accommodate someone else?" Victoria snapped, rolling her eyes.

Jonee had not been introduced to the feisty side of Victoria and was visibly taken aback.

"And furthermore," Victoria raised her voice, turned and glared at Reds and Dominique, "if a customer is paying, I can spend the entire night in the room if I so desire and I don't need permission from any of you."

The women fell silent. Reds looked shocked as if she'd just been falsely accused.

Kareem appeared in the doorway of the lounge and beckoned Victoria. The lounge was strictly off-limits to customers, but with her eyes, and wearing one of her Nana's stern expressions, Victoria defied any of the women to say a word.

"Is it possible to see you outside?" Kareem asked as Victoria walked him to the lobby. "Can we go out sometime?"

She wanted to shout an emphatic yes, but realized that an involvement with Kareem could only add more confusion to her already complicated life. Victoria smiled sadly and shook her head no.

"I can respect that," he said. "I understand. So, uh, I guess the only way I'm gonna get to see you is if I come back here?"

Victoria nodded.

"When are you working again? Will you be here tomorrow?"

"No. This isn't my regular shift. I'll be here Monday night after five," Victoria said, while thinking: *Damn, Kareem must have money to burn.*

"Okay. I'm gonna try to get back on Monday." He brushed his hand across her face. "So tomorrow is your day off?"

"Yes. Why?"

"Just wondering." Kareem touched her chin with his finger. "Wanted to know, just in case you change your mind about going out with me."

"Yo, Kareem," his friend called from the lobby. "Come on, man. Let's roll! I've been out here freezin' my ass off while you in there tryin' to fall in love."

Kareem kissed Victoria on the cheek. She watched as he and his friend disappeared out the door.

Victoria made careful steps as she returned to the lounge. Trying to stay grounded wasn't easy for someone who was walking on air.

Chapter 11

V ictoria taught Jordan their telephone number, now it seemed every time she picked up the phone, he was on the other end. He'd call from the sitter's house immediately after being dropped off, then he'd call again early the next morning, awakening her long before she was ready to start the day. The endless phone calls were driving her crazy and Victoria could only pray that the novelty would soon wear off.

Around 10:30 Sunday morning, Victoria arrived home to a dark, silent apartment. The closed blinds did not allow any sunlight to filter in, making the apartment tomb-like, which Victoria, suffering from sleep deprivation, was grateful.

Though creaky and badly in need of a new mattress, Victoria's bed beckoned her. She couldn't wait to throw back the covers, slide in, and hopefully sleep uninterrupted for at least three hours. She'd have to call Charmaine and ask her to keep Jordan for another hour or two. She'd offer to pay extra, of course.

Peeling off layers of outerwear: hat, coat, scarf, and gloves, Victoria headed for the hall closet. As she passed her bedroom, she noticed that the red light of the answering machine blinked ominously. She was tempted to ignore it; she didn't want to hear anything from anyone. But she couldn't. There may have been an emergency; suppose something had happened to Jordan.

In a sudden panic, she pushed down the button to review the messages. There were three—all from Jordan. "Hi Mommy. Do you know who this is? It's me!"

While listening to the second message, Victoria could hear Jordan's friend, Stevie giggling in the background. "Hey Mom, when are you coming to get me?" And finally, the third: "Mommmmy! Hurry up! What's taking you so looong?"

Victoria erased the messages. She was annoyed and felt harassed; she held her babysitter responsible. Charmaine knew that she wasn't scheduled to pick Jordan up until noon, so why did she allow him to call incessantly?

There was no emergency; her son was okay, so Victoria forced thoughts of Jordan from her mind. She was in no mood to venture back out into the cold, nor was she in any condition for Jordan's high-spirited shenanigans.

Victoria pulled off her boots, then her socks and, as the tension gradually left her feet, her entire body began to relax. She slipped out of her jeans, but when she pulled her sweater over her head, she was overcome by the strong stench of cigarette smoke and other odors she associated with Pandora's Box. Aiming for the clothes hamper, she slung the offensive sweater out into the hallway. It reached its mark.

Victoria couldn't get into bed fast enough, but as tired as she was, she knew she wouldn't get a wink of sleep if she tried to crawl into bed without taking a shower.

Musing mindlessly she ran the water in the bathroom, she found herself thinking of Jordan, and tried to steer her thoughts in a different direction, but couldn't. She thought about the urgency in his voice, and his desire to be in his own home bothered her.

Abruptly, Victoria shut off the water, redressed, (substituting the befouled sweater for a clean one), threw her coat on and, feeling like a martyr, she trudged back out into cold, gray morning.

Mercifully, she didn't have to climb the stairs to Charmaine's third floor apartment. Soon after ringing the doorbell, like magic, she heard

Charmaine's door creak open and a few seconds later, Jordan and Stevie were bounding down the stairs. Dressed in a robe and slippers, Charmaine plodded slowly behind the rambunctious boys.

"Good morning," Charmaine said cheerfully as she swung the door open wide. "Good Lordy, it's cold out here. Hurry up, Jordan. I can't be holding this door open and letting all the heat out." She shivered dramatically and laughed.

Victoria grunted in response. It was as close as she could come to laughter. Barely keeping her eyes open, she was too exhausted to find anything funny.

"He ate a big breakfast: juice, pancakes, bacon and eggs," Charmaine said.

"Thanks, Charmaine." Victoria said flatly, hoping her eyes reflected the depth of her gratitude. In her current state, there was no way that she could possibly throw together anything remotely resembling a well-balanced meal. Charmaine was a lifesaver and a saint.

The twenty-degree temperature did not affect Jordan. In fact, he seemed invigorated by the blustery weather. On the walk home, Jordan took long running slides on the sheets of ice that covered the pavement.

"Look at me, Mommy! I'm ice skating."

Victoria tiptoed around the slippery pavement with her shoulders hunched against the cold, and her face buried in the scarf around her neck.

"Be careful, Jordan," she called out in a muffled voice.

Jordan's high level of energy continued at home. He zipped from room to room, yelling Mommy this and Mommy that.

They had been home for less than five minutes, and already Jordan had started to get on Victoria's nerves. The boy never walked calmly to get from point A to point B. He thumped, jumped, and ran everywhere.

Suddenly Victoria remembered the video she'd bought from Rover that was stuffed in her workbag. Eureka! She could calm and distract Jordan with a movie while she got a few desperately needed hours of sleep.

Rover didn't have Disney movies or any other kiddy movies, but he persuaded Victoria to buy an old movie he claimed to be a classic called *Robocop*. Rover said the movie was a futuristic thriller about a cop turned robot who keeps the peace in Detroit. He assured Victoria that Jordan would enjoy it, but warned that there was some violence.

Victoria had never seen the movie, and thought that it sounded incredibly stupid. But what did she know? It was action-packed and she'd be granted some uninterrupted sleep.

There was a pang of guilt for exposing her son to a movie that had violent scenes. She had to push away the thought that she was condoning and perpetuating Jordan's growing interest in guns.

Victoria took a quick shower and fell into bed. Throughout her fitful sleep she heard over and over gunshots and screams accompanied by haunting music. When she awakened around one o'clock, she was horrified to find Jordan riveted in front of the TV. The policeman who would become a robotic officer of the law lay in a pool of blood, one limb blown away, his body riddled with bullets while a band of depraved criminals whooped and hollered in demonic glee.

It was the kind of scene that could scar a child for life.

"How many times have you watched this, Jordan?" Victoria grabbed the remote and pushed pause.

"I don't know."

Victoria recalled hearing the music in her dreams. "Did you rewind this part over and over?

Jordan's eyes twinkled as he nodded vigorously.

"But this is horrible, Jordan. Do you like this?" She pointed to the frozen screen.

"It's okay, Mommy." Jordan patted his mother's arm reassuringly. "After they kill 'em, he gets to be Robocop."

"Did you watch anything else? Any cartoons?"

"Just Robocop," Jordan said with pride.

Victoria stopped the VCR and pushed eject. He'd seen quite enough. She needed her head examined for allowing an innocent child to view something so evil. She shook her head, to rid herself of the terrible thoughts. She couldn't allow herself to become introspective, for if she examined herself too closely, she'd come to realize that she'd brought the tape home as a sort of bribe. She was neglecting her son—again. At first it was her music career that drove her, that permitted her to give him only small portions of herself, only snatches of her time. She'd reasoned that she'd make up for it later, providing him with a privileged life would nullify the neglect. Since she'd accepted that there'd be no privileged life, no happy ending, no pot of gold—she should have spent more time with Jordan. But she didn't. Most of her time was spent at that scandalous place where she did unspeakable things for enough money to pay some bills and keep them afloat.

A few hours later, Victoria played Uno with her son and then a few rounds of Old Maid.

"Okay, Jordan," she said, putting the cards back in the pack. "Why don't you go play in your room?"

Jordan raced into his room but immediately returned with a board game. "Let's play Sorry, Mommy." Wearing an impish grin, he began setting up the game, as if the sight of the colorful board and pieces would compel his mother to play.

"I'm blue. What color do you wanna be?"

Victoria groaned; she hated playing Sorry. With a weak smile she chose red and listlessly rolled the dice and pushed the red piece around the board.

When the game ended and Jordan squealed for more, Victoria put her foot down. Enough was enough, she was beginning to feel abused. How much quality time did she owe her son?

"Why don't you go in your room and play with your Legos?" Victoria suggested in a pleading tone.

Jordan's lips curled into a pout. "I don't want to. Please, Mom. Can't we play again?"

"Jordan! Leave me alone! I don't want to play any more games!" Her tone was sharper than she intended. Her eyes welled up and as she watched Jordan slink off to his bedroom, she was reminded of the troubled relationship she had with her own mother. Tears burned her eyes. She'd make it up to Jordan. Perhaps she'd order pizza or something later on.

Victoria's own mother, whom she called by her first name, Zeline, had always kept Victoria at arm's length. Victoria had been born when Zeline was just sixteen, and Zeline happily handed Victoria over to her own mother, who insisted that Zeline complete high school unencumbered by the responsibility of a child. There was college after high school, and Zeline, a bright student, had several choices. Wanting to put distance between herself and her unwanted child, Zeline chose UCLA and seldom came home to visit. Philly was too far, airfare too high.

Victoria spent her childhood in a perpetual state of waiting for the mother she hardly knew, but loved to the point of worship. Each time Zeline disappointed her, Nana attempted to soften the blows by assuring Victoria that her mother was busy preparing a better life for the two of them. But Victoria often overheard Nana on the phone with Zeline. Her voice a low grumble, accusing Zeline of neglecting Victoria.

Finally, when Victoria was eight, Zeline sent for her. But juggling a new teaching career, dating, and raising a small girl alone proved too troublesome for the inexperienced, unwilling young mother. Victoria was sent packing back to Philadelphia and back to her Nana, whose love, though abundant, could never fill the empty space, heal the hurt, or end the belief that she was flawed, defective, and unlovable.

To this day, those feelings lingered.

Nana had been the link between Victoria and Zeline. Zeline had called Victoria a few times since her Nana's death, but their conversations were awkward and brief.

Victoria held a passionate belief in reincarnation and wondered about the karmic ties that bound her and Zeline. She suspected that something awful must have occurred between them in a previous life; something still unresolved that would have to be confronted in the next.

Victoria shuddered at the thought of another round with Zeline.

Hours later, after having eaten too much pizza, Victoria felt bloated and guilty as sin. She surveyed her image in the mirror, checking to see how much damage the pizza had done and was relieved to find her body unchanged. If she planned to keep it that way, she knew she would have to get back into a regular exercise program and figure out a way to fit a low-fat diet into her crazy work schedule.

Eating nutritiously was not a top priority at the massage parlor. Victoria had fallen into the habit, along with the other girls, of ordering greasy fast food from a twenty-four hour nearby restaurant that made around-the-clock deliveries.

Victoria gave Jordan her undivided attention. She listened intently and responded appropriately to his incessant childish chatter. It was maddening, but she forced herself to interact with her son until bedtime.

After Jordan had gone to sleep, Victoria was finally able to focus on the honey-coated feelings that had been flitting in and out of her mind all day. Pleasant sensations coursed through her body, prickling her skin and now softly tickled the corners of her mouth, curving it into a smile.

Victoria clicked off the TV and curled up on the sofa. She closed her eyes and began reviewing the images from the previous night. There was no order to the succession of scenes that played in her mind: Kareem's lips touching hers, her hands exploring his muscular body, the sound of his laughter.

But Kareem was a customer, not a potential love interest, she sternly reminded herself. Still her thoughts made her feel good; it was harmless fun. Folly. Entertainment.

Besides, thinking about Kareem was far more pleasant than contemplating her future. The eviction date loomed and though she had saved more than enough money to make a down payment on a new apartment, she needed a good credit rating to move into a decent place. Her credit was awful, and it would take a fortune to pay off her debts.

Chapter 12

Motivated by the encounter with Kareem, and the promise of seeing him again, Victoria spent eight torturous hours having her hair braided in an African braiding salon. The final hour was the worst. She sat with fists balled, toes curled and her face contorted, while the braider, unaware of the excruciating pain she inflicted, chatted annoyingly in her native tongue with another braider.

During that final hour, Victoria fought the urge to scream, and bolt from the chair. But suffering, in one form or another, was often a requirement in the black woman's quest for glamour, particularly when associated with hair, and so Victoria endured the pain.

Sporting her new 'do, Victoria returned to work looking and feeling like the proverbial Nubian queen. However, her regal aura began to dissipate after an hour of sitting in the lounge, waiting.

The smoky room, it seemed, was a single shade of lifeless gray: the walls, the sofa, the carpet, and the mood of the seven women who waited for customers.

Victoria wondered if perhaps a few plants placed here and there would brighten the place. But no…nothing green could survive; there were no windows, no sunlight.

"Is it always this slow here?" asked Allegra, a gaunt, blue-eyed newcomer to Pandora's. Allegra, however, was not new to the business. She twirled her ponytail nervously as she waited for a response. Her question was ignored. No one, not even Victoria, felt inclined to respond. No sense in encouraging the girl to cut into their money. It was better for everyone if she left in disgust, never to return.

Wanting to establish that she was not like the rest, that there was a distinct difference between herself and her unrefined co-workers, Victoria was usually polite to the parade of transient new faces that passed through the door of Pandora's. But not today. Her thoughts were completely absorbed with the thousands of dollars she needed to pay off her debts and repair her credit.

Miquon was back, despite predictions that she'd never again be permitted to work at Pandora's. When she entered the lounge, Allegra asked again, this time with a frown, and in a whining tone, "Is it always this slow here?"

Miquon stopped abruptly and placed a combative hand on her hip. "If you usta things moving faster than this, then you need to take your narrow ass on back to wherever you came from. Don't be coming up in here complaining. I came to make some money, so don't be talkin' all that negative shit. Whatchu tryin' to do—jinx my night?" Miquon's head rotated on her thick neck fast enough to cause whiplash.

Allegra uttered a vague sound of indignation.

Rolling her eyes hard, Miquon plopped down on the loveseat next to Victoria. She sat too close for comfort, mumbling to herself and deliberately invading Victoria's space. Victoria inched away but Miquon shifted her position, and her ample derriere took up even more of the loveseat.

Victoria couldn't help noticing the tacky black and white checks that looked like miniature floor tiles, painted on the tips of Miquon's squared-off acrylic nails. Even worse, a nail was missing from the index finger of one hand and the middle finger of the other.

"You gotta match?" Miquon inquired, impatiently waving a cigarette at Victoria.

"I don't smoke." Victoria's eyes were riveted to the two fingers clipping the cigarette. Stripped of its nail, Miquon's index finger looked sickly—vulnerable.

"So whatchu sayin'?"

Perplexed, Victoria frowned.

"Lotta people don't smoke, but they still carry matches. You need matches to smoke weed, don'tchu?"

"I don't smoke weed, either," Victoria said, regretting immediately that she had opened her mouth. It was foolish to expect Miquon to respond logically.

"I mean...damn...the way your face broke all up, you'da thought I asked you if you smoked crack! Don't make no damn sense the way some bitches always gotta have attitude."

The average working girl would have challenged Miquon on the B word; Victoria chose to ignore it. Looking for somewhere else to sit, Victoria scanned the room, but all the seats were taken. When she caught Allegra's eye, Victoria shook her head, giving the girl a one-victim-to-another kind of look. Refusing to commiserate, Allegra sucked her teeth, and turned her head.

Chelsea, Lauren, and Sydney were squeezed miserably on the sofa.

Jonee, who morphed daily from one outlandish persona to another, was draped entirely in black. She sat perched like a raven on the arm of Allegra's chair. Earlier, Jonee had discovered that her favorite wig was missing from her workbag. Stolen, she claimed, as she wagged an accusing finger and insisted Rover do a bag search. Rover refused.

Jonee's attire seemed to match her mood. She wore a long black wig with severe bangs, a flowing sheer black negligee that was cut so low, two black-berry nipples peaked out. A black snake bracelet winded its way up her arm, and her down-turned lips and clawed nails were also painted black.

They were a cheerless group, and Victoria realized that joining them would not lift her spirits.

"Anybody gotta light?" Miquon bellowed.

The girl was crude beyond belief! Victoria considered paying Rover a visit, but decided against it. He was too needy, and would probably try to talk her ears off. She was better off stuck with Miquon.

Chelsea threw Miquon a lighter. Miquon curled her lips around the cigarette as she lit it. A thick cloud of smoke hovered near Victoria. The odor filled her nostrils, and when her eyes began to burn, she had no choice but to seek refuge in the office with Rover.

"And what did you come to pester me about?" Rover asked gruffly, though Victoria could tell that he was pleased to have her company.

"What's the matter, Rover? You look beat."

Rover's eyes were bloodshot, and he was badly in need of a shave. Victoria was surprised to see specks of gray mixed in the stubble.

"Dominique, the so-called manager on the midnight shift, called out sick last night. Probably too high to come in…so I had to work her shift."

"You've been working around the clock?"

Rover nodded his head, and sighed deeply. "I had a two-hour nap."

"That's a shame," Victoria said in earnest. "Doesn't the owner have anyone else to cover? What would happen if you were both sick?"

"I never get too sick to count money." Rover chuckled. "But I wish Gabrielle could find a more reliable manager for the midnight shift." He paused in thought, and then continued. "Trouble is, she don't trust nobody but me. Gabrielle and me go way back. Believe me, I'd work all three shifts if I could. Just to make sure she gets every dollar she's entitled to. Those girls rob her blind on the midnight shift.

Victoria pondered Rover's remark and decided that Gabrielle could afford to lose a few bucks. How much damage could a missing fifty here or there do to Gabrielle's take?

Excluding the forbidden tips, Gabrielle collected half of the earnings of every girl who worked for her. For that reason, Victoria felt unsympathetic.

"I heard you knew Gabrielle when she was working in the business. That true?" It wasn't like Victoria to pry, and she felt downright naughty. However, there were many rumors swirling about and she didn't know what to believe. She was more than just a little curious about the mysterious Gabrielle.

"Yeah, I knew her then, but not the way the girls tell the story. I was never one of her customers."

Victoria raised a dubious brow. Was Rover insinuating that he and Gabrielle had been romantically involved? Rover was a nice guy, but from what she'd heard, Gabrielle was out of his league.

"I used to drive for this Italian guy, whose name I won't mention." Rover pronounced it Eyetalian. "It was rumored that he was in the mob. I don't know. I mind my own business. Anyways, he was one of the owners of the place where Gabrielle used to work—a place called Foxes on 13th and Arch. It's not there anymore; there's a restaurant there now. That entire area used to be the red-light district. Massage parlors, strip joints, peep shows, go-go bars, you name it. Back then, there was a lot of money in prostitution." Rover looked wistful.

But the bright, curious expression on Victoria's face vanished immediately when Rover used the word prostitution, and was replaced with downcast eyes and a brooding darkness.

Rover noticed but pretended not to. "After the Convention Center was built, that area became respectable," he continued. "A few bars are left, but they don't have the topless dancers." He ran his hand over the stubble on his face. "For some reason, the peep show's still on the corner…the owner must have City Hall connections, I guess. But everything else is gone."

"You were telling me about Gabrielle's boyfriend," Victoria reminded him.

"Oh yeah." Rover chuckled. "He was married. Spent a lot of time with his wife and kids. But every Wednesday, he took Gabrielle with him to the casinos in Atlantic City. I drove." Rover stopped abruptly, and cautioned with his finger. "Now this is between you and me."

Victoria nodded enthusiastically.

"For lack of a better name, let's call the Italian guy, Frank. Frank would promise Gabrielle that he'd take her to dinner or to see a show, but once he hit the blackjack tables…well, suffice to say, the romantic portion of the evening ended. Gabrielle would get bored standing around watching, so Frank would give her money, sometimes as much as a grand, to do whatever she pleased. At that point, my role would switch from driver to…I guess you could say…escort. We'd go catch a lounge act, have a few drinks, get a bite to eat…go shopping. I'd be right there with her when she tried on clothes in those fancy designer shops. She valued my opinion, too. Never bought nothing I didn't give a nod to." Rover's voice reflected his pride. "Anyways, that's how we became friends. Passing time and hanging out together. Waiting for ol' Frank to call it a night."

"So I guess it's true that Pandora's is really owned by this Frank guy?" Victoria asked.

"As far as I know, this is Gabrielle's business. A gift from Frank. The license is in her name and all the money we pull in goes directly to her."

"Yeah, but she's just a front, isn't she?" Victoria spoke with authority, but was only repeating information she'd overheard in the lounge.

Rover shrugged. "Gabrielle's doing all right for herself. She retired from the business at twenty-five. She drives a Mercedes, has quite a spread somewhere in Jersey, and a place in the Bahamas...Now how many girls do you know in the business who have sense enough to get out before it's too late?"

Too late! Too late for what! Victoria wanted to know, but didn't ask, deciding that Rover probably had dozens of horror stories about girls who wore out their welcome, stayed in the business too long. Victoria exclaimed, instead, "A spread! What do you mean? Gabrielle lives in a mansion?"

Rover lived in a dank, dark basement at Pandora's Box, but he nodded proudly as if he resided at the mansion with Gabrielle.

Although Victoria suspected that Rover was exaggerating, she was troubled by the possibility that she was contributing to someone else's lavish lifestyle.

Chapter 13

S everal hours later, Victoria found herself in a most unfortunate position—lying beneath an amply endowed black man named Bernard.

"I'd like to see you," he had said with a warm smile when he selected Victoria from the swarm of women who'd greeted him at the door.

Standing there in the lobby, he'd seemed so well adjusted, giving no indication that behind closed doors he'd behave like something that should be caged.

Bernard had perfected a technique that prolonged the session. Thrusting deeply and rapidly, he'd build up a momentum, and maintain it for an excruciatingly long time. Seconds away from what seemed an appropriate time to climax, he'd suddenly stop, take a deep breath, exhale with an appalling groan, then, feeling revitalized, the onslaught would begin again—all the while producing a violent flow of perspiration that fell like torrential rain.

The sheet was soaked. Victoria's entire body was soaked. She was drowning in a lake of sweat. There was moisture everywhere except on the condom. Victoria was in such discomfort, she considered replacing the dried-out condom with a freshly lubricated one, but changed her mind. More lubrication would make the experience more pleasurable for

Bernard, give him a second wind—the session could drag on indefinitely. She'd just have to tough it out with the old condom.

As the relentless pounding continued, Victoria could feel an inner rage building. She imagined herself shoving Bernard off, and with all her might, kicking him clean across the room.

Victoria was two seconds from hysteria; she had had enough. Squirming, she pushed away the sweaty shoulder that was pressed into her chin.

"Hurry up!"

Bernard stopped pumping and scowled down at her. Drip, drip.

"Yeah, all right, baby. Just a few more minutes." The sweating and pumping resumed.

She turned her head from side to side, frantically trying to dodge the droplets of perspiration. But when she realized that her brand new beautiful braids were being saturated with Bernard's revolting sweat, she shrieked. "That's it. Your time is up!"

Bernard stopped mid-thrust, but remained on top of her. He propped himself up with clenched fists.

Victoria lay immobilized. Her head lay between his rigid arms and menacing fists. An expression of sheer terror twisted her face. Bernard was either unaware, or simply didn't care that Victoria couldn't move, her braids were pinned down by his fists.

"What's my problem? You talking so much shit, my jimmie done went soft," Bernard roared. Spittle gathered in the corners of his mouth.

Even in a semi soft state, Bernard still had one hell of a whopper. The condom clung so tightly; it looked like a layer of thick dry skin.

A burning mixture of mascara and perspiration blinded Victoria; she was emboldened by the pressing need to wipe her eyes.

"Get the hell off me!" With surprising strength, she pushed Bernard off and wiped her eyes.

"My time ain't up," Bernard said, eyeing his watch suspiciously.

"Oh, yes it is! You've been in here for an hour; I'm leaving." Still rubbing her stinging eyes, Victoria leaped from the bed. With one hand she groped around the room, snatching up her shoes, camisole, panties, and purse.

Bernard blocked the path as she reached for the door. "You got a lot of game. I'll give you credit for that. But you got to be crazy if you think you gonna leave me like this." Bernard glanced at his watch again, with a smirk. "I got ten more minutes. Maybe if you worked with a little more enthusiasm, we could both get outta here." He grabbed Victoria's wrist, squeezing it tight.

Too shocked to speak, but suddenly able to clearly see, Victoria stared, her mouth gaping, at the big hand that gripped her wrist.

"I paid good money for this. Now if you can't get me off, then give me my money back!" As spoke those angry words, he pointed at Victoria's purse, which was tucked snugly under her arm. She had only half his money, and didn't intend to give it back. The other fifty dollars belonged to the house, and was in the office safe, mingled in with the thousands of dollars collected for the past week.

It occurred to Victoria that she should scream for help. But she didn't. Screaming for help seemed incredibly undignified, and would provide the women in the lounge too much fun at her expense. She'd have to quietly handle the situation on her own.

Victoria tugged, but Bernard tightened his grip.

"You messin' with the wrong one, bitch." Bernard bent slightly so that they were face-to-face.

Victoria whimpered, which inspired Bernard to work himself up even more.

"Don't play with my money!" He spoke through clenched teeth, tightening his grip with each word. "I will fuck you up over my money!"

Quaking in fear, Victoria accidentally dropped a shoe. Bernard was distracted, he shifted his gaze to the floor.

In a series of swift motions, she yanked her hand away, pulled open the door, and tumbled out into the hall. Bernard started after her, but realizing that he was naked except for the condom, he retreated.

Victoria clutched her belongings in front of her (which included a single shoe) and streaked naked up the hall. She darted past Rover's office and burst into the bathroom. Turning the lock, she fell against the door.

As her racing heart began to slow down, she caught a sudden, unpleasant whiff. She looked around the bathroom, sniffing wildly at the air. But to her amazement and disbelief, the odor emanated from her! A disgusting, musty, funky, smell of sweat—men's locker room sweat! Bernard had left his scent; it was all over her. Nothing was worth this, she told herself. No amount of money—nothing.

There was a shower stall in the bathroom, used mostly by customers. Victoria had never used it. It looked unsanitary, and needed a thorough scouring. The sight of the accumulated film made her flesh crawl. It would take at least an hour-long shower to remove the stench of Bernard, but under the circumstances, a wash-up at the sink would have to do.

As she pumped soap onto a paper towel, she felt the vibration of heavy footsteps. Her heart began to pick up speed. She could hear Bernard's voice, a low disgruntled rumble. She could also hear Rover talking softly, in placating tones.

Would Bernard overpower Rover? Victoria wondered. Could he break down the flimsy bathroom door? If so, what would he do? Beat her up? Strangle her, while in a horny rage?

How could something like this be happening? Why didn't he just leave quietly? The man was causing a commotion over ten lousy minutes. She'd been brutalized by his big, impaling appendage for forty minutes. Forty minutes of torture was long enough.

Sequestered in the bathroom, Victoria prayed that Rover would resolve the unfortunate situation without demanding to hear her side of the story. Her heart wouldn't stop thumping; she could feel an anxiety attack coming on. If she were forced to look at Bernard's mean, sweaty face again, she'd surely lose her fragile grip on sanity, and topple over the edge.

Angry, pounding footsteps stomped down the hall. The next sound Victoria heard was the slamming door. Bernard was gone! Victoria was so relieved, she was practically giddy, but she remained in the bathroom, cowering behind the closed door.

Rover tapped on the door. "All right, Pleasure. The coast is clear. You can come out now." There was laughter in his voice.

Wearing an embarrassed smile, Victoria cracked the door, and peeked out.

"Did you give him his money back?" She was past caring about the money, but didn't know what else to say.

"No way! I'm not in the habit of handing out refunds to someone who's tied up a room for damn near an hour. Now, in the future, if a customer is giving you a hard time…just leave the room. I'm here to protect you girls."

"I tried, but he grabbed me."

"Then you should have screamed. Nine times outta ten, these fellas don't want to make any real trouble. They want to slip in and out of here as fast as they can. They have wives, families. They can't afford to make too much of a fuss."

"I pity his wife," Victoria said, shaking her head and imagining the grisly horror of having to tangle with sweaty Bernard and his gargantuan penis night after night-for free!

Chapter 14

A few of the girls who'd made money, openly counted their take at the end of the shift, flaunting big bills in the solemn faces of those who were going home empty-handed. Victoria, however, feeling compassionate, tallied her earnings with a hand tucked discreetly inside her purse. She counted three hundred dollars. Not bad for a night that had begun so slowly, and with regard to her encounter with Bernard—violently.

As feared, the new girl, Allegra, was the moneymaker of the night. Highly skilled in the art of separating men from their assets, she shamelessly displayed her sizeable earnings. Oblivious to the covetous glances of Miquon and Chelsea, Allegra pranced about, displaying a thick wad of money that was strapped to her thigh by a pink lace garter.

There had been times when Victoria had chosen to stay on for the next shift because her earnings were insufficient, but she had yet to experience the humiliation felt by the women who didn't even break luck.

The customers were mostly undesirables: men who had to pay for sex. That they were responsible for causing such feelings of inadequacy in someone as intelligent and as pretty as Chelsea was incomprehensible.

"Are you okay, Miquon?" Chelsea asked.

Miquon screwed up her lips, and then gave a reluctant nod.

"Are you gonna stay, and try to make some money on the next shift?"

"Can't."

"Why not?"

"My babysitter don't mind if I'm a little bit late, but she ain't tryin' to watch my kids all night long. Ain't like it's guaranteed that I'm gonna make enough on the next shift to pay her double time. Nah, I ain't stayin'...I'm gittin' up outta here."

"Do you have money for a cab?"

"Nope. Gotta pay my sitter; I'm gonna have to hop on SEPTA." Miquon paused, bit her lip contemplatively, and then said, "I can't believe this shit. I been on suspension...ain't had no money. My first day back, and I gotta leave here broke."

Chelsea shook her head.

Wearing a grave expression, Miquon prepared to leave, packing her workbag as if in slow motion.

As much as Victoria disliked Miquon, it saddened her to see her with her spirit broken. She wanted to say something encouraging, or offer her cab fare, but a survival-of-the-fittest attitude existed at Pandora's, and for some reason, offering money to anyone who failed to break luck was frowned upon.

Poor thing, Victoria thought as she watched Miquon dragging her heavy workbag down the hall. She gripped the handle with one hand, and with the other she clutched her street clothes, and coat. Miquon mumbled to herself as she ambled toward the bathroom. Victoria couldn't recall Miquon ever requiring privacy while getting dressed. She seemed to delight in defiantly exposing her stretch marks, cellulite, and flab. Shame and disappointment must have driven her out of the lounge, Victoria concluded. Then, feeling magnanimous, Victoria decided to stealthily slip Miquon fifty dollars.

Victoria waited a few minutes, and then tapped on the bathroom door.

"What!" Miquon asked, sharply.

"It's Pleasure. Can I come in?"

"Yeah, when I'm finished," Miquon said, with much attitude. "Damn, can't have no privacy in this joint."

Undaunted, Victoria tapped on the door again. "Miquon, I want to talk to you."

Miquon sighed heavily, then unlocked and cracked the door.

Victoria offered a smile, which wasn't returned. Through the open space Victoria could see Miquon's personal possessions in several piles on the floor. She was shocked that Miquon would scatter her personal things on the dirty bathroom floor.

"I just wanted..." Victoria fell silent as her eyes roamed to the piles on the floor.

"Yeah!" Miquon bucked her eyes. "Whassup?"

Appalled, Victoria spotted several familiar articles among Miquon's things: Sydney's Lancôme bag, Arianna's sequined demi bra, and Lauren's treasured silk Indian robe. A platinum wig, balled inside out, was undeniably the hair that on that very night had been stolen from Jonee.

Miquon was a kleptomaniac! A mean-spirited thief! She couldn't even fit the robe or the bra, and she'd look absolutely frightful in the pale-colored wig.

"Never mind," Victoria said, lips pursed.

"Crazy bitch," Miquon muttered with a resentful look as she banged the door shut.

Victoria rushed back to the lounge. The room was in chaos. Allegra was crying into her hands. Chelsea provided comfort, patting Allegra's thin back.

"What happened?" Victoria asked. Lord, there was never a dull moment at Pandora's Box.

"She lost her money," Lauren said.

Allegra lifted her head, revealing angry blood-shot eyes. "I didn't fuckin' lose my money!" she screamed. "One of you thievin' bitches stole it!"

"Don't call me a bitch," Lauren said. "You're the fuckin' bitch, you stupid ass. Can't even hang onto your own damn money."

Allegra shook off Chelsea's arm, sprang up from her seat, and advanced toward Lauren.

"You're calling me stupid? I heard you got dumped by some nigger from India...now who's stupid?"

The spectators, black and white, gasped at the *N* word.

Lauren swung at Allegra, but missed. Allegra grabbed a hank of Lauren's long hair, quickly wrapped it around her fist, and yanked it before pulling her into a headlock, and taking a bite out of her cheek.

At the sound of Lauren's blood-curdling shriek, Rover bounded down the hall, covering it in just a few, long strides.

And as Rover, Chelsea, and a few others struggled to separate the two women, Miquon slipped past the lounge. With Allegra's money stuffed in her bra, she was out the door, her swift and silent departure announced by the chime of the bell.

Victoria darted into the waiting cab.

As if aware of Victoria's urgent need to put distance between herself and the massage parlor, the cabbie hastily pulled away from the curb, made a bold U-turn, weaved into the far right lane, and raced up Market Street.

Beginning with the ravings of her first customer and ending with Lauren and Allegra's fistfight, the evening had been fraught with mayhem.

The cab zipped past 30th Street. Victoria caught a glimpse of an attractive couple, laughing and holding hands as they rushed inside the train station. They looked so happy, so normal. She felt a twinge of envy and slumped into her seat.

Victoria was lonely, but hadn't realized it until now. Being in the company of the unending stream of men who patronized Pandora's seemed to replace the desire for a normal relationship.

A crystal clear image of Kareem surfaced. That night with him. Something had been awakened that night, something that proved she was a normal woman capable of normal feelings for a man. And the quick but sharp pain that shot through her heart at the sight of the couple was a reminder that the desire blazed as strong as ever. But where was Kareem? She'd waited for him to come back, but he hadn't. Oh, what difference did it make? He was just a customer. All he could offer was a warped version of a love affair; a pseudo relationship confined within the walls of Pandora's Box. And like the Greek mythological story, inside Pandora's there was only malice, discontentment, violence, and resentment.

Victoria hung her head in anguished resolution. Nothing good could come from Pandora's. Victoria lifted her head, recalling the end of the story. As Pandora closed the lid on the box, which contained all the evils of the world, she found hope lying on the bottom. And there was hope for Victoria, too. She would not allow herself to remain trapped inside Pandora's. Just as soon as her affairs were in order-one more month, two at the most-she'd work out a plan to restructure her life, and she'd put this wretched experience far, far behind.

Chapter 15

Sheena was back on the midnight shift after a fifteen-day hiatus. She looked terrible. Her complexion, which used to be a rich mocha, was now a baffling grayish hue, a greasy red bandana concealed dirty, matted hair, and she was skinnier than ever.

It was not unusual for Sheena to disappear for days, sometimes for up to a week, but never had she been gone for over two weeks; her money never lasted that long.

Unlike her co-workers who competed at a breathless pace for as many sessions as their bodies could endure, Sheena needed only one session, or one sucker (as she put it) to make enough to get high. Sometimes it took days for her to break luck, but she would wait patiently, sleeping most of the time.

A few faithful customers came to see Sheena. Her regulars. Those straggling few were remnants from her pre-drug era, and came to see her a couple times a month.

It was hard to believe that the tall, twenty-eight-year-old woman once filled out a size twelve. Over the last few years she had dwindled down to skin and bones, and even a size three fit her loosely. A sad semblance of her former self, Sheena looked downright unhealthy. Sick. Like she had contracted *something*.

The other girls, prettier and certainly shapelier, were mystified by the loyalty of Sheena's customers.

The black girls at Pandora's Box usually profited from both black and white clienteles. Black men, however, were the major contributors to their income. Sheena had no black customers; her regulars were all white. Ordinarily, the black men who came to call, were desirous of someone soft with sumptuous curves. Sheena, with her skeletal appearance did not merit an appraisal and was, therefore, dismissed on sight.

Rumors about Sheena swirled: she did it without a rubber; she never asked for a tip; she was into anal sex. No one knew for certain what Sheena did privately, but they did know that at the conclusion of a session, Sheena was out the door, and she wouldn't reappear until her money and credit ran out at the place where she got high.

Six women were working the midnight shift: Dominique, Reds, Kelly, Milan (a pretty newcomer with brand new breast implants), Sheena, and Victoria—too many women for a Monday night.

Victoria recounted the four hundred dollars she'd made from the previous shift, and mentally added that to the twelve hundred she had at home. Sixteen hundred was close to what she needed to move, but she'd asked to work the midnight shift because she needed an additional thousand dollars to make a down payment on a new, but inexpensive compact car. There was a dealership on Passyunk Avenue that cared not a whit about bad credit. A car would make apartment hunting a lot easier.

Victoria had never met Sheena, and nothing she had heard about the unfortunate girl prepared her for the bedraggled creature lying curled up on the sofa. In a subconscious gesture, Victoria clutched her purse to her chest. Sheena didn't look capable of making one dollar, and Victoria did not intend to share any portion of her earnings with this seeming derelict, who more than likely was also a thief. There was absolutely nothing that distinguished Sheena from any of the vagrants roaming the streets. Victoria couldn't imagine why Sheena was allowed on the premises.

Then, reminding herself to not be judgmental, Victoria tried hard to look upon Sheena with pity.

Sheena hadn't bothered to put on any make-up, and had tossed her ratty, used-to-be curly wig on top of her dirty work bag. She looked dog-tired as she curled up on the sofa.

"Whatchu doing, Sheena? Preparing to camp out for the night?" Dominique inquired, scowling.

Sheena's mouth twitched into a smile.

"You got some fucked up timing. As you can see, it's crowded as hell. Why'd you have to drag your ass in here tonight?"

Sheena mumbled something, and then burrowed deeper into the coat she was using as a blanket.

"And you got the nerve to sprawl your ass out, takin' up the whole damn couch."

Sheena drew up her knees to provide some space, hoping to avoid being banished from the sofa to an uncomfortable chair. Then, jolted by a sudden recollection, she shot up straight.

"Guess who I saw?" Sheena said, excitedly.

"Who?" Dominique and Reds asked, simultaneously.

"Bethany." Sheena's voice became a whisper as her frail body slumped into its original position, fatigue overpowering her desire to engage an audience.

"Where did you see Bethany? I thought she was still locked up in that crazy house in West Philly," Dominique said, smoothing her slick hair.

"She's out, 'cause I was with her and Fred all last week."

"Where?" Dominique asked, raising her voice.

"Um…we was in North Philly."

"Doing what?" Reds chimed in. She held a curling iron poised in mid-air.

"Gittin' high!" Sheena announced with uncharacteristic sass, accompanied by a circular neck move.

"What!" Dominique and Reds shouted in unison.

"That bitch is hittin' the pipe again?" Reds directed her words to Dominique.

"What did she say about the baby, Sheena? Does she know the people from that funeral parlor called here damn near every day for about two weeks?"

"Bethany ain't say nothin' about the baby, and I didn't want to bring it up," Sheena said, clearly regretful that she'd opened her mouth.

"Well, you should have. We were feeling sorry for Bethany, thinking she was in the nut house, and she out gittin' high with you!" Dominique said.

"We even took up a collection for the funeral and gave the money to Fred," Reds added. "I didn't want to believe it, but I'm starting to think there's some truth to the story that they killed that child! Damn, they didn't even have the decency to bury their own kid."

Dominique shook her head in disbelief. "So what about the money we gave for the funeral...what happened to it?"

"I don't know nothin' about no money," Sheena said, shrinking back into the couch.

"The twenty dollars a piece we all chipped in for the baby's funeral—the funeral that never was," Reds said, ticked off.

"So, our money just went up in smoke?" Kelly asked mid-nod, scratching.

"Our money!" Dominique hissed. "You didn't give up a cent, and you know it. And don't try to act like you're any better. You may not be a smoker, but your get high in a way that's just as fucked up. Shooting that shit up your veins is probably worse."

"I have a habit, I admit it," Kelly said sorrowfully. "But at least I'm trying to get help. I'm on the list for the methadone program, and..."

"Yeah, yeah, yeah," Dominique interrupted. "We've heard that story before. Give it a rest, Kelly. I don't feel like hearing your bullshit tonight."

In feigned bewilderment, Kelly threw up both her hands.

Dominique was an imposing figure as she stood over Sheena, glowering. "Let me get this straight. You're saying all our hard-earned money went up in smoke? Just like that?" The question was accompanied by an extravagant wave of her lean, muscular arm, and a snap of thin fingers. "Is that what you're saying, Sheena?" Dominique dropped suddenly to her knees, meeting Sheena eye-to-eye.

Sheena looked away from Dominique's reproachful gaze.

"And you was gittin' high with Bethany and Fred? You helped them fuck up our money?"

Sheena recoiled into a knot. Tsks, sighs, and other utterances of disapproval sounded in the room. Dominique shooed Sheena from the sofa. The eyes of the others, filled with condemnation, followed the gaunt, jittery girl as she scurried to a corner on the floor where she made a pallet with her coat. On the floor, cushioned by the ratty old fur coat of undeterminable species, Sheena lay under a dingy polyester robe that barely covered her long body. She curled into an even tighter knot as she attempted to keep her legs and feet beneath the flimsy fabric.

The stories that circulated around the death of Bethany's son had just started to die down, now they would begin anew, but with a different twist. Bethany had become a folk hero of sorts, a noble mother who, unable to cope with the loss of her child, had sank into the depths of despair, the result being a nervous breakdown. But after tonight, her name would be forever tarnished. Bethany would be labeled a baby-killer, and the ever-changing story of her son's death would be told inside houses of ill repute throughout the city for years.

As it turned out, Monday night wasn't bad at all. The doorbell rang three times in quick succession during the first hour. As expected, Milan, with her demanding attention breasts, got the first session. Dominique got the second, and a ferret-faced black man who wore a grimy gray uniform chose Victoria.

Inside the room, the wiry little guy paid the fee.

"I've been on the road all night; I'm a truck driver," the man said, rubbing his forehead wearily.

"Hmm." she felt no sympathy for him, and did not intend to engage in mindless chatter.

When the truck driver stripped down to his underwear, Victoria was hit by a pungent body odor. He smelled like he'd been driving for a week. Why was it so rare for customers to come in fresh and clean? She had seen enough dingy, threadbare boxer shorts to last a lifetime. Most of the customers were married. Victoria couldn't imagine how their wives tolerated them, permitted them to crawl into bed so rough and ashen, so unclean.

With his thumbs beneath the elastic waistband, the truck driver was about to shed his boxer shorts. "The shower is at the end of the hall," Victoria informed him.

Disappointment shone in his eyes. "You want me to take a shower?"

"I certainly do," she said, with her arms folded across her chest.

In record time, the man returned. He was dripping wet, and wearing a sheepish grin. As he briskly dried himself, Victoria wasn't surprised when she caught a whiff of the same acrid scent. He was as funky as before. She also noticed that his shoulders and back were dotted with unsightly black bumps. Victoria sighed, and rolled her eyes in disgust. Oh, well, it was his loss! She tended to be extremely cold and abrupt with customers who didn't practice good hygiene.

Without a word, and with minimal eye contact, she pointed the grinning ferret to the cot. She surveyed him and unfurled a condom.

"What do they call you? Precious?" the truck driver asked with an unattractive, crooked smile.

"Pleasure."

"You're a pretty girl. Either one of those names fits you to a tee."

Shuddup and stop trying to be nice, she thought as she covered the condom with a generous amount of KY jelly. She straddled him, trying to avoid touching his rough thighs. A full body condom was what she needed.

"Your skin is so soft," he said, running a sandpaper hand over her shoulders. Victoria groaned, then pushed down on the lubricated condom, careful not to permit his knotted pubic hair to brush against her own neatly-trimmed pubis.

She bounced up and down mechanically, and after only a few seconds, the man cried out. "Ugh!" It was a mournful sound. Wearing the doomed expression of a drowning man, he reached out and fondled her breasts. Victoria looked at his callused hands scornfully, then smiled when she felt his shudder, a prelude to his orgasmic moan. Hallelujah!

The man redressed quickly. "Thank you, Precious," he said. Victoria didn't bother to correct him. He reached for her hand, and she pulled away. But he was quick. Quite unexpectedly, the truck driver forced money into her balled fist.

"Thank you, so much, Precious," he repeated, his rheumy eyes filled with warmth.

Victoria couldn't bear it. She'd treated him so shabbily; she didn't deserve a tip. She thanked him, and stuffed the bills in her purse, too embarrassed to look at the amount.

❦

After he left, she peeked inside, and was shocked to discover that he'd given her an extra two hundred dollars, more than she'd ever been tipped. She felt so ashamed. Then she reminded herself that nice or not, the man had a lot of nerve coming there expecting to copulate without even bothering to take a decent shower. Hmph. She deserved that extra money. The truck driver had made a pit stop at Pandora's with the same urgency of someone pulling over to make a restroom stop.

Still, Victoria was disgusted with herself. The things she put up with for money. It was downright revolting. Her poor Nana must be turning over in her grave.

But those self-deprecating thoughts retreated to the corners of her mind the instant she heard the peal of the bell.

Chapter 16

Muhammad looked distinguished and somewhat afro-centric in a black cashmere coat and black and bronze kofi. He gazed at the women—studied them, as he stroked his chin. His eyes, resting on Milan's breasts, grew wide. But under the glare of three ready-to-be indignant black women, he shifted his gaze to Victoria, selecting her with a confident nod.

It was now four-thirty in the morning; Victoria felt fatigued. Working two shifts was grueling. Still, she couldn't have been more pleased to do business with the well-groomed gentleman. He was a godsend after the grungy little truck driver, and a tip from him would give her the rest of the money she needed toward the down payment on the car.

He undressed, and placed his kofi on top of his clothing. Victoria was surprised that the kofi concealed a balding head—a rather misshapen head, at that. Instead of holding onto the remaining tufts of hair, he should have shaved it all off, and gone completely bald. It would have given him more dignity.

"Why don't you join me?" He patted the cot he lounged upon, lowering his eyes seductively. Victoria thought the gesture looked a tad feminine.

"Would you like a massage with oil?" she asked, sitting down next to him.

"No, let's not waste time with preliminaries."

Victoria nodded. She didn't feel like giving him a rubdown, anyway. In fact, she didn't feel like doing anything. If she had it her way, she'd just extend her hand, take his money, thank him kindly, and bid him a fond adieu.

Muhammad inched closer; he ran his fingers through her braids. "I chose you because you had that look."

"What look?" she asked, suddenly interested. She could use an ego boost.

"The look of a freak who can get real down and dirty!"

She gagged, and then gasped in shock, fingers fluttering to her heart. "Moi?" How could he think such a thing? Compared to her sleazy cohorts, she should have appeared innocent and untouched—a virgin, for Chrissakes. What had made him decide that she was his best bet for a down and dirty deed? And God only knew what that might be.

Unfazed by her incoherent protests, Muhammad continued. "Yeah, I like a woman to give me all her nasty stuff..."

Her what? Instead of running toward the door, Victoria opted to give this seemingly normal sick-o, the benefit of the doubt. Perhaps he was only kidding, making awkward small talk. Besides, she had already counted the guaranteed fifty and was flirting with the idea of getting a hundred-dollar tip. Greed was a terrible thing! She decided to hear him out, hoping that he was actually in the market to purchase normal, old-fashioned, missionary position sex. Maybe he had to rely on filthy, perverted dialogue to get it up.

"So, what do you have for me?" Muhammad ran his fingers up and down the front of Victoria's beaded G-string. She noticed with a twinge of irritation that his nails, which were too long, shimmered from several coats of clear polish. Unwelcome thoughts of Justice Martin and his glossy nails crowded her mind, filling her with sudden rage, which she directed toward the customer as she roughly pushed his hand away. She could just see the precious beads flying every which way, if Muhammad snagged them with his long, stupid nails.

"Do you have something for me?" Muhammad asked, his voice softly seductive.

"What are you talking about? What am I supposed to have?" It was late; she was tired. What a jerk Muhammad was turning out to be. Why didn't he just get to the point?

In the same sexy voice, Muhammad said, "I was hoping you might have a little pee-pee for me."

Silently, Victoria screamed obscenities. She wanted to pummel him with her fists, scratch out his eyes, and kick him in the balls. But she was too weary. Drained.

"I'm not into that," she said finally, and without emotion. "You can have your money back, or I can send someone else in."

"No problem," he said, shrugging. "Look, I tried to look out for you... tried to give a sistah some play. I should have known better. Black women have so many hang-ups...so inhibited. Then you wonder why brothas cross over."

Victoria stared at Muhammad. She could think of a million retorts for the pervert, but it was pointless to debate the issue, her loud sigh would have to suffice. "Do you want your money back or not?"

"No. Send in the white girl. The one with the big..." He made a lewd gesture in front of his chest. Victoria sucked her teeth.

On her way back to the lounge, after informing Rover that the customer wanted to switch to Milan, the door to the middle session room opened.

Victoria froze. Her hand flew to her mouth as she stifled a gasp. Dominique stood in the doorway; her nude body glistened from oil. She was strapped with a monstrous black dildo that was also slathered with oil.

"Hey, Pleasure, you wanna make a quick fifty bucks?"

"Doing what?" Victoria asked, appalled.

"Nothing. Just watch me work this mothafucka." Dominique opened the door wider, revealing the unfortunate man inside the room. He was on his hands and knees.

"He was talkin' a lotta shit a few minutes ago, so I had to whoop his ass. Come on in, let me show you how to train a dog."

Victoria hesitated briefly, then decided that getting paid to watch Dominique working her craft was more appealing than being in the presence of someone who wanted to ingest urine.

"He's being a good doggy now, ain'tcha boy," Dominique said, patting the man's head. The customer imitated a whimpering dog and nuzzled Dominique's hand. "Good boy, that's my good boy," she cooed.

Victoria was fascinated. She'd never observed an S&M session. She supposed that Muhammad's request could be viewed as S&M, but his desires were beyond her capabilities; she was not into playing any games that involved body fluids. Not her own, or anyone else's.

"Come on boy, turn around. I know you want it doggy-style."

The customer turned quickly on all fours, and impatiently wagged an imaginary tail.

"Oh hell no!" Dominique said, pushing the man away. "I don't give up the dick that easy. You got to show me what a good dog does."

The man quickly turned around and scampered toward her. Dominique forced the dildo into his mouth. The man made a choking sound, his eyes watered as he tried to pull away. "What the fuck! Are you refusing to suck my dick? Huh?" She kicked him in his side. He yelped, and scrambled to a corner.

"Get over here, goddamit," Dominique ordered. The customer didn't budge.

"You better obey me, you fuckin' mutt." Dominique advanced toward the man, slowly. She grabbed a hank of his stringy brown hair and pulled him out of the corner. With an oil-slick finger, she parted his lips. Once again, Dominique forced the dildo inside his mouth. He slurped and gagged as she cursed him with every thrust.

The novelty of the act began to wear off. Victoria shifted her position and checked the time. Sensing Victoria's waning interest, Dominique launched into the next phase of the exhibition. "Get the money, you mangy dog." There was a glazed over look in Dominique's eyes. "Get the fuckin' money before I choke your ass." She jammed the device in deeper.

The customer began heaving, his eyes wild. "Don't you throw up, you bastard. Throw up and I'm gonna make you lick up every drop! Now go get the fuckin' money! "

He scooted across the room, naked and on all fours, then with his teeth, he retrieved a fifty-dollar bill from beneath a pile of clothes on the floor. Crawling, he brought the money to Victoria. Self-consciously, she accepted the money.

At the end of the tawdry session, Victoria rushed from the room, feeling diminished for having viewed such depravity. Dominique, she concluded, was as sick as the poor customer.

The other girls often laughed about the weird things that some men requested, and Victoria had the impression that most of the girls only pretended to dispense punishment. Not Dominique. She wasn't pretending; the deranged woman was completely involved.

Chapter 17

B y the end of February, Victoria had given in and accepted the friendship Jonee (whose real name was actually Jonee) extended. Being with Jonee was fun, in certain settings. But Victoria regarded the friendship, like her new profession, as only temporary. She doubted that she'd ever stop feeling embarrassed by Jonee's garish attire, and her limited worldview.

One wintry evening, the two women made an impromptu decision to get away to a warm, sunny locale. Her utility bills were paid up-to-date, and she had saved enough to find a new place, and only needed a little more to make a down payment on a car, but the payment agreement she'd worked out for the huge recording debt would keep her at Pandora's a little longer than she'd planned. She deserved a vacation; she needed to get away. Plus, taking a vacation would distract her from constantly thinking about Kareem, who, despite their magical, practically spiritual sexual encounter, had never returned.

"Let's go to the Jamaica," Victoria suggested.

"Okay, Mon. No problem," Jonee said, and laughed.

Victoria laughed with her, and then stopped abruptly.

"What's wrong?"

"I was thinking about Jordan. I'll feel guilty leaving him with his sitter while I'm having a ball in Jamaica." Victoria paused, in thought. "I know…why don't we take our kids with us?"

"I can't take Alec out of school."

"Isn't spring break coming up soon?"

"Not until next month. The end of next month."

"Okay, let's put the trip off until spring break. Instead of Jamaica, we should take the kids to Disney World."

"Disney World!" Jonee squealed. "Now that's whassup! I've never been to Disney World, and I'm not waiting for no spring break. Alec's a good student; he can afford to miss some time."

The night before their five-day trip to Orlando, Victoria agonized, hoping that for once Jonee would relax and dress down. Victoria mentioned pointedly that she planned to free herself of beauty rituals during their vacation. No make-up, no fancy hairstyles, or flashy clothes. She hoped Jonee would take the hint, and tone down her look.

But no such luck. The next morning, Jonee showed up at the airport gussied up, face painted, and flinging a bright maroon weave that hung down her back. She was toting knock-off Louis Vuitton luggage; a matching duffel bag was slung over her shoulders.

"Pleasure! Pleasure!" Jonee yelled when she spotted Victoria. She grabbed her son's hand and rushed toward Victoria and Jordan.

Victoria was mortified. Repeatedly, she had asked Jonee to refrain from using her alias while out in public or in front of Jordan.

Jonee greeted Victoria with a bear hug. "I can't believe we're going to Disney World! I think I'm more excited than Alec."

Victoria fought the urge to fan her face. Jonee smelled like she'd taken a bath in the fake designer cologne that she wore at work. Jonee and most of their colleagues preferred the fake stuff, claiming they didn't want to waste their good fragrances in a whorehouse. The faux cologne of choice was contained in an aerosol can, and the girls generously sprayed up and down the length of their bodies, fumigating the lounge. The strong scents, combined with cigarette smoke, often sent Victoria running out of the lounge, choking and gasping for breath.

"Hi, Alec. This is my son, Jordan," Victoria said nudging Jordan forward. "Jordan, say hi to Alec." The two boys mumbled, "Hi," but clung to their mothers, shyly checking each other out.

Long navy blue nails brushed strands of the maroon hair from her face. Jonee was either unaware or unconcerned that clumps of dried gel made it obvious that she or some jackleg beautician had tried to blend her badly-in-need-of-a-perm hair in with the straight, store-bought hair.

In stark contrast, Jonee's six-year-old son, Alec, was tastefully dressed in Osh Kosh. Alec, with his soft curls and creamy complexion, was obviously biracial. He was a well-mannered little guy, a first grader at a private school on the Parkway. Victoria couldn't help wondering what the school staff thought when Jonee showed up looking like a floozy, dressed in one of her outlandish outfits.

Jonee was an enigma. She strutted around like the last of the great hoochie mommas, without an ounce of good taste, yet she had the foresight to invest in her son's education. Go figure!

Victoria's half of the trip was financed with a portion of the money she had intended to move with. On the appointed court date, the aging landlady sent a well-dressed attorney in her place, alleging that her failing health prevented her appearance.

Victoria described the condition of her apartment and claimed that she had withheld the rent with the hope of forcing the owner to make the necessary repairs. A female judge listened sympathetically as Victoria rattled off a long list of problems: missing ceiling tiles, exposed pipes, doors off hinges, broken faucets, leaky pipes, no smoke detectors or fire extinguishers, and an inoperable oven. Appalled, the judge looked from the nattily-attired attorney to Victoria, who looked slightly unkempt. She hadn't been able to find the time to sit through another agonizing eight-hour rebraiding and her hair was looking kind of rough. The judge demanded that the negligent owner make the necessary repairs.

"That place is unsafe for anyone to inhabit, let alone a young child. Shame on your client," the judge admonished. Looking over her glasses, she turned to Victoria. "Should the owner not comply in the future, be aware young lady, that you are not to withhold rent without going through the proper channels. You are required to put the rent into an escrow account."

Blinded by the flaming Orlando sun, Victoria fumbled in her purse for a pair of sunglasses. Jonee's designer sunglasses had been affixed to her face since their departure from Philadelphia. The boys, excited by the change in climate, hastily discarded their winter gear before hopping into a waiting cab outside the terminal. According to the travel agent, the temperature in Orlando in February was expected to be in the high seventies. The high nineties seemed more accurate.

There was plenty of room in the back with Victoria and the two boys, but Jonee slid in the front seat.

"How ya doing, Pedro?" Jonee asked flirtatiously.

The Hispanic cabbie smiled and said, "I'm fine, thank you." The name Antonio DeJarnette was boldly printed on the identification card posted on the dashboard.

"Boy, it's hot! What's the temperature today?" Victoria asked the cab driver.

"High eighties," he said, with a great deal of pride.

As the cab glided along, Jonee squealed like a child, pointing to the palm trees lining International Drive. Jonee's lack of sophistication usually embarrassed Victoria, especially when they were out in public. Once, while dining in Chinatown, Victoria shrank in her seat, mortified when Jonee gleefully screeched, "Ooh, look at that!" as the waiter, making careful steps, carried a flaming meal to patrons seated at a table nearby.

But here in Orlando, Victoria wasn't bothered at all, she was glad that Jonee was happy, and found her unguarded expression of joy refreshing.

Their entrance into the hotel lobby caused quite a stir. All eyes were on Jonee as she and Victoria registered at the front desk. Two bellhops—one black, the other Hispanic, gawked and elbowed each other. Victoria shifted her gaze downward, certain they were making lewd comments. Jonee encouraged the lustful admirers with puckered lips that spread into an inviting smile.

After Victoria and Jonee finished filling out the forms, two young men practically fell over each other trying to get to Jonee's bags. It was just the kind of negative attention Victoria had hoped to avoid.

After they had unpacked and settled in their rooms, the boys, who had become quite chummy, convinced their mothers to accompany them to the arcade they'd spotted in the hotel lobby.

"We're not staying too long, fellas," Victoria said, glancing at her watch. "The next shuttle to the Magic Kingdom leaves in an hour."

Jordan and Alec scampered about; they seemed content playing one video game after another, without giving a thought to the Magic Kingdom, or any other theme park that Victoria was impatient to visit. Jonee leaned sexily against the change machine, engrossed in flirtatious banter with the pimply-faced game room attendant. She didn't appear to be in much of a hurry either. Victoria wandered unhappily behind the boys, dispensing change on demand.

As a child, during a summer visit to California, Victoria went to Disneyland with her mother. But the memory did not evoke joy. Zeline had complained of a headache, exacerbated by the long lines, the heat, and all the walking. They had only gotten as far as Fantasyland, and Zeline was ready to leave, promising to return before the end of Victoria's stay. They never did.

A late lunch in the hotel's rather formal dining room did not go over well with the boys; they wanted McDonald's.

Unhappily, Jordan pushed peas around his plate, mixing them in with congealing mashed potatoes. Except for the roast beef, Alec's food was untouched also. Victoria beckoned the waitress for the check.

"We've missed two shuttles. The last one arrives at four. It's probably too late to start out for the Magic Kingdom. We'll have to hang out at the hotel tonight," Victoria said, apologetically.

"That's cool," Jonee said.

"There's a pool in the basement. Who wants to go for a swim?" Victoria asked.

"I do!" Jordan and Alec both shouted.

"Okay, but afterward I want you both to get a good night's sleep so we can get an early start in the morning." Victoria paused, scanning one of the many tourist pamphlets. "Wait a minute," she said, excitedly. "We can go to Sea World. It's not far, and later we can have a Polynesian luau-style dinner. Won't that be fun?"

Jonee screwed up her face. "Are there rides and things at Sea World, or just a bunch of fish?"

"Rides? No, but the boys will love it." Victoria unfolded the Sea World map. "Look!" Victoria said, trying to sound upbeat. "There's entertainment. See!" She pointed to a picture of a dolphin twirling a ball. "A dolphin show, an exhibit…and the kids are allowed to feed the dolphins."

"I'm tired," Jonee said, stretching. "I came here to see Disney World, I wasn't planning on messin' with no fish… so I'm gonna have to pass."

"Come on, Jonee," Victoria whined. "They're not just ordinary fish. We'll see dolphins, sharks, and…" Victoria looked down at the pamphlet, her eyes widened. "And Shamu the Whale!"

Jonee sucked her teeth. "I told you, I'm not tryin' to see no sharks or whales. Why you trying to cram so much in one day? We got five whole days, don't we?"

"Only four after today," Victoria replied.

"Look girl, I just want to chill tonight. Eat dinner in my room and watch a movie. I don't feel like a whole lot of rippin' and runnin'."

Victoria was crestfallen.

"Why you gotta look so sad? Girl, go on to Sea World. I'm not stopping you."

"Okay, Jonee. If you change your mind, we'll be in our room for the next half hour or so."

"Don't hold your breath. But look…you can take Alec if you want to. He likes sharks and whales, don'tcha, baby?" Jonee patted her son on the head.

Knowing that Alec would be good company for Jordan, Victoria agreed to take him along.

After the trip, Alec ended up crashing in the room with Victoria and Jordan. Jonee picked him up around two in the morning, explaining that she was sound asleep and hadn't heard them knock when they returned from Sea World.

The first morning in Orlando, Victoria awakened early. Excited as Jordan, she couldn't wait to explore Disney World, the Epcot Center, Universal Studios, MGM Studios—she wanted to do it all.

On their way downstairs to breakfast, Jordan grabbed his denim jacket.

"Oh no, baby. We don't need our jackets. It's hot!"

Tossing his jacket aside, Jordan grinned.

Victoria picked up the phone to call Jonee.

"Good morning," Victoria said cheerfully to Jonee's sleepy hello.

"Rise and shine! Jordan and I are dressed and on our way downstairs to breakfast. The buffet started at seven." The buffet breakfast was included in the package and Victoria wanted to take advantage of it.

"I know you trippin'. I'm not getting up this early for no damn buffet. We're on vacation. Remember? I'm staying in bed, and I'm calling for room service."

"Get up, Jonee." Victoria dragged out her name. "The first shuttle leaves in an hour."

"Girl, I'm 'bout sick of hearing about when these shuttles are pullin' out. Why you wanna leave so early? Damn!"

"The Magic Kingdom is huge. It takes a couple of days, at least, to see all of it." Victoria couldn't keep the whine from her voice. "So, we'll wait for you in the dining room, okay?"

"Yeah, all right," Jonee mumbled.

Victoria and Jordan walked to the elevator. A white family of four, dressed in summer attire: shorts and sleeveless shirts, waited by the elevator. Victoria smiled a greeting. The mother responded with something of a facial contortion, and drew two freckled children closer to her. The father, perusing a guide to Orlando, became instantly engrossed.

"Hmph!" Victoria snorted, wishing there was a way to take back her smile.

Turning her attention toward Jordan, Victoria scowled. She wondered if she should have dressed him lighter. Would the heavy sweatshirt be too warm? Then reminding herself that white people were notorious for jumping into summer attire way before the temperatures required it, she relaxed. In Philly, white people threw down their convertible tops and headed for the Jersey shore at the first signs of spring, while black people, far more cautious, didn't shed their jackets until the beginning of June. And black people most certainly did not step foot on the beach until late, late June.

As the elevator descended, the white family chatted noisily, as if the elevator was an extension of their hotel room. Victoria spoke to Jordan in a hushed tone-requisite elevator etiquette, she believed.

"What's wrong, Jordan?" she whispered for the second time.

"I'm not hungry, Mommy. I don't wanna eat breakfast."

"You'll get hungry later, so let's eat now," she said, firmly. As they stepped out of the elevator, she coaxed him with one hand toward the impressive buffet table; the other hand removed his cap. Jordan looked at his mother, knitting his brows in confusion.

"You don't eat with a cap on," Victoria explained, but Jordan's expression did not soften with clarity. His mother was imposing a new rule.

Victoria surprised herself. Influenced by the elegant atmosphere, she instantly took on Nana's old-fashioned rules of etiquette.

Jordan refused to touch his eggs, bacon and pancakes. He ate a couple spoonfuls of cereal, then wrinkled his face, and poked out his lips.

"Knock it off, Jordan. Do you want to spend the entire day in the hotel room? That's exactly what you're going to do if you don't straighten up," Victoria said, unconvincingly.

Jordan slouched in his seat and continued frowning.

Victoria held Jordan with an unwavering gaze of disapproval. She was giving him the ultimate kids' vacation, and he had the nerve to pout. What an ingrate! And where was Jonee, she wondered, as she glanced at her watch for the thousandth time. Victoria's attitude was rapidly changing from enthusiasm to aggravation.

Finally, Jonee breezed into the dining room with Alec. She wore dark sunglasses, skintight pink capris with a tiny top that stopped at her navel.

Jonee insisted on dressing like a streetwalker; no wonder they were getting sidelong glances everywhere they went. Granted, Jonee was slim. She weighed no more than one hundred pounds, but her rear end was large, out of proportion to her size, and it protruded. It stuck out like an afterthought, and a longer top would have been more appropriate for a family outing. Victoria exhaled, and waved Jonee to their table.

The Magic Kingdom was a magical experience, indeed, rendering the bumpy morning start a vague memory. The boys were enthralled by the parade of Disney characters that marched along Main Street. And Jonee was having a ball! Victoria's body shook with laughter as she watched Jonee running down Main Street with a pack of kids, in hot pursuit of Disney characters.

Not once during their entire stay did Victoria wear a drop of make-up—not even lipstick. Jonee wore enough for them both.

Each morning Victoria and the boys ate a buffet breakfast in the hotel dining room, while Jonee spent the time painting her face and diligently applying false eyelashes. Victoria couldn't imagine why Jonee bothered with such a time-consuming, tedious task. One morning, Jonee's lengthy make-up ritual caused them to miss both the eight and nine o'clock shuttles. Jordan and Alec were inconsolable as they watched the little van pull off without them.

On that day, Victoria drove herself and the boys to Universal Studios in a rental car, leaving Jonee at the hotel, alone with her silly lashes—all day.

The primary purpose of the trip to Orlando was to spend quality time with their kids, not to pick up men, as Jonee's come-hither look suggested. But Victoria kept her thoughts and opinions to herself; she had learned to tread lightly on the subject of Jonee's appearance or behavior.

On their last night in Orlando, Jonee asked Victoria to baby-sit Alec overnight.

"I have a date," Jonee whispered. Her eyes danced with excitement. "Got two customers lined up, and I'm charging vacation rates. Two hundred a piece—plus tips. Girl, you know I'm not about to turn down that kind of money."

Unable to speak, Victoria could only gape at Jonee and shake her head. Jonee was conducting business from her hotel room. Soliciting customers in Orlando—family-oriented *Orlando*? Instantly, an image of the father of the unfriendly family that Victoria had encountered at the elevator flashed across her mind.

It occurred to Victoria that Jonee had been enjoying a lot of free time during their vacation. Tonight probably wouldn't be the first time she'd used her room for illicit activities. The woman had stooped lower than Victoria thought her capable. But without uttering a sound of condemnation, keeping her feelings to herself, Victoria agreed to baby-sit. By the time Alec arrived in pajamas, Victoria's emotions had run a full range from shock, disgust, and anger at Jonee to total sympathy for the sweet little boy. Clearly, Jonee's priorities were skewed; her child deserved better.

❦

The temperature in Orlando had shot up to the nineties, and so they returned to Philly clad in summer attire, purchased from a strip mall near the hotel.

"We're just getting back from Florida. You wouldn't believe how hot it was," Jonee explained to the bundled-up, harried travelers at Philadelphia International Airport, who didn't appear the least bit interested.

Weary of Jonee, and seriously contemplating ending the friendship, Victoria was relieved when Jonee's luggage appeared on the revolving rack.

"Do you want me to wait for you?" Jonee asked.

"No, go ahead. Who knows how long this will take."

"Okay, well...I'll see you at work. Alec, tell Jordan goodbye."

Suddenly shy, the two boys blushed and raised their hands in an awkward farewell.

"When are we going back to Disney World, Mommy?" asked Jordan, sporting Mickey Mouse ears.

"We're not even out of the airport yet, and you're already asking to go back," Victoria admonished, but was secretly tickled that Jordan had had such a good time, he wanted to return to Orlando.

"Is our plane going right back to Disney World, Mommy?"

I'm not sure, honey. I don't think so. The plane probably needs to be refueled before it takes off again, and I'm sure the pilot needs to rest before he flies the plane again."

Jordan's face lit up. "I want to be a pilot. Can I Mommy, please?"

Victoria chuckled. "Sure, Jordan. You can be anything you want to be."

"Can I fly my airplane to Disney World everyday? Can I, Mommy?"

"Of course, you can. But pilots don't just fly to Florida. They fly all over the world."

For the past week, Victoria had lived a normal life; she'd been a good mother who devoted much time and attention to her child. But Jordan's innocent little face looking up at her, his words filled with hope, had reminded Victoria of her own lost dreams.

"When can I start, Mommy?"

"Start what?" she asked, distracted.

"Start being a pilot."

Victoria lovingly cupped her son's face. "You can start preparing now. We'll get lots of books about airplanes, and when you're a little older you can take flying lessons."

Their luggage finally appeared. Jordan dragged a large net bag filled with Florida oranges while Victoria carried the luggage with one hand, and squeezed her son's small free hand with the other. She tightened her grip with each step, silently willing Jordan to never accept defeat as she had.

Chapter 18

Victoria was sorry she'd responded to Rover's eight-a.m. call of distress. He'd said that he needed her to fill in for Zoe, the only black girl allowed to work the morning shift.

Victoria wasn't scheduled to return to work for two more days. Unpacked luggage, stacked in a corner in the bedroom, implied that she was still in vacation mode-mentally unprepared for the frenetic energy at Pandora's Box.

"You'll be perfect on the morning shift," Rover had said. "We have a nice clientele. Mainly businessmen who prefer the classy type…like you."

Victoria should have followed her instincts, but instead she allowed Rover's flattery, along with her own greed, to uproot her from her warm, safe bed.

Victoria entered the lounge and was hit with a feeling of foreboding. Oh God! Not an anxiety attack. It had been months since the last one.

Perhaps her anxiety stemmed from her lack of familiarity with the four white girls she'd be working with, though she recognized one of them, Georgette, as the person who had greeted her when she came in for her interview with Rover.

The personalities of the morning shift, Victoria noticed, were very different from those on the second shift. They were an alert and peppy group—energized Barbie dolls, chatting amicably, though clearly ignoring Victoria. The Barbie dolls were dressed and made up before Victoria had even figured out which restaurant would deliver the coffee necessary for her to function. If her sluggish movements were indicative of her ability to make money, then she was headed for big trouble.

Fueled by indignation, Victoria mustered the energy to flip her braids dramatically and turn up her nose, sending the message that she was unfazed by their silent treatment. Across the room, she noticed a menu tacked to the wall. She sauntered over. There was a five-dollar minimum for delivery. She scanned the breakfast selections, but nothing looked appealing, everything was high-cholesterol, and higher fat. Victoria used the pay phone to order a large coffee and a bagel—no butter, totaling three dollars and tax. What the hell, she'd just have to pay the extra money, she certainly wasn't going to try to find out if any these bimbos wanted to place an order.

The first customer of the morning arrived before the coffee, but Victoria joined the bevy of girls at the door anyway. A professional-looking white man, who wore a suit beneath a trench coat, and carried a briefcase, stood in the lobby, smiling. Grey eyes flicked with interest from girl to girl, but there was cool indifference when he noticed Victoria.

Racist, she muttered to herself, then abruptly spun around and returned to the lounge to wait for the delivery guy. There was no point in standing around trying to dazzle the customer with a hard-to-hold fake smile when he had shown no interest in her.

The man selected a tall, slender blonde named Diana, who resembled the late British princess uncannily. Diana smiled smugly at her competitors before she swept off, leading the man and his briefcase up the corridor. Victoria was mildly amused by the reactions of those who weren't chosen. They streamed back into the lounge red-faced and pouting. Amanda, who was as tall and slim as Diana, but past her prime, chewed her lower lip furiously.

The bell rang. Victoria rushed to answer it with the seeming assurance that the caller was for her. As expected, it was the guy from the deli. She handed the young black man a ten-dollar bill and waited for change. The pleasant looking, chubby-cheeked fellow could hardly conduct the money exchange as he gawked at the nearly-nude women who had rushed to the door, then swiftly retreated, en mass, back to the lounge.

Violated, apparently, by the black man's roving gaze, the white women huffed indignantly and cloaked themselves with robes, sweaters, towels—anything that covered their exposed body parts.

"What kind of place is this?" he inquired, whispering.

Despite the young black man's shameless interest in Caucasian women, buoyed by a desire to further provoke her co-workers, Victoria responded with a wink. "This is a whorehouse."

"Damn," he exclaimed, prolonging the word. "I thought something freaky was going on up in here. How much to get with one of y'all?" He craned his thick neck as far as he could, looked past Victoria, as if her presence was inconsequential, and ogled the disinterested white women in the lounge.

Victoria shook her head. What was wrong with some black folks? This moron was practically drooling. Didn't he realize that his behavior perpetuated the myth that all black men desired and preferred white women? An annoying image of Justice Martin's white secretary flashed in Victoria's mind. Uncharacteristically, Victoria snatched her change—a five-dollar bill the delivery guy held out trance-like, as he surveyed the lounge.

"It costs more than a coffee peddler could ever afford, so hit the pike, you sell-out!" She slammed the door in his startled face, feeling justified in not giving him a tip.

"What did that black guy ask you, Pleasure?" asked a little waif who had not, until that moment, spoken a word to Victoria.

"And you are?" Victoria asked in a haughty voice.

"Lara," she said, in a matching waif-like voice.

"And why should I indulge your curiosity? Hmmm?" Victoria asked, feeling really bitchy.

Lara looked shocked. Her mouth curved into an uncomfortable smile that twitched.

"Why don't you just mind your business? Think you can do that?"

A hush fell over the room.

"What's your problem?" Lara turned and faced the stunned spectators. "Jeez, I just asked her a simple question."

Exhilarated by the tension she created, Victoria plunked down into the flower print chair. The room was so quiet, the squeak from the plastic lid seemed amplified when she lifted it from the Styrofoam cup.

Coffee, the calming elixir that it was, enveloped her with tranquility as soon as she took the first sip. She was suddenly very sorry for her harsh treatment of the delivery guy. She even felt sorry for Lara. With softened eyes, she glanced over at Lara, expectantly. Lara, however, pursed her lips and shifted her gaze. Oh well, I tried, thought Victoria as she gulped the coffee.

"I can spot an implant a mile away; every other woman at my gym has them," Georgette declared. "She's definitely had some work done. I mean it's so obvious. She goes away for a month and then comes back—sticking out to here!" Georgette extended her arms in front of her chest.

"I don't know," said Amanda. "Her boobs were already big. Why would she need implants?"

"To make more money."

Victoria simply did not care about whom the two women gossiped—another vain white woman, she supposed. She wished they'd conclude the senseless discussion so she could organize her thoughts, get centered.

The next time the bell sounded, it was a well-dressed, kindly-looking older man, with shiny white hair. He kept the front door ajar while he communicated something to his limo driver. The man held his hat in his hand and spoke the King's English perfectly. Victoria smiled and posed enthusiastically. The customer looked like an excellent tipper.

But again, Diana was selected.

While Diana was busy, the waif broke luck with a skinny, awkward kid, not more than a teenager. Georgette got the next customer, occupying the last of the three rooms.

Though she couldn't get a full view, Victoria studied her reflection in the bathroom mirror. She admired her teal camisole, and then frowned.

As pretty as it was, the camisole and high cut panties weren't working for her. She was getting really sick of jumping up and down, smiling and posing for nothing. One never knew what these stupid customers wanted, but clearly, she needed to change. Victoria put on a scarlet, sheer netted teddy with marabou feather trim and strutted back into the lounge, invigorated.

Victoria and Amanda were alone in the lounge the next time the bell chimed. Victoria prayed that she would be selected; her ego couldn't endure any more rejection. Victoria appraised Amanda as they both went to the door. Amanda was attractive and slender, but her body was not nearly as toned as Victoria's. Her face, though still pretty, was not perfect; it was marked with tiny lines, and there were crow's feet gathered at the corners of her eyes. Noticing Amanda's worst feature—her flat, sagging derriere, Victoria felt a surge of confidence as she walked to the door, quietly chanting positive affirmations.

An enormous grin spread over Victoria's face when she opened the door to discover one of her regulars, the amorous professor. What a relief! Now she wouldn't have to put up with the smug attitudes of her white co-workers who felt superior and believed that black women couldn't make money with the day-time clientele who were considered to be far more selective than the men who frequented Pandora's Box at night.

Surely, a higher power was instrumental in this little coup. Victoria said a silent thank you, acknowledging the miracle.

"Hi!" Victoria said, her smile filled with gratitude. She was not only grateful, but also extremely flattered that the professor had gone through the trouble to find out that she was working the day shift. Victoria was so filled with the wonder of the moment she didn't notice the professor's sheepish expression.

"How are you, Michael?" Amada asked.

Michael? Victoria actually looked behind the professor to see if someone else had come in.

"Would you mind very much having a seat and waiting for me, Michael? All the rooms are filled right now, but one should be available in a few minutes."

"I don't mind at all," the professor said, smiling lovingly at Amanda, without so much as a glance at Victoria

Victoria looked from Amanda to the professor like they were speaking a foreign language. This had to be a mistake. The professor was Victoria's customer—her regular, for crying out loud. But when Amanda and the professor gave each other a quick peck on the lips, Victoria knew there was no mistake. She knew well, his penchant for kissing. Ugh! And to think she had allowed it, for the sake of keeping him as a regular.

Livid, Victoria stormed out of the lobby and up the hall to the office, where Rover was setting up a display of snacks, condoms, beauty supplies, and feminine products.

"Rover, I want to leave. I'm not making any money. I'm just wasting my time being here—and I can think of a million other things I could be doing besides watching other people make money."

"You can't leave, Pleasure. You know the rules. If you leave, I'll have to suspend you, and who knows—Gabrielle may fire you."

"Fire me! This isn't even my shift! I came in as a favor to you...and I'm just sitting around doing nothing but suffering."

"Don't you think you're being a little dramatic?" Rover asked, looking mildly amused. "It's not even noon yet."

She glanced at her watch; it was five minutes to twelve.

"Give it a chance, Pleasure. You'll make some money."

"I don't think so." Victoria sighed in exasperation. "Why can't I just leave? Who's going to miss me? None of the airheads on this shift will, I can assure you of that. Nor will these customers—a bunch of bigots. I hate this shift!"

Rover squinted at his display, with his head cocked to the side. "Oh, I got something new you might wanna try." He handed Victoria a small plastic squeeze bottle.

"What's this?"

"Hand cleanser. Fights bacteria without water. Just rub it on your hands."

"No thanks," she said, handing it back. "I prefer soap and water."

"Yeah, but this will protect you from germs during those in-between times, when you can't get to the sink right away. The girls are buying it up faster than I can stock it."

"Good for them. I said I don't want it. Now stop trying to change the subject. How come this nonsensical rule doesn't apply to Sheena? She gets up and leaves whenever she's good and ready? Kelly does, too. And they're both addicts, dammit! Now I ask you, is that fair?"

"The world's not fair," Rover said, mechanically. "They both have drug habits; Gabrielle takes that into consideration."

"Well that makes a lot of sense," Victoria replied facetiously. "They can leave to go get high, but I can't leave to take care of my son who, by the way, was shuttled off to a babysitter for no reason that makes sense to me. I feel like a negligent mother sitting around here listening to the drivel from those idiots in the lounge, when I could be spending time with my child." Victoria's chest heaved with indignation after her tirade

Rover made the motions of playing a violin. Victoria chuckled involuntarily.

"But you really don't need me here, isn't that obvious?" she asked, still laughing. "Rover, let me go home." She whined playfully, dragging out the last word.

"Be patient. Everyone has a bad day every now and then. Every day can't be Christmas."

His words were scant consolation. Victoria didn't like the feeling of being low man on the totem pole. She didn't like being regarded as insignificant, as a nonentity.

"Your luck will change. If you don't break luck on this shift, you know you'll make a killing on your own shift."

"I'm living in the moment, Rover. I want to make money now, not in some distant, obscure future. Besides, I'm off tonight, remember? I'm still on vacation."

Victoria sank dejected onto the cot, focusing her attention on the TV screen as the News at Noon theme song began. Forgetting her troubles, Victoria smiled as she watched a clip of the black mayoral candidate. He was looking boyishly handsome in sweats, smiling and waving at the cameras, as he and a couple of handsome brothers jogged along Kelly Drive. Victoria leaned forward. One of the black men—the tall one—looked familiar. The smile left Victoria's face, her heart thumped wildly as she waited for the camera to pan in again. It was the opportunist himself, Justice Martin! Smiling broadly, he jogged with the soon-to-be mayor.

The reporter queried the candidate, who was now jogging in place. Victoria turned away from the images and tuned out their voices. She couldn't bear to watch Justice looking so decently All-American. He, the devil's spawn, who had ruined her life, was happily living his own, hanging out with the future mayor. No doubt, a photograph of that Kelly Drive run would grace a wall in Justice's office the instant the voters elected the candidate mayor. Sickened, Victoria stood up to return to the lounge. She wondered if the future mayor was aware of the low-life company he was keeping.

As the day wore on, the situation at work continued to deteriorate. Victoria was without a single session, while the four white girls hopped in and out of the rooms, gabbing merrily with each other. After being overlooked repeatedly by the entirely white, blue collar, and professional daytime clientele, Victoria stopped going to the door.

She had planned to hang out in the office with Rover until quitting time, but he informed her that the girls had to stay in the lounge. That was new information. She usually had to dodge Rover; he was always trying to lure her into his office to chat.

Amanda, who, amazingly, had more sessions than Diana did, gave Victoria pitying looks, while the others, deeming Victoria unworthy of acknowledgment, ignored her. Victoria mistrusted Amanda and refused to meet her gaze.

"Are you okay?" Amanda asked.

A sarcastic, "Paleeze!" was Victoria's only response. Like Miquon on her worst day, Victoria was feeling more than disgruntled.

As much as Rover loved Gabrielle, he hated her wicked side. She had so much going for herself. Why was it so important for her to control the girls who worked for her? He was following Gabrielle's explicit instruction when he called Pleasure to replace Zoe. To accommodate the occasional client who preferred women of a darker persuasion, Gabrielle scheduled only one black girl on the morning shift. Black girls did well on both the other shifts, but it was common knowledge that the daytime hours belonged to Caucasians. No one knew why.

Disenchanted after a couple of days on the morning shift, the average black working girl quickly wised up and switched to evening hours. But Zoe, light-complexioned, with auburn hair of her own, in addition to an assortment of blonde wigs and a variety of pairs of contact lenses ranging from hazel to sky blue, was determined to survive on the morning shift. Married, Zoe led a dual existence. In the beginning of her new career, Zoe had gone home empty-handed every day. But she persevered and managed to build up a respectable clientele. She didn't make a killing, but the money she earned provided her with the extras she desired. As soon as she'd gotten comfortable with the lifestyle, Gabrielle pulled the rug out from under her, insisting that she work the midnight shift, knowing full well that Zoe did not have the flexibility of the other girls. When Zoe refused, Gabrielle called personally to inform the uppity girl that she should not report to work, that her services were no longer required.

Gabrielle told Rover that Pleasure's popularity had gone to her head. She needed to be brought down a peg or two. How dare she leave work for over a week to take a Florida vacation? Even if she never set foot on the premises again, there was only one Queen Bee at Pandora's Box, Gabrielle had screamed at Rover. "ME!"

Chapter 19

At 3:30 p.m. Victoria awakened grumpily to the annoyingly high-pitched cartoon voices coming from Jordan's bedroom, fused with the shrill sound of the alarm clock.

"Jordan, turn that TV down," she yelled as she got out of bed. The volume decreased a decibel. Still half asleep, she shuffled into the kitchen and poured hazelnut beans into the coffee grinder and pressed the switch. The pleasant aroma jolted her into awareness. Having recently acquired a taste for gourmet coffee, she had an extensive collection. An assortment of expensive-looking bags that boasted a variety of fancy flavors: Toasted Maple Walnut, Godiva's Raspberry Truffle, Kona Hawaiian, Jamaican Blue Mountain, and Pumpkin Pie completely concealed a can of Maxwell House that hadn't been touched in months.

She wondered, idly, if the week would end with her topping the two grand she'd earned the week before. The memory of the profitless day that she spent on the morning shift was fading fast. On the five o'clock shift Victoria made money hand-over-fist! Images of crisp green money folded neatly in her purse gave Victoria a palpable rush.

She looked around in wonder at her new lifestyle. Everything inside her once dilapidated apartment looked and smelled brand new. Kitchen appliances glimmered and gleamed. Tags still adorned the stacked, apartment-sized washer/dryer she had bought from Sears. And hallelujah for that! Gone were the days of loading weeks' worth of dirty laundry into trash bags and then lugging the load into the gloomy laundromat.

After the owner had made the necessary repairs to the apartment, Victoria had gone on a nonstop spending spree. Every stick of old beat up furniture was tossed out and stacked curbside in a shabby heap and replaced with stylish new furniture, paid for in cash.

The freshly-painted living room walls were decorated with prints of colorful African American and Caribbean art, and an Andrew Turner original in an ornate gold frame was proudly hung above the buff-colored leather sofa.

Loony Toon characters raced across the curtains and walls in Jordan's redecorated bedroom. His new bunk bed was an elaborate piece of work with attached dresser drawers, a pullout desk, and a toy bin. The room was filled with new toys, books, and Jordan's very own TV and Playstation 2.

Parked outside was Victoria's new car, a metallic gold compact that she adored. Her income provided these new pleasures. Her child, like any other, she rationalized, deserved to live in a decent environment with bright, colorful playthings. It was her responsibility to make sure that he was never, ever deprived again.

She smiled to herself. Perhaps those accustomed to the rich highlife would scoff at her version of newfound wealth. Still, she was amazed and grateful for all her shiny new acquisitions. She had once believed that there was nobility in being poor-in suffering and sacrificing, but she now believed that it was shameful, sinful even, for anyone to endure the wretched existence of her former life.

Victoria poured a second cup of coffee, stirred in the nondairy creamer and sugar, and, with cup in hand, she padded back to the bedroom. Passing Jordan's room, she caught a glimpse of him aiming the remote at the TV-channel surfing. "Jordan! That's enough TV. Read a book while Mommy gets ready for work."

"Aw, Mom. I wanna watch *Arnold*."

"What did I say, Jordan?"

"But I can't read all the words."

"Try sounding out the letters the way I taught you."

Jordan emitted a sound of displeasure, which Victoria chose to ignore. She didn't have time to chastise her son; she had to start putting her work attire together. She picked up and examined the oversized pink nylon bag that was used to haul her essentials back and forth to work. When she unzipped that bag, the pungent distinctive scent of Pandora's Box was unleashed—that now familiar combination of cigarette smoke, hair spray, body spray, and sex.

Inside the bag were five outfits that she had taken to work the night before: four pairs of heels, stockings, thigh-highs trimmed with lace, a garter belt, cologne, make-up, a couple of wigs (one red, one blonde), a curling iron, a vibrator (to please her more kinky clientele), dozens of condoms that she bought by the case at Drug Emporium, a lubricating gel, body lotion, costume jewelry, baby wipes, a silk robe and slippers, a CD player (to mute the bickering and daily skirmishes among the girls) and, for inspiration, *Acts of Faith* by Iyanla Vanzant.

With spirits high, Victoria slung the heavy bag effortlessly over her shoulder as she locked her apartment door. She quickly dropped Jordan off at Charmaine's. There was money to be made—she could feel it.

Victoria pressed the doorbell at Pandora's; Arianna opened the door. Without cracking a smile or uttering a word of greeting, Arianna swirled around and returned to the lounge. Victoria's high spirits vanished. She had not expected to see Arianna; she thought she was the only black girl scheduled to work that night. For the past month she had managed to avoid the insufferable girl, scheduling her own workdays around Arianna's schedule. But it appeared that Arianna did not adhere to any schedule; she just came and went as she pleased.

It was common knowledge that she only came to Pandora's to drum up business for her own recently-acquired establishment. Jonee had seen an ad in the Adult Services section of the *City Paper*, announcing the opening of Tatianna's Boudoir. Jonee was certain that Arianna and Tatianna were one and the same. "Girl, I knew her when she got in the business about five years ago. We were both working at the peep show at 13th and Arch. Back then she used the name Tatianna. She was only sixteen, but pretended to be twenty."

Arianna's beauty could not be denied. Amazingly, five years in the business had done no visible damage to her looks. The corrosion and deterioration, Victoria imagined, was occurring on the inside and expressed itself as contempt for the customers and loathing for her co-workers, and more than likely-for herself.

With determination in her stride, Victoria entered the lobby, the hall, and then the lounge, encouraging herself to remain undistracted by Arianna's presence. However, as she watched Arianna prancing back and forth, wearing a straight black wig that accentuated her exotic look, and a sheer slinky gown, Victoria started counting her losses: the money she'd spent on parking and the babysitter, all for naught. Her night was ruined; she wouldn't make a dime. Not with Arianna competing with her.

"S'matter, Pleasure?" Sydney asked sheepishly.

"Nothing's the matter," Victoria snapped.

"Don't get upset with me. I didn't put her on the schedule." With a lift of her chin Sydney indicated the doorway that Arianna had just swished through.

Embarrassed, Victoria felt hot all over. It was preposterous to her that a silly twit such as Sydney could read her so well. She'd entertained a few wicked thoughts about Arianna, but had regarded her with indifference, never speaking an unkind word about her.

Arianna returned to the lounge; the doorbell rang before she'd even taken a seat. The caller, a newcomer who said his name was Rex, selected Arianna without hesitation. To keep her bottom lip from protruding childishly the way it did whenever she was disappointed, Victoria pressed her lips together firmly.

The next customer didn't arrive until nine o'clock. He chose Sydney. A few minutes later the bell sounded, and again, Arianna was chosen. Victoria and the others sat in stony silence while Sydney and Arianna conducted business. After their sessions, the two women returned to the lounge, talking animatedly about the huge tips they'd received.

In an effort to drown out their cheerful chatter, Victoria pulled the CD player from her bag and clicked on Jill Scott. Admittedly Scott was a superior talent, but Victoria was far too agitated, too envious of the singer's success to relax and enjoy the music. She popped the CD out and scrounged around in her bag, searching for music that fit her mood. She pulled out a Billie Holiday CD. Perfect!

"Pleasure." Lauren nudged Victoria.

Victoria reluctantly removed the headphones. "What?"

Lauren leaned in and spoke in a whisper. "I want to tell you about Gabrielle's party."

"Who?"

"Our boss, Gabrielle! You've never met her?"

"No. She communicates with me through Rover. I thought that was how she communicated with all the girls."

"Oh no. Me and Gabrielle have been friends for a long time," Lauren boasted.

"Friends?"

"Yeah, we're good friends. Last week she called here just before I got off and invited me to her party—said she would send a limo for me."

"Oh really? So you weren't invited, you were summoned!" Victoria felt bitchy. She was having a bad night and Lauren was bugging her, so she felt entitled.

Lauren's face turned a shade paler. "No. She sent an invitation weeks in advance, but Rover lost it and forgot to tell me."

"So, what happened at the party?"

"I jumped at the chance to go to her party because I was really mad at Raj… Uh, I'll give you an update on Raj a little later." Victoria groaned at the thought of another drawn out tale about Lauren's elusive Indian lover.

"Gab sent a stretch limo to pick me up."

"Oh, she's Gab now," Victoria teased.

"It was fabulous," Lauren continued, beaming. "Stocked with champagne. I started feeling a nice buzz before we even got to the bridge."

"Where does Gabrielle live?"

"Somewhere in Jersey."

"I've heard. Where in Jersey?"

Lauren shrugged. "I wasn't paying attention. Somewhere near Cherry Hill. You should see her home. It's unbelievable. A mansion! I've never seen anything so beautiful—not in real life. Gab's house looks like something you'd see on *Lifestyles of the Rich and Famous*!"

Lauren's wide-eyed naiveté embarrassed Victoria. She wondered why Lauren didn't realize that she and the rest of the stable at Pandora's had helped put Gabrielle in her mansion.

"I didn't even see most of the house because the party took place in the pool area."

Victoria shook her head and crinkled her brow. "You got in the pool? I'm shivering just thinking about going swimming this time of the year." White folks were truly a mystery.

Lauren let out a long, exasperated sigh. "What are you, a moron? We weren't outside. Gab has an indoor pool, a sauna, and a Jacuzzi!"

Victoria didn't take too kindly to being called a moron, but she restrained herself from retaliating with a verbal jab of her own.

"When I got there, Gabrielle gave me a quick tour. Her bedroom is beyond belief. Her bed is huge and round. Mirrors on the ceiling like they have at Inn of the Dove, and…"

"Who else was there?" Victoria interrupted, still peeved by the moron comment.

"Nobody. Just Gabrielle and her maid."

"Her maid?" Victoria smirked.

"Yeah, but she's not your run of the mill type maid. She acts more like Gab's assistant. She's young. Looks Hispanic…a really pretty girl."

"And when did the guests arrive?"

"Shortly after I did. Rich Italian guys," Lauren said, emphasizing the word rich. "They reeked of money. You could smell it. It was in their skin, their hair, and their clothes. Being around all that money and power made me realize how powerless Raj is. I had to face the fact that Raj's family controls him. I need someone who can help me get out of this rotten business." Lauren looked away, deep in thought. "You know, Gabrielle always says a man puts a girl in the business and a man will take her out."

"What's she mean by that? Is she talking about a pimp?"

"No. Gabrielle is saying that a girl ends up in the business when the man she depends on lets her down. For instance, my dad remarried when I was twelve. His wife hated me. She was so jealous of my dad and me. She put him in a position where he had to choose and he chose her. I got rebellious at around fourteen, kept running away. Don't ask me how I got started or who turned me out, it just happened. But think about it, Pleasure…if my dad had been there for me, I would have stayed home where I was safe. It would have never occurred to me to try to survive out on the streets."

"Lauren, you made a conscious choice to leave home. Your father didn't force you to—uh—do what you're doing. Subconsciously, you wanted to hurt him for what you perceived as his betrayal, but you really can't blame him for your decision." Victoria spoke softly, patiently, reasonably, and, as far as Lauren was concerned, patronizingly.

Ignoring the lecture, Lauren continued. "Gab said that while she was six month's pregnant, her son's father married a girl who lived right across the street from her. The pain and humiliation almost drove her crazy. He didn't have anything to do with Gab or their son after he was born. Gab said there were plenty of times when she'd be out with the baby, pushing him down the street in his stroller and her kid's father and new bride would drive right past them without so much as even blowing the horn. After that, Gab started hanging out with the wrong crowd and ended up turning tricks. But that all ended when Joey Rocco set her up with her own business."

Both women were silent for a moment. Victoria broke the ice. "But in a sense, Gabrielle is still in the business. Isn't she really just a front for that Rocco guy? I've heard that this place is owned by the mob."

Lauren looked around nervously; her eyes swept the room.

"What's the matter? Is the room bugged or something?"

"One never knows," Lauren responded in a whisper, eyes still bouncing around the room. "Gabrielle is way too smart and too business-minded to front for anyone. She already owns Pandora's, and now she's gonna open another place on Locust Street. A real classy place. Only the best girls will be allowed to work there. No druggies, none of the older girls, and only a very few black girls."

Victoria felt stung by Lauren's last remark. Still, it was useless to engage in a discussion of discrimination and racism in a place where nothing made sense anyway. Changing the subject, Victoria asked: "How old are you, Lauren?"

"Twenty-two."

Victoria sadly shook her head. "How long have you been…you know—doing this?" She couldn't bear to use the distasteful terms the other girls used so freely: turning tricks, hookin', or being a hoe.

"Since I was sixteen. I started out trickin' on the streets. Jumping in and out of cars down on Kensington Avenue. Gabrielle got me off the streets."

"Really!"

"Yup. I'll never forget it. Gab picked me out of a crowd of about six or seven girls. Most of them were druggies. She drove up in a Benz and handed me her card-told me I was too pretty to get myself all messed up out there. She said I could make a lot more money in a safe environment if I called the number on the card. I did and the rest is history," Lauren concluded with a shrug.

"You're grateful to Gabrielle for exposing you to this?" Victoria waved her hand, indicating their dismal surroundings.

"Yes. Believe me this is better than trying to make it out on the streets. And if this place is so bad, then why are you here? And while it's on my mind, how old are you and how long have you been getting paid for services rendered?"

Victoria was unprepared for the sudden interrogation.

"I'm…uh…twenty-five and my uh, reasons for working here are personal. This is a temporary situation. I certainly don't plan on making a career out of it. I can't tell you how shocked and disgusted I am every time I hear one of the girls expound on the principles of what a good hoe should or shouldn't do. That is not how I define myself."

"A hoe is a hoe! And as long as you're here fucking and sucking like everybody else, it really doesn't matter how *you* define yourself…does it?"

Insulted, Victoria slapped the headphones back on, turned up the volume and closed her eyes. The music, however, did not block her jumbled thoughts. How did she define herself? She simply didn't know. She had to admit she was getting much too comfortable at Pandora's. Selling her body was becoming far less difficult than it had been in the beginning. She was caught up in the money and the things it could buy. Money was freedom; money was the medication that dulled her pain. And Victoria wasn't quite ready to let it go. But that didn't mean she was like the others who aspired only to being good hoes. She was embarrassed to admit, even to herself, that she still had hopes and dreams of music, her unrequited love.

Chapter 20

Rover reluctantly shifted his gaze from the color TV screen to the black and white monitor that revealed the activity in the lobby. He watched with little interest at the girls' futile attempt to tantalize an Asian customer. Rover recognized the customer and figured the guy would probably walk. He was one of Bethany's regulars and had been looking for her for weeks.

His eyes shot away from the monitor and returned to the more interesting happenings on the TV screen. Despite the poor quality, he loved homemade porno. No federal guidelines, no enforced wearing of condoms to ruin the mood. The camera panned in for a close-up; Rover was on the edge of his seat. The blonde was about to take it in the rear, but to his surprise and complete disappointment, the guy mounting her, with his needle dick, wasn't equipped to do any kind of real damage.

"Hey watch it!" The man on the tape cautioned, covering his face. "Keep that fuckin' camera away from my face." Rover frowned at the man's fleeting image. He was one of Gabrielle's big-shot associates—a grease ball from New York.

Gabrielle's laughter and a chorus of rough male voices could be heard in the background cheering for the man they called Danny.

The screen darkened briefly, and then Gabrielle appeared. The shock of her sudden appearance caused Rover to gasp. She was dancing provocatively, then stopped, laughed, and beckoned someone. Now her back was to the camera as she swayed and undulated to a silent rhythm. A beautiful woman with dark, wavy hair entered the scene, approaching Gabrielle from behind. She was much taller than Gabrielle and had to bend to embrace her. As the woman kissed the back of Gabrielle's neck, her long, dark curls fell and covered her own and Gabrielle's face.

Rover watched mesmerized as the two women moved together seductively. His body ached with urging. Fingers that stroked the rough stubble on his chin involuntarily traveled down to his crotch.

The camera shifted back to the blonde and the big shot. Rover was about to rewind to Gabrielle and the dark-haired woman when he heard footsteps hurrying toward the office. Arianna burst into the room, impatiently waving the Asian's money. Rover froze, wearing an alarmed deer-in-the-headlights expression. He recovered and tried to stop the tape, but clumsily pushed all the wrong buttons.

Arianna's eyes gleamed with excitement. Lauren was on the screen with two men. A man without a face was mounting her doggy-style, while she gave head to another hairy, faceless torso.

"The camera's kind to Lauren; she looks great! Who're her co-stars? I assume those studs don't want their faces associated with their miniature dicks." Arianna chortled.

Rover laughed nervously. "I was thinking the same thing. That girl looks just like Lauren."

Arianna flashed a cold smile. "Nice try, Rover. I'm not retarded and I have perfect vision. I wonder what Lauren would think of her look-alike?" She met his eyes challengingly, and without hesitating she stepped out into hall. "Hey, Lauren," she called. "Come here, I want to ask you something."

"Does your customer want a double?" Lauren called out happily, half-trotting down the hall.

"She's just kidding, Lauren," Rover said. He tried to spread his lips into a smile, but it came off looking more like a grimace. "Just kidding, go on back to the lounge."

Cranky from sitting idle for too long, Lauren stopped in her tracks. "You fucking assholes. I'm not in the mood for this shit." Clutching her robe, Lauren swished furiously back to the lounge.

Rover cursed himself for his carelessness. He shouldn't have played the video until his shift was over. Gabrielle would have his head for this. With a thumping heart, he logged in Arianna's session.

Arianna smugly held out her hand for the fifty dollars she was entitled to.

Hoping to buy her silence, Rover laid four fifty-dollar bills in her open palm and looked upon her with pleading eyes. Without acknowledging the bribe, Arianna tucked away the money, collected her customer, and as always, was in and out of the session room and back in the lounge in record time.

In an effort to gauge Arianna's mood, Rover paid close attention to the silent monitor. The next customer-a sallow-faced, skinny white kid, looked startled by the flock of women who surrounded him. Momentarily forgetting his own troubles, Rover observed the lobby and chuckled. The women were circling the poor kid hungrily, licking their lips like he was prey.

As Sydney mouthed the sales pitch, Rover kept his eyes fixed on Arianna. He was distracted when the kid pointed a bashful finger, indicating Sydney as his choice. Rover observed as looks of indignation and narrow-eyed suspicion formed in the faces of the women. He braced himself for the string of hissing accusations that the angry women would surely bring to his office. Sydney would be accused of dirty dealings of some type. It never ceased to amaze him how such coarse and hardened women so often behaved like little snot-nosed kids.

Fully aware that she was being watched, Arianna turned her face to the ever-watchful eye of the camera. Rover squinted at the tiny screen, hoping to find a hint of a truce in her gaze, but her eyes were filled with contempt. Though somewhat shaken, Rover was not at all surprised.

Back in the lounge, Arianna snatched off her wig and flung it in her workbag and vigorously brushed her own thick, curly hair. She stopped brushing suddenly and scowled at a Pepsi can on the plastic end table next to her chair that someone had been using as an ashtray. Angrily, Arianna sent the can clattering to the floor.

After securing her catch in the middle session room, Sydney returned to the lounge to get some essentials from her bag. Oblivious to Arianna's glare, she hummed a merry tune while rifling through the bag. When Sydney left the room, Arianna shifted her gaze to the remaining girls. She looked at each girl slowly, individually, with poisonous eyes, then snatched up her leather satchel and abruptly left the lounge. Curious glances and shoulder shrugs followed her departure.

To Rover's relief, her long furious strides moved Arianna quickly past his office and into the restroom at the end of the hall. But his relief was short-lived. He nearly dropped the stack of bills he was counting when she reappeared, seemingly from nowhere, swathed in black designer wool.

"It's too slow in here tonight; I'm leaving. I have better things to do with my time than just sit around with a pack of losers." She flung a handful of business cards across Rover's desk. Rover looked with great suspicion at the cards that were embossed with fancy hot pink script: TATIANNA'S BOUDOIR.

"You know you can't leave until the shift's over," Rover said in a placating tone.

"Oh really? Watch me! Not only am I leaving—I'll be back tomorrow on any shift I choose."

At a loss for words, Rover nervously scanned the schedule that was taped to the wall near the desk. "You're not on the schedule tomorrow. You know I can't let you work unless I clear it with Gabrielle."

"I'm not interested in the details of how you arrange it—that's your business," Arianna said, pointing a lacquered pearl-colored fingernail. "I want you to distribute these cards for me. Give one to every customer that walks through the door…but no young drug-dealer types. I don't want any riff-raff in *my* place." With narrowed eyes, she added, "Don't fuck this up, Rover."

"How can I give out your cards when I don't even have much contact with the customers? And you know Gabrielle is bound to find out."

"That's your problem, so stop sniveling. Pandora's Box makes tons of money and you're going to have to figure out how to direct some of it my way."

Rover nodded grimly.

"Do you want to know what Gabrielle *will* find out if I don't start getting my share of her clientele?"

Listening in rapt attention, Rover sat up straight. He looked into eyes that were dark and unblinking and waited for the next horror to unfold.

"Lauren's going to be pretty damn upset when I tell her that I witnessed her getting skewered on tape. She's going to run screaming to Gabrielle."

"But I didn't…"

"Shut up, Rover!" Arianna snapped. Resting the heavy satchel atop the desk, she leaned in close. "I overheard that poor fool bragging to Pleasure. The girl would not shut up about the fantastic time she had hobnobbing with Gabrielle's rich friends." Arianna paused. "Curiously, she made no mention of her film debut. I wonder why?"

Her voice was thick with sarcasm. "Could it be that she allowed herself to be taped because she thought the video was a naughty little secret between her and her so-called friend, Gabrielle. How do you think Lauren will feel when she finds out that Gabrielle passed the tape on to you-for your freakish pleasures? To keep you occupied during your long, boring day."

Rover flinched. Arianna picked up her business cards and began straightening them into an orderly pile.

"I bet there's even more to the story," she continued, wearing a satisfied smile.

She paused again, eyes gleaming as if she were savoring every torturous moment. Rover could hear his heart pounding and found the sound of it most unsettling. He never went around looking for trouble. That wasn't his make-up. He hadn't bothered a soul, so why oh why, he wondered, was this evil bitch trying to ruin his life?

"I think…" Arianna whispered knowingly, "that Gabrielle used Lauren to make a dirty movie for her Mafia boyfriend. I bet that tape's been copied and distributed all over the East Coast."

Rover felt his face flush; he dropped his head in defeat.

"I hate to disappoint you. I know you assumed that Gabrielle made the tape just for you… A gift! A little something to jerk off to." Arianna shook her head in mock sympathy. "You really are a pathetic man." Arianna hurled the words like rocks. "You're not even a suitable slave because your mistress Gabrielle won't even take the time to properly train you. What does she do? Instruct you via videotape?" She threw her head back and laughed cruelly.

It was sadly true. Rover could have easily cried. Gabrielle's mistreatment of him was shameful. He worked ridiculously long hours for so little pay. He did whatever she asked him to and more, anticipating her every need. But she was never satisfied. He was chastised daily over the phone. There was no appreciation. And worst of all, Rover hardly ever saw her. Using the back entrance, Gabrielle popped in once or twice during the week to collect money, always irritable, always in a rush. When she did stay to go over the books, Rover was banished to the basement or sent out to run an errand. But she had arrived earlier that day, wearing a smile and patted Rover on the head. "I have something for you, sweetie," she said and handed him the tape. "Be very, very discreet. Don't let any of the girls see this." Rover had considered the gesture to be a turning point. No longer would they be merely employer and employee. They'd become fast friends again. He'd be her confidante—and over time she'd come to realize that love as loyal and as deep as his was more valuable than anything money could buy.

Arianna, hateful bitch that she was, threatened to permanently damage his relationship with Gabrielle. Well, he wouldn't let her. He'd have to come up with a plan, a way to keep Arianna quiet.

Chapter 21

Heads turned as Arianna rushed past the lounge. Victoria, still seething, didn't give her a glance.

With a self-important air, Arianna punched numbers on her cell phone as she headed toward the heavy glass door that opened into the lobby. Before opening the door, she paused, pulled an earring from her left lobe and covered it with the phone. "Bethany, it's me," she whispered into the phone. "I think I may have some work for you tonight, so stay near the phone. I'll call you when I get home."

"Are you leaving, Arianna?" Kelly asked. The only response was the sound of the banging door.

The tension lifted. There was renewed hope; perhaps there was money to be made after all. Miracles were known to happen. During the waning minutes of a shift, there was sometimes a sudden, inexplicable rush of customers.

"Who has a dollar? It's time to get some customers in here!" Sydney exclaimed.

Kelly pulled out her money, but had only two fives.

Lauren quickly produced a crinkled one-dollar bill. "Get outta here." Sydney said, turning up her nose. "You know it only works if it's a new dollar bill."

"How would you know, Sydney? You never saw Bethany do the dollar trick."

"Well, I heard about it."

Victoria looked at the three women like they were from Mars.

"Whenever it was slow, " Kelly explained. "Bethany usta take a dollar and write all our names on it, then she'd burn the dollar in an ashtray. Immediately-like magic, a trick would ring the bell."

"That's not how she did it," Lauren said, rolling her eyes to the ceiling. "She only did it that way if we only had a dollar between us. Usually, we'd each put in a dollar and write our own name on it. Bethany would chant some shit she learned at that occult shop on South Street, and then she'd burn all our money together. And believe me, that little spell really worked. We'd all get sessions!"

"Didn't she burn a green money candle, too?" Kelly asked.

"Sometimes. She'd light the candle, mumble something, and let the candle burn a while—and bam! The tricks would come out like crazy! It'd be standing room only in the lobby!"

Victoria quickly pulled out a crisp one-dollar bill and handed it to Lauren, who seemed to have taken over the activity from Sydney. It sounded crazy, but it was worth a try. Since no one else had a dollar, Lauren wrote each woman's name on Victoria's bill. Victoria hoped that providing the money gave her an edge over the others for the next session.

Fifteen minutes later, the bell sounded. A potential customer, a scowling, beady-eyed man, looked the girls over one by one. Unimpressed, he sighed and shook his head. "Any big girls working tonight?"

"What is this, pervert night?" Sydney hissed before retreating to the lounge. Victoria threw up her hands in exasperation, and began to follow Sydney back to the lounge. Kelly and Lauren remained standing. Suddenly curious as to which woman the customer would perceive as a *big girl*, Victoria stood in the doorway to observe the interactions.

Showing signs that she needed a fix, Kelly fidgeted and impatiently shifted from foot-to-foot. She sidled up to the man. Towering over him, she stuck her tattooed bosom directly in his face. "Come on baby, don't you wanna play?" The man responded with a thin smile. Undaunted, Kelly revealed a pink nipple. She licked her fingertip and rubbed the exposed flesh. Looking a bit more interested, the customer stroked his chin.

Competing with a strung-out Kelly was not easy, but Lauren seemed determined to at least try. Admittedly, Lauren could stand to lose a few pounds. At work she wore outfits that accentuated her good points and hid the areas that needed work, but it was surprising that her ego allowed her to compete as a *big girl*. Victoria had to admit that under such desperate circumstances, she too would have flaunted extra poundage—if she had any.

Lauren loosened the sash around her black satin robe, allowing the man to see her bodily flaws (flabby thighs and a fat tummy) in a two-piece bra and G-string.

"I was looking for...you know—someone really big," he explained, stretching out his arms. The man shifted his body to turn and leave, but before the turn was complete, he was suddenly held in the grip of Kelly's determined green eyes. When she cast her gaze downward, his eyes followed, resting on her hand, which pulled back flimsy material, and completely uncovered the furry mound of her pubis.

"Okay, I'll take you." He pointed to Kelly, and then followed her to the first room.

A few minutes later Victoria got lucky. The cloud around her had finally lifted. Maybe there was something to that dollar trick after all! Her customer was a slight man with bushy brows, a beard, and thick mustache. His abundant facial hair seemed ill-suited to his narrow face.

"How are you feeling tonight?" Victoria asked cheerfully as she led him inside the first room.

He groped around in his pant pocket and pulled out two hundred dollar bills. "I usually see Zoe during the day and I give her this," he held up the money," and when she's really nice, she gets fifty dollars more." The sight of the money excited Victoria. "I guess she doesn't work here anymore," the man said sorrowfully. "You see, we had an arrangement and...."

"An arrangement?" Victoria said nervously, sensing that the money he held would never cross her palm.

"We had a good relationship. She trusted me, and I felt the same…and, uh, she didn't make me wear, uh, anything. I just can't feel anything…"

"You'll have to wear a condom with me!" She felt like throwing a hizzy fit, but managed to maintain her cool. "I can send someone else in if you'd like. Who would you like to see?"

"The thin girl," he stammered. "Light brown hair."

"Sydney?"

"I guess. But, before you send her in, would you please find out if she's an agreeable girl."

Enough was enough. Victoria could feel herself about to commit an assault on the stupid man. "You must be nuts," she exploded. "I'm not asking anybody anything. It's bad enough you came in here waving money in my face, knowing you were going to ask me to put my life at risk?"

Raising an unruly brow, he asked. "Do you think I have AIDS or something? I'm clean. I don't have any diseases. I'm a married man, and if I'm willing to trust you…"

Victoria shook her head, astounded that a married man, probably with kids, would walk into a brothel and argue about using protection. "I'll ask the manager to get Sydney or one of the other girls," she mumbled.

Victoria poked her head in the office. Rover was sitting at the desk counting money. "Rover, the guy in the first room wants to see you."

"Is there a problem, Pleasure? Did he give you a hard time?" There was concern on Rover's face.

Victoria smiled wearily. "No, not really. He's wants something that I'm not willing to do. Not only that, he wants to involve me in finding *an agreeable girl*," Victoria mimicked the customer.

"Okay, I'll go see what he wants." Rover pushed back his chair and stood up. He grabbed two of Arianna's cards and slipped them into his shirt pocket.

After conferring with Rover, the customer left a few minutes later, whistling merrily as he went out the door.

As the women who were scheduled to work the midnight shift began trickling in, the room became crowded with activity and the atmosphere changed from tranquil to tumultuous.

"Hey, Pleasure. Are you gonna stay for the next shift?" Lauren inquired.

Victoria shrugged. "I don't know, I'm getting tired—and disgusted. I should just give up, go home and come back tomorrow."

"If you're gonna stay you better hurry up and let Rover know before the schedule is full. I overheard Rover on the phone with Miquon about an hour ago."

"Oh no. Is she coming in?"

"I don't know. He told her he'd call her back to let her know if she could work tonight."

Victoria was not left to wonder long. A few minutes later Miquon pushed through the door, holding a grease-stained paper bag in one hand and her large cloth workbag in the other. Her dark hair was shiny from the gel that covered and hardened little curls.

Miquon unzipped her tight jeans. Everyone in the room looked the other way as she pulled, tugged, and wriggled out of them. Wearing only a sweatshirt and baggy, unattractive cotton panties, she plopped down into the empty chair that Lauren had occupied. Miquon was not concerned that Lauren's sweater was draped across the chair, a clear indication that Lauren would be returning to the seat.

Miquon began unpacking the canvas bag, and pulled out a variety of personal items that included queen-sized lingerie, a large jar of petroleum jelly, a CD player, headphones, a thin comb with a long dagger-like handle, a bandana, and a pair of boots. Various items of clothing were piled on top of another chair while her remaining belongings were spread out on the floor.

She tied the bandana loosely around her head and completed the look by sticking the pointed end of the comb beneath the curls on the top of her head. The comb protruded like a macabre feather worn on the head of an angry Indian squaw.

"Why are you wearing a scarf, Miquon? Are you planning on going somewhere?" Sydney's tone was thick with sarcasm.

"Why don't you mind your fuckin' bizness; don't be worrying about what's on my head! 'Cause I ain't even tryin' to mess up my hair, pullin' clothes over my head." Miquon snatched the comb from her hair, and used the narrow end to angrily dig into her itching scalp. She brushed away the dried particles of hair gel that fell to her shoulders. With each scratch she grimaced and groaned; it was hard to tell whether she was in ecstasy or pain.

While applying petroleum jelly to give some shine to her legs, Miquon stopped mid-stroke and reached for the greasy brown bag. She tore open the paper that covered a tuna hoagie; the strong smell of onions, peppers, and tuna lit up the room. Oblivious to the odor, Miquon munched noisily.

Unable to stand another second of Miquon's obnoxious behavior, Victoria bolted from the lounge. In the restroom she quickly changed into her street clothes. She mouthed the words good luck to Lauren on her way out the door.

The chilly night air felt more like winter than spring. Victoria breathed in deeply, hoping the cool air would help dissipate the sense of disillusionment gnawing at her. It was unfathomable to have been confined inside Pandora's, an insulated world of perversity, for so many hours and have nothing to show for it.

She buttoned her jacket, prepared to brave the two-block walk to the lot where her car was parked. There was not a sound or sign of life on the empty street. She gazed warily over her shoulder. Up ahead, a row of cars was parked along the street. From her vantage point, the cars appeared empty; the owners were probably masturbating inside the adult theater.

The dim streetlights barely illuminated the street. Victoria groped inside her pocket, until she felt the smooth, cool security of a small container of mace. With shoulders hunched, she walked quickly down the street. Then, startled by a horn honk, she stopped suddenly and reached for the mace container. Concealed behind tinted glass, the driver of a dark blue jeep lowered the window. "Whassup, Pleasure?"

Fear shook her insides. With a hand pressed against her chest, she looked up and discovered that the voice belonged to a very handsome, familiar face. "Kareem! You scared me half to death." Her tone admonished him, but her eyes were smiling.

"Sorry 'bout that. I was gonna come in there to see you." He nodded in the direction of Pandora's Box. "But then I remembered you got off at midnight...so I just chilled out here." Kareem looked even more adorable than she remembered. The corners of her mouth twitched, but she bit the inside of her bottom lip, controlling the urge to smile.

"Well I'm just amazed at your ability to remember my schedule after— let's see now—how many months ago? One...two...three?" She teased, counting on her fingers. After the horrendous night she'd just endured, she was surprised that she was even capable of being playful. It felt good. Real good.

"Yeah, I was tryin' to get back with you, but something came up. I had to go out of town."

"Yeah, yeah, yeah," she said, laughing. "Well it's nice to see you again, Kareem, but I told you...I don't see customers outside of work." Kareem flinched at the word, customer.

"I'm not trying to see you like *that*," he said, his dark eyes offended. Then, recovering quickly, he smiled. "I thought you might be hungry or something. Maybe we could stop and get something to eat. That's all. Nothing else."

She didn't say anything for a moment, and then assumed a sassy stance with her hand on her hip. "I'm not hungry."

"Then how about a drink?"

"Now that's tempting. Hmmm. I don't know..." A burst of cold air chilled her; she pulled up her collar around her ears.

"Why don't you think about it inside? It's nice and warm in here." Kareem patted the passenger seat. She drew in her breath, and reminded herself not to be charmed. Vivid memories of their night of passion reminded Victoria of how Kareem had ignited feelings that ran deep inside her, and then disappeared. She had to keep things in perspective and be very careful with him.

Victoria climbed inside the roomy Lincoln Navigator, and wondered how Kareem could afford such an expensive vehicle. The leather interior, and the state-of-the-art dashboard that lit up like a spacecraft impressed her. The huge luxury vehicle made her compact car seem like a toy, like one of the Hot Wheels Jordan pushed around. She drew back her hand when she touched the seat. "The seat is hot!" she exclaimed.

"Is it too warm? You can turn it off if you want."

"No, no. It feels good. Mmm. Very nice, Kareem."

Kareem quickly looked away, and started flipping through a stack of CDs, but Victoria had already caught an expression of boyish pride that told her he appreciated the compliment. He pushed a button that changed a rap CD to a slow tune by Maxwell. Persuaded by Maxwell's sultry falsetto, Victoria allowed her shoulders to relax, and got comfortable in her seat.

"I guess a drink won't hurt. But let's not go too far. My car is parked around the corner on Chestnut Street."

"Cool. I know a spot you'll like. It's quiet and the kitchen is still open—in case you get hungry."

Enjoying the music and the smooth ride, Victoria closed her eyes as they cruised along Walnut Street. The ten-speaker sound system gave the music an almost surreal quality. From the corner of her eyes, she stole glances. She noticed that although Kareem still sported designer labels, this time his look was softer-more GQ. Not as thuggish as before.

The club was situated on a small cobblestone street near Penn's campus. Though she lived in the area, she had never noticed it, but apparently the place was popular with college kids.

Kareem and Victoria squeezed through a throng of rowdy students.

"It's not usually this busy!" Kareem yelled over the noise. "But, it's spring break…" Scanning the room, he spotted an empty table. "Come on, I see a couple of seats." Kareem was almost a foot taller than Victoria; she didn't see a thing, but she smiled sweetly and nodded as Kareem squeezed her arm and maneuvered her through the crowd.

It was a romantic setting. Rose buds in a crystal vase. Candlelight. The table was positioned in a cozy corner toward the back of the room, far away from the noise. For some reason, Victoria felt as if the setting was orchestrated, as if perhaps Kareem had arranged it all. She didn't care. After they were seated, Kareem beckoned the waitress.

In an instant, a pretty, young waitress appeared at their table, pad in hand. "Whatcha havin'?" she asked, cheerfully. Overworked and over-whelmed, she still managed a wide smile that revealed perfect teeth. Victoria found herself thinking that a girl as pretty as the waitress would make a killing at Pandora's. She returned the young woman's smile, grateful that the she was waiting tables instead of competing with her at work.

Victoria ordered white wine; Kareem ordered a Coke. "I don't drink," he explained when Victoria lifted a brow.

"You look a little young to be a recovering…"

Kareem laughed heartily, cutting her off. "No, I'm not an alcoholic. And I'm not on any twelve-step program. I just don't like the taste, so I don't drink it."

Unable to come up with a clever remark, Victoria simply smiled.

"But since we're getting personal, let me ask you a question." Kareem paused, then asked, "What's your real name?"

"Victoria," she replied, relieved. She had been braced for a difficult question that began with: "What's a nice girl like you…"

"Victoria," he repeated. "That's nice, but I wouldn't have guessed it."

"Oh no? What would you have guessed? LaKeisha? Quineesha? Or Tyreesha?" she asked, laughing. So often her laughter was a fake response to something a customer said. It was refreshing to laugh in earnest.

"No, I thought your name would be something like…Angel."

"Angel?" she repeated, making a face.

Looking at her with soulful eyes, Kareem said, "Yeah, Angel." He paused, then shook his head. "Because I feel like I'm in heaven."

Caught off guard, Victoria blushed, and then lowered her gaze. She struggled to control the modest smile that threatened to become a ridiculous grin.

Kareem was a smooth operator. He knew exactly what to say. Victoria tried to suppress a smile, but couldn't. Then a look of worry clouded her eyes. What was Kareem after—a free session? How many times had she heard the girls at work expound on the qualities of a good hoe. It seemed that the worst thing a working girl could do was to fall in love with a trick, and give up the goods without monetary exchange. The stupid girls who engaged in this practice always ended up disgraced and ashamed when the relationship ended. The trick always returned to the place where he met her. But he'd ignore the foolish girl who'd sold herself cheap. Ready for a new challenge, he'd select someone who'd demand hard cash—up front.

Victoria did not aspire to become a good hoe, but she cringed at the thought of Kareem showing up at Pandora's and eagerly paying her nemesis, Arianna.

She'd have to be very, very careful, indeed.

But she was perplexed by thoughts of the time they had spent together. She was certain they had shared more than just a night of passion. Their lovemaking had been special; something deep and meaningful had transpired between them.

Feeling self-conscious, Victoria turned the wineglass to her lips and took several sips. She studied her hands, but not knowing what to do with them, she began nervously fiddling with the vase.

Without a word, Kareem extended an open palm, compelling her to look at him. Victoria lifted her gaze; she suddenly wanted so badly to trust someone again. She took a deep breath, and on a leap of faith, she gave him her hand. Instantly, currents, sensations, coursed up her arm. Their fingers entwined. She was caught up in the whirlwind of a touch so intense and as powerful as actually making love.

Chapter 22

Mommy!" The urgency in Jordan's voice jerked Victoria from a deep sleep.

"What is it, honey?"

"We don't have any more cereal."

"Can't you eat something else? There's some strawberry yogurt in the fridge; why don't you eat that?" Victoria stroked her son's face, hoping he'd cooperate. She wasn't ready to leave the warmth of her bed.

"Yogurt?" Jordan wrinkled his nose.

Victoria threw off the comforter. "Okay, all right. I'll fix pancakes."

Jordan yelped with glee.

Trudging into the kitchen, Jordan on her heels, Victoria couldn't help thinking hateful thoughts about her son's babysitter, Charmaine. The woman had disrupted her sleep earlier that morning when she brought Jordan home at seven in the morning—two hours earlier than she was supposed to.

"Girl, my beautician called last night to tell me that she had an early morning cancellation. You can see how bad my hair is looking, so you know I'm gonna be there as soon as she opens the door," Charmaine had said, laughing.

Victoria saw no humor in being awakened. She waited for Charmaine to mention returning the extra money she'd paid her, but Charmaine just signaled her son Stevie to follow her out the door. Victoria made a mental note to deduct the money the next time she paid Charmaine.

After Charmaine left, Victoria, still groggy from lack of sleep, had emptied a box of cereal into a bowl, added milk, placed it in front of Jordan and practically dove back into bed.

But cereal wasn't enough; Jordan was still hungry. She forced herself to become alert as she measured the ingredients for pancakes. Then, pouring batter into the hot skillet, her thoughts drifted to Kareem. Since the night they'd gone out for a drink, the night that had ended on her doorstep with a cautious kiss, Kareem had called every couple of days. "Just checking in," he'd say.

Awkward silences made their first telephone conversations choppy, without rhythm, but they soon progressed to lengthy, intimate discourse. Victoria was relieved to find out that Kareem did not sell drugs. He told her that he and a partner had recently formed a production company that handled rap artists.

"What's your partner's name?" she asked, stiffly.

"Max Kleinberg. He's Jewish, and he's down with rap."

Relieved that he didn't say Justice Martin, Victoria added with a chuckle. "Your partner's Jewish, and he's down with money!"

"Aw, that's cold. Why you hatin'?"

"You left that wide open. I couldn't resist."

Despite the staying power of rap music, Victoria still held onto the notion that except for Philly's own Will Smith, rappers were nothing more than thugs who were paid incredible amounts of money to spew venom onto borrowed tracks. But she kept those thoughts to herself.

Victoria encouraged Kareem to talk about himself, his work. His enthusiasm and drive were refreshing and reminded her of how she used to be. She offered little personal information, and Kareem didn't pry. The topic of her former marriage was not worth mentioning, and as far as work was concerned, what tidbit could she share? *I met a really weird guy at work today; he offered to tip me an extra fifty if I walked on his back with spike heels...oh yeah, and he also wanted to lick the bottom of my shoes!* It was doubtful that Kareem would be comfortable listening to banter such as that, and since she couldn't guarantee that she'd be able to keep her emotions in check if she discussed her past life as a singer, her contribution to their conversations focused on Jordan-the funny things he said and did, her hopes for his future.

Victoria and Kareem sometimes talked for hours at a time, but there was no mention of when they'd get together again. They were being cautious, and there was so much left unsaid.

After clearing away the breakfast dishes, Victoria napped undisturbed until noon. Feeling refreshed and invigorated, it occurred to her that she should tackle the chore of grocery shopping while she had the energy. Donning a pair of jeans, a Gap sweatshirt, sneakers and dark shades, Victoria pushed a shopping cart up and down the aisles in the supermarket. With his arms draped over the side of the cart, Jordan stood on the bottom rack and rode along. Ordinarily, Victoria would shoo her son from the cart as soon as pushing him became burdensome, but preoccupied with thoughts of Kareem, she hardly noticed the extra weight.

A sharp turn into the coffee aisle caused Jordan to yelp with glee as he clung to the cart wide-eyed and grinning as if he'd just survived a wild roller coaster ride. "Do that again, Mommy!"

There was enough coffee at home to last a year; still, Victoria inspected the containers of coffee beans. Cinnamon Viennese was a new discovery, but the bin was empty; there was only decaffeinated left. Victoria turned up her nose; decaf lacked the kick she needed to get her day started. She spun the shopping cart around and gave it a forceful push. Jordan was delighted to be in motion again as he and his mother speedily left the coffee aisle. Victoria stopped suddenly in front of the pasta and spaghetti sauce. Instead of scanning labels, she pulled her cell phone from its leather case and began pushing numbers to check her answering machine. There was only one message, and it was from Kareem.

"Hey, gorgeous. Sorry I missed you, too." Kareem said in response to her recorded message that began with: *Sorry I missed your call…* "Hit me up on my pager when you get this."

Victoria had to admit that she was quite smitten. And it was time to do something about it. She was ready to take their relationship to another level. There was absolutely nothing to fear. Kareem's awareness of her profession was a good thing, she reasoned. It absolved her from the burden of having to lie about what she did for a living. She didn't expect him to approve, but his pursuit of her was evidence that he had accepted it.

"Why are you smiling, Mommy?"

"Because I'm happy." She cupped her son's face and kissed him.

Victoria controlled an urge to page Kareem right there in the supermarket. She had a lot to say but decided to wait until she got home and could talk privately.

All interest in grocery shopping ended. Victoria scanned the items that were in her cart, trying to determine if she'd forgotten anything important.

"Can I have this, Mommy?"

Lost in thought, Victoria glanced at Jordan, who was holding a box of Fruit Roll-Ups. She muttered a vague response, which Jordan interpreted as consent. He tossed the box into the cart, and a large bag of caramel corn as well.

"This is fun, Mommy," Jordan exclaimed as he and his mother, both slinging groceries into the cart, sped up and down the remaining aisles.

At home, Victoria quickly put away the groceries, and then paged Kareem. Sorting through the ton of piled-up laundry gave her something to do while she waited for his return call.

Though she was waiting for the phone to ring, the sound of it made her jump.

She answered with a nonchalant: *Hello*, and had no idea why she found it necessary to play games.

"Whassup?" Kareem asked. It was his standard greeting.

"Hi, Kareem," she said, sounding surprised, as if she hadn't just paged him. More games.

"I'm stuck in Baltimore right now, but I'll be back in Philly tonight. So, look here..." Kareem paused. "I miss you, girl."

His declaration took her completely off guard; she was too flustered to think of an appropriate response. The first thing that popped out of her mouth was, "What are you doing in Baltimore?" in a thin, whining voice that she instantly regretted.

"I'm trying to take care of some business," Kareem replied. "One of my acts is booked to play down here, a young brotha called Indecent. I'm dealing with some contract issues with the promoter. Hopefully, we'll be able to work things out. But, I didn't call you to discuss my problems. You working tonight?"

"No!" she lied. She was on the schedule, but wouldn't hesitate to call out.

"Think we can get together?" There was a nervous crack in Kareem's voice. "I know you said you don't go out with…"

"Kareem," she interrupted him. "We can get together; I'd love to see you tonight."

"Sounds good."

"I'll pick you up around eight. Do you have a favorite restaurant?"

"Why don't you choose," Victoria suggested. Then in a sultry voice, she added, "I'm open to new experiences. Surprise me."

Chapter 23

Victoria was no longer upset with Charmaine. In fact, she couldn't thank her enough for agreeing to baby-sit for Jordan on such short notice.

"Your hair looks nice, Charmaine."

"Thanks." Charmaine proudly patted her new 'do. Her hair was pulled back into a thick French roll. The style was attractive, but did nothing for Charmaine's round face. Her beautician probably expected the style to have a slimming effect.

After agreeing to baby-sit, Charmaine asked with widened eyes and screwed up lips that suggested concern, "Are you working again tonight?" It seemed to Victoria that Charmaine's curious face had become an enormous circle with smaller circles filled in.

"No, I'm not working. Actually, I have a date," Victoria said, beaming.

"Well, you go girl. It's about time. Now you can start wearing some of those expensive clothes I know you been buying." Victoria looked surprised. "Honey, I don't miss much. I see you coming home carrying bags from Macy's, Bloomingdale's, and what's that other one...Neeman somebody."

"Neiman Marcus," Victoria said, laughing.

It was true. Victoria's closet was overflowing with expensive outfits she had never worn. Her date with Kareem was a perfect opportunity to wear one of her favorite dresses, a Nicole Miller black sheath. The dress was cut low in the front, and for maximum exposure, there was a long slit in the back. Seamed stockings would add an extra sexy touch, and show off her long shapely legs.

Victoria hustled Jordan to Charmaine's at five o'clock, then rushed to get a manicure and pedicure at the nail salon on Baltimore Avenue.

Admiring her shimmering oyster-colored nails, Victoria returned home at twenty after six. To set the mood, she clicked on the stereo and popped in *Voodoo* by D'Angelo. She filled the bathtub with warm water and peach scented bubble bath. Humming along with *Send It On*, she padded into the kitchen to uncork a chilled bottle of Pouilly-Fuisse and poured herself a glass. Sipping wine and harmonizing with D'Angelo, she returned to the bathroom. She carefully placed the wineglass on the side of the tub, lit a peach-scented candle, and deeply inhaled the delicious aroma that wafted through the air.

Victoria stripped out of her clothes, pinned up her braids, and eased down into the soapy water. A warm glow relaxed her body; she took a few more sips of wine before easing her head against the bath pillow. Behind closed eyes she saw a beautifully vivid image of Kareem—naked. Hot and excited, she sat up straight, splashing water from the tub as she fanned herself, then reached for the wineglass. She couldn't recall the last time she'd felt so exhilarated, so happy.

Victoria listened with a smile as D'Angelo belted out the question, *How Does It Feel?* She slid back down into the tub, knowing she'd get the answer to that question tonight.

❦

"You look beautiful."

Victoria managed to look both shy and seductive as she looked across the table at Kareem. "Thank you," she said, meeting his gaze. Then she looked around admiringly at the posh, dimly-lit room that was accentuated by displayed artwork. Adding to the ambiance were flowers and foliage that hung from exposed beams. Soft jazz played in the background.

"A friend recommended this restaurant. I wasn't sure if I was capable of offering a new dining experience to someone as sophisticated as you." There was a glint of mischief in Kareem's eyes.

The modest, downcast angle of Victoria's eyes revealed that she was flattered, but she made no immediate response. Kareem was so smooth, she wasn't sure if he was being playful or sincere. After a long pause, she said, "This is lovely, Kareem. Your friend has exquisite taste."

"True. I have to give my man his props. But you have to admit...I have pretty good taste, too."

Victoria looked surprised.

"It's obvious." He laughed. Then his tone turned serious and low. "Look at you. You're beautiful—intelligent. And no joke, Victoria...I can't believe I'm sitting here with you. "

The fear that Kareem was toying with her prevented Victoria from enjoying his compliments completely. Searching for a glimmer of deception, she looked into his eyes and stared intently. Reflected in his eyes were raw emotions that matched her own. She saw yearning and hope...a willingness to love.

Feeling safe enough to peel away a protective layer of nonchalance, Victoria said in a whisper, "For whatever reasons and for however long, I'm glad that you're in my life, Kareem."

Kareem didn't miss a beat. "And I'm going to be here as long as you want me to."

The desire for physical contact had never been so strong. It was on the tip of her tongue to say: "*Kareem, I want you now!*" Her eyes darted around the room at the other diners and she was reminded that they were not alone. More than anything, Victoria wanted to hold and be held by Kareem.

Mercifully, the waiter appeared with the entrée before the reckless words escaped her lips.

Suddenly awkward after the revelation of feelings, Victoria became pensive. She didn't know how to respond to Kareem's words. Her thoughts became troubled as she gazed at Kareem, his beautifully-chiseled face, the flawless toffee skin, the heavy dark lashes, and the silky brows. And she knew—had memorized—every contour of his hard, muscular body. Yet she and Kareem pretended that the relationship that was developing was something fresh and pure. When in reality, their meeting and union had been a tawdry, sordid affair. Victoria was hit with a wave of self-disgust. Their encounter had been an exchange of sex for money. An elegant dinner in a fancy restaurant could not change that.

Throughout their meal, Kareem tried to keep up a steady stream of polite conversation, while Victoria, hardly eating, pushed food around her plate, murmuring one-syllable responses. Affected by her mood and keenly aware that the one-sided conversation was not likely to improve; Kareem gave up, and became somber himself.

The arrival of the dessert cart seemed to give Kareem renewed hope of lifting Victoria's spirits. He enthusiastically pointed to the array of attractively presented, decadent pleasures. He tried to cajole Victoria into trying a sliver of this or a bite of that, but her woebegone expression did not change. They left the restaurant in a cloud of gloom that neither could explain.

Kareem shook his head, as if he could not understand how he had so abruptly fallen from favor.

The jeep roared toward the eastbound ramp of the Schuylkill Expressway. Silent, Kareem and Victoria both pretended to be absorbed in the music from the radio.

Knowing that she was responsible for creating the tense atmosphere that existed, Victoria wanted to say something that would clear the air, but the words would not come.

Kareem pulled up to the curb in front of Victoria's apartment.

"Thank you for dinner, Kareem. Everything was wonderful." Victoria's smile was tinged with sorrow.

"What's wrong, Victoria?"

"I don't know. It's hard to express. I probably just need some time alone to sort things out."

"Why? Did I say something to offend you?"

She shook her head. She wished she could say something to remove the confused hurt from his face.

"For awhile, everything was flowing perfectly. Then all of a sudden, you just shut down." Kareem waited for Victoria to respond.

Victoria looked up, her lips parted as if to speak, and then she sighed and shook her head, offering no explanation.

"Victoria," Kareem said in a sharp tone. "Why can't we talk about whatever's bothering you? You know I'll listen and try to understand." Kareem swallowed and looked at Victoria with pleading eyes. "Don't shut me out."

Without planning, Victoria leaned toward Kareem and placed her head on his shoulder. She felt world weary, listless, and weak. Kareem put a protective arm around her and kissed the top of her head. Moved by the gesture, Victoria tilted her head, offering her lips. But instead of a full kiss, Kareem gently brushed her lips.

"I've had a long day. As a matter of fact, the past two days have been crazy. So look, I'm going to call it a night. I'll call you tomorrow."

Like a spoiled child, Victoria was so self-absorbed she had ruined their evening, created problems where none existed, and had totally forgotten that Kareem was under a lot of stress. He'd asked her out so he could relax and unwind. Her sudden mood swing had caused him more angst. She was thoroughly ashamed of herself.

Wordlessly, Victoria got out of the jeep. Her heels rapped the pavement as she rushed toward the steps that led to her apartment. With the motor running, Kareem sat behind the wheel and watched as Victoria disappeared behind the steel security door.

Chapter 24

A massive maple tree shaded the quaint little house that was graced by neatly-trimmed hedges and blossoming roses. Below the windows, flowers that were set in brightly-colored wooden boxes danced in the breeze. The structure had the innocent appearance of a dollhouse and blended in with the other well-tended homes on Naudain Street. There was no hint of the bawdy activities that went on inside.

A man who had parked his car a block away, made hesitant steps toward the front door. He checked the address that was scrawled on a piece of paper before pressing the doorbell.

Arianna reached for the buzzer, admitting the fourth customer of the day. Prices at Tatianna's Boudoir started at two hundred and fifty dollars. The money that Arianna expected to receive from the gentleman at the door would bring her a total of at least one thousand dollars. That money would be tripled by the end of the night if none of her scheduled clients cancelled.

Arianna sat behind an elegant oak desk in a room that was put together tastefully with the assistance of an interior decorator. Large ferns in ceramic pots were placed carefully for just the right amount of sun. Philodendra and spider plants dangled from the windows, and a crystal vase filled with a bouquet of freshly-cut wildflowers adorned the desktop, adding a splash of brilliant color to the room's muted color scheme.

"My name is Joe," the man said, without bothering to part his lips into a polite smile.

Preferring transactions that did not require friendly social interactions, Arianna wore a stoic expression and did not extend a cordial greeting either as she surveyed the man.

His weathered look suggested that years of outdoor activity had taken a toll. Icy blue eyes were starkly contrasted against his tanned leather skin.

"You called yesterday, right?" Arianna asked. Joe was a name that was commonly-used by customers who wanted to conceal their true identity. She wanted to make sure he was the Joe she was expecting.

"Yes. I have a two o'clock appointment." The words came out staccato. "I requested someone submissive." Joe looked at Arianna suspiciously. His expression suggested that he was doubtful that Arianna would fit the bill, that he did not intend to waste money on the arrogant young lady who sat before him.

"Is my appointment with you?" he inquired gruffly.

"Of course not," Arianna responded sardonically. "Your submissive will be here shortly," She emphasized the word submissive. "You're a little early, so why don't you have a seat? Would you like a drink while you wait?" She waved her hand in the direction of a brass cart with a glass top that was set up with an assortment of top shelf liquor.

"No thanks." He glanced impatiently at his watch and handed her three hundred dollar bills.

"Thank you," Arianna said without emotion as she slipped the bills inside an envelope in the middle desk drawer. "Bethany will be with you, and as I said, she'll be here shortly. Your session is for one hour and will take place in the downstairs chamber." Arianna's eyes glimmered. She was proud of her fully-equipped dungeon.

Joe sank into an overstuffed sofa, and then scooted to the edge. Ignoring the carefully arranged magazines displayed on the coffee table in front of him, he kept his cold eyes fixed on the front door.

Arianna wondered if Bethany enjoyed being submissive or had she been reduced by her crack habit to do anything for a quick hit. Then with a wry smile, she thought, as long as Bethany took care of the difficult customers who wanted things that Arianna chose not to do, she didn't really give a shit what motivated the trifling girl. Bethany was so trifling she had smoked up the money that was collected for her baby's funeral and because of that, she couldn't even get her job back at a seedy place like Pandora's Box.

Fifteen minutes later, Joe sighed audibly and shot Arianna an accusing glance. The sigh and a succession of heavy foot taps as he clasped and unclasped his hands clearly indicated that his patience was wearing thin. Arianna appeared not to notice the man's discomfort as she wrote in a ledger, spoke to potential clients, and made appointments over the phone. But she was livid. She was on the verge of telling the foot-tapping asshole to take his money and get lost. He was working her last nerve.

Finally, Bethany arrived—disheveled and twenty minutes late. There was smudged black mascara and liner around her eyes, traces of make-up from the night before. Her thin, oily hair was pulled back with a dingy white scrunchy. She wore a wrinkled sweatshirt, a faded pair of black jeans. The Nikes on her feet, beat up with filthy laces, had seen better days.

Wearing an embarrassed grin, Bethany said to the man, "Give me a few minutes to change. I'll be right with you."

Arianna glared at her, then turned to the stone-faced client.

"I assure you, sir, I do not condone tardiness. If you'd like to see some-one else at another time, it's not a problem. I can give you a full refund."

Bethany's eyes widened. She owed her dealer half of the one hundred dollars that Arianna had promised for the session.

After losing her job at Pandora's, Bethany started turning tricks in cars on Twenty-second Street in North Philly. Charging only twenty dollars for a blowjob and sometimes less if the competition was stiff made it next to impossible to earn a hundred dollars on most nights. The dominance sessions that Arianna offered lasted only an hour and always paid well. Besides, the spankings and other physical abuse she endured dulled the continuous emotional pain almost as effectively as crack. On the occasions when a customer chose to torment her mentally by spitting at her and calling her names like bitch, whore, cum slut, and worthless white trash—she couldn't disagree. What kind of mother, she asked herself repeatedly, bore four children and ended up with none.

"That's okay. She'll do," Joe said. He rolled his eyes heavenward.

Bethany tossed him a look of gratitude, which he returned with vacant, dead eyes.

"Bethany will be with you in a moment," Arianna said, managing a slight smile. "You can come with me."

Looking regal in a flowing crepe dress, Arianna cast Bethany another disapproving glance, then escorted the client past two sunny Victorian-style bedrooms and across shiny parquet floors to a stairwell that led down to the basement.

When Arianna returned upstairs the sight of Bethany slouched on the love seat offended her.

"I am so humiliated. How dare you come here late and looking like shit? Please get off my furniture."

Bethany sprang up. "I'm really sorry, Arianna. I overslept and..."

"Shut up, Bethany," Arianna snapped. "Look, you're almost a half hour late and I had to return half his money," she lied. "Needless to say, if you want the session I'm going to have to deduct half of your pay."

Bethany swallowed and nodded her head.

"So what does he want to do? Greek?" Bethany asked, ready to get the session over.

"I don't know if he's into Greek. I don't care. If he wants Greek included in his session, then so be it. He asked for a submissive and I booked your worthless ass for the session because you told me you'd do it." Arianna looked upon Bethany with murderous eyes. "Listen, Bethany, I've had it up to here with you. You're late and your appearance makes me want to throw up. So if you're no longer interested in complying with the desires of my customer, then just get the fuck out."

Arianna's harsh words, coupled with the way her lips were twisted, made Bethany flinch. "No, no. Uh, it's cool," Bethany stammered. "I was just wondering before I went down there if you knew what he wanted to do."

Arianna sighed, then dramatically held up her wrist and stared at her Movado bracelet watch. "I'd love to chat, Bethany, but..." Bethany about-faced and headed for the stairs. Like a lamb to slaughter, Bethany gripped the railing and descended slowly.

Chapter 25

Victoria did a double take when she arrived at work and saw a young black girl languishing on the sofa in the lounge. At first glance, the girl looked to be no more than fifteen or sixteen, looking closer, it was apparent that she was a little older—eighteen, at least. The girl was the color of mocha and wore emerald contacts that gave her an eerie feline look. Her dark hair was streaked with blonde, pulled back with a curly artificial ponytail. Tiny swirls of hair were plastered to her forehead and hardened with gobs of gel. She wore a gold lamé halter and skirt set; the skimpy skirt barely covered her tiny butt. The girl lit a cigarette and puckered berry-colored lips as she blew out long streams of smoke in a manner that informed everyone in the room that she was not to be fucked with.

"Girl, it's gonna be a mess in here tonight," Jonee warned in a hushed voice as she nudged Victoria and cut her eyes in the direction of the nubile vixen.

"What kind of mess? What are you talking about?" Victoria asked with an edge in her voice. Although the presence of the young girl did not bode well, Jonee's doom and gloom talk was unsettling and annoying. Victoria had been on edge and testy ever since her botched date with Kareem two nights ago.

"That little hoochie's gonna get all the money tonight."

"Why do you say that? She looks like a child."

"Duh! That's what I'm talking about!" Jonee waggled her finger and twisted her neck around to emphasize her point. "That chile looks like a little girl dressed up like a woman. The tricks are gonna take a look at her and lose their minds. What do you think they fantasize about? I'm telling you, Pleasure, not ne'er motherfucka in here—black or white, is gonna make a dime tonight. "

Victoria sighed resignedly and made a mental count of the girls working. There were six including the young girl—three black and three white. Too many for a Monday night. She should have stayed home and tried to patch things up with Kareem.

"She cleaned up on the morning shift. Everybody went home broke." Jonee continued to rage. "Even the blondest blonde with the biggest tits couldn't make any money. She should have took her greedy narrow ass on home, but nooo…she wants more money. Fuckin' bitch!"

Victoria had a vision of the horrible time she'd had when she worked the morning shift and had left empty-handed. "She made money on the morning shift?" Victoria asked, incredulous. "I thought only light-skinned girls…"

"Chile, please," Jonee interrupted with a wave of her hand. "How many times do I have to tell you: there ain't no accounting for the taste of a trick!" On a roll, Jonee continued, "Miss Thang brought out the freaky deaky in all those morning shift businessmen. If you think I'm lying, go ask Rover to let you see the sheet from this morning. Hershey's name is all up and down the page."

"Hershey?"

"Yeah, that's what she calls herself," Jonee replied, her lip curled in a snarl.

Overcome by what she felt was irrational fear, Victoria felt a sinking sensation in the pit of her stomach. She couldn't afford to sit around without making any money when she only had two hundred dollars to her name.

Ever since she'd started working at Pandora's Box, Victoria had spent money as quickly as she made it. Sometimes it seemed to her that the money was something vile and she had to get rid of it. Besides the home of her own that Nana had wanted for her, there wasn't another thing that she needed for herself or Jordan. And so that very morning, after tossing the idea around for weeks, Victoria put thirty-five hundred dollars into a high interest one-year certificate of deposit, never doubting that she could make the money back quickly.

It was the first step toward securing their future. The purchase of the CD had given her the adrenaline rush that she needed. She had planned to buy another with an even higher interest rates, and perhaps call a financial advisor to find out how to sock away some of her tax-free dollars. Those thoughts had motivated Victoria to once again leave the sanctuary of her apartment to sell her soul at Pandora's Box.

Engrossed in her thoughts, Victoria caught only the tail end of something Jonee whispered.

"What did you say?"

"I said we have to figure out a way to get her out of here."

Involuntarily, Victoria shot a guilty glance at Hershey. Seeming to suspect that Jonee and Victoria were whispering about her, Hershey shifted her position on the couch and arched her back like a cat ready to attack. Narrowing her eyes at Victoria, Hershey drew up her lips. The sight was so disturbing, Victoria eagerly accompanied Jonee into a vacant room to talk privately.

Still wearing her street clothes, Victoria dragged her workbag into the room and began rummaging through it, pulling out and examining one outfit after another.

"I'll tell you one thing," Jonee said. "If the gov'ment don't do something about welfare reform, this place is going to be swarming with hot-to-trot hoochies just like Hershey."

Victoria looked at Jonee quizzically.

"That's right! Those bitches getting kicked off welfare ain't prepared to hold down no job. They done got accustomed to getting paid to watch soap operas and run they mouths on the phone all day. They got bad habits and no type of work ethic. They can't handle the responsibility of holding down no job-especially a job that's only paying minimum wage."

Victoria was hesitant to get into a political discussion with Jonee, who tended to be overbearing and inflexible in her opinion. "So what is your suggestion?" Victoria asked, treading lightly. "The welfare system has failed, change was necessary."

"The gov'ment created that monster. Why should the rest of us suffer? Let 'em stay on welfare. What difference does it make? This country can afford it with all the money politicians waste on dumb shit." Jonee paused as she unraveled a new pack of cigarettes. Victoria watched Jonee use a long, navy blue, clawed nail to effortlessly extract a cigarette from the pack.

Jonee lit the cigarette and dragged deeply. "In my opinion," she said through a puff of smoke, "if you want welfare reform, then you have to take care of the next generation and educate 'em. 'Cause public schools in Philadelphia ain't turning out nothing but drug dealers, welfare recipients, and…and hoes like us!" Jonee laughed as she spoke the last few words, but Victoria didn't laugh in turn. She was in deep thought. Though spoken crudely, Jonee's comments provoked thought.

Victoria's anxiety deepened as she thought about Jordan's future. She regarded Jonee as crude and unrefined, yet Jonee had made her keenly aware that Jordan's early education could not be left to the public school system. She had thousands of dollars in designer crap in her closet and not one penny toward her son's education. She had planned to register him for kindergarten in the neighborhood elementary school. It hadn't occurred to her to start shopping around for a private school.

"So what do you think we should do?" Jonee asked, anxiously.

"About what?"

"About getting that little winch out of here!"

"I'm not comfortable with that, Jonee. I don't like the karmic implications."

"The what? Oh no! Here you go again talkin' that hoodoo shit."

Victoria laughed a deep hearty laugh. "Karma is cause and effect. There are consequences for our actions that determine our destiny. I can't knowingly…"

Jonee interrupted, humming the theme music from *The Twilight Zone*. Victoria and Jonee shared thigh-slapping laughter. The sound of it alleviated the tension as it echoed in the meagerly furnished room.

"All right, girl," Jonee said. Wearing a wry smile, she continued, "I don't want to have to worry about that karma mess or anything else following me around, so have it your way. We'll just sit tight and watch while Miss Chocolate Candy Bar makes all the money." She gathered her purse and glanced at her image in the mirror panels. "Hurry up and get dressed. I'll save you a seat in the lounge."

Victoria selected an aqua teddy with interwoven metallic thread that she'd worn before and had made lots of money. Perhaps she could recapture the magic. As she admired her image, her thoughts drifted to Kareem. He had promised to call, but hadn't. After all her sulking and pouting she couldn't blame him. She should have at least made an attempt to convey her confused feelings, but instead she became morose and ruined the good time Kareem had planned for them.

But it was probably for the best, Victoria surmised. Her life was so complicated, out of balance, and unfocused. She grimaced, imagining that the imbalance in her life had changed the color of her aura to some dark, murky, unpleasant hue. Yes, it was best, she concluded, not to involve Kareem or anyone else in her disordered life.

The doorbell sounded as soon as Victoria was seated comfortably in the lounge. Pushing past Lauren and Sydney, Jonee led the pack to answer the door. Hershey advanced slowly with a predatory gaze fixed on the door. Her movements resembled a cross between slithering and sashaying, which made Victoria distrust the girl. In an effort to put distance between herself and Hershey, Victoria did not leave her seat until she heard Jonee begin the sales pitch.

Harvey, an old Jewish man who'd been patronizing Pandora's faithfully for years, was in the lobby, holding a bundle of gladiolas. Harvey owned a shop on Jeweler's Row and was known to be an excellent tipper. He'd been seeing Lauren regularly for months, but like most customers, Harvey was fickle and apt to change his favorite girl at any time. Desiring to win him over, the girls who knew him offered their most alluring smiles and provocative poses. Harvey grinned, exposing a mouthful of ill-fitting dentures. Unaware of Harvey's reputation, Victoria gave a thin smile; Harvey looked like the type who preferred white girls. Hershey wore a serious expression and assumed a sort of B-girl stance, with her legs apart, her fists balled, arms crossed in front of her.

Parkinson's disease or some malady brought on by age, along with the excitement of being in the company of six tantalizing, young women, caused Harvey to tremble and shake uncontrollably as he considered his choices.

Apparently tired of standing still, Hershey suddenly broke from her pose. "My name is Hershey, the baby chocolata, whatever you want, you know that I got-a..." The words came out in a syncopated rhythm that was so unexpected and startling, mouths gaped and then, gasps, tsks, and nervous giggles were heard. Undaunted, Hershey continued, writhing snake-like to the beat. "So, baby, come with me—and I'll take you to ecstasy..."

"Hold up!" Jonee commanded. "What the fuck is up with that shit? This ain't no Rap City." She inched closer to Hershey. "And who you 'spose to be? Lil' Kim or somebody?"

Hershey's lips curled back in a snarl. "You better back off bitch, and get your old ass out of my face."

"*Old ass!*" Jonee and Victoria both exclaimed, though Hershey was referring to Jonee only. Being a lot older than she admitted, Victoria was personally offended. The words struck like a sudden slap; Jonee looked staggered by them.

"Who you calling old ass!" She lunged at Hershey. But Hershey was ready. She had been fighting her entire young life and was programmed for battle mode at all times. Both hands flew up; her fingers were curved in a clawed position. In an instant, sharp nails slashed Jonee's face, leaving four angry red stripes down each cheek.

Rover viewed the fight on the monitor and made it down the hall in several bounds. As he grappled to separate the two hissing and spitting brawlers, Lauren stealthily maneuvered a distressed Harvey away from the ruckus to an empty session room.

Breathing heavily, Harvey eased down into the hard chair. He extended to Lauren the flowers that he clutched in a trembling hand.

"I'm sorry you had to be in the middle of that fight. The black girls are always fighting. They really give this place a bad name." Motivated by the anticipation of a healthy tip, Lauren lovingly caressed the sparse hair on the top of Harvey's head. "I'm going to ask the manager to give us some extra time," she cooed. Her hand left his head and began stroking and smoothing out the wrinkles on his face. "So. if you pay me now, I can go take care of the books while you get undressed and relax."

Harvey nodded. He looked grateful for Lauren's tender concern. "You're such a pretty girl. A *sheyna meydele*," he said in Yiddish. "And you're a good little girl, too." Harvey pinched Lauren's cheek. Feeling better, he winked at Lauren as he handed her the fee. "Go. Put those flowers in *vater* before they *vilt*. I have a surprise for you later."

Warmed by the thought of an extravagant tip, Lauren left the room smiling.

Carrying the flowers and the money for the session, Lauren entered Rover's office. She was surprised to find Victoria there, pacing nervously. Curious about what was going on, Lauren handed Rover the money then slowly wrote her entry on the lined sheet of paper on the desk.

"You gotta vase, Rover?"

Rover gave her a you-gotta-be-kidding look.

Lauren shrugged. "Well, hold onto them for me until my session is over." Rover didn't bother to respond.

"Oh yeah, I need some condoms," Lauren lied to prolong her stay. "The gold pack," she added, remembering that Rover hadn't brought them up from the basement.

"Okay, give me a second, Lauren," Rover said absently. He returned his attention to Victoria.

"Pleasure! Read my lips—the answer is No!" Rover said, forcing a stern expression.

"Why can't I give her a ride home? She can't pay for a cab because she hasn't made any money. And I didn't bring any money with me, otherwise I'd pay for the cab."

"Jonee is suspended because she started the fight. Don't get involved. If she doesn't have cab fare, she can just get on the bus. And don't tell me she doesn't even have the price of a bus ride."

Victoria appealed to Rover with pleading eyes. "Rover, she doesn't want to be seen in public with her face looking like that. And she's in a lot of pain. Can't you bend the rules, just a little? It shouldn't take too long for me to drive her home—I'll jump on the expressway and be back before I'm missed."

"Rules are rules. I don't make them; I just enforce them. It's your call. If you leave without permission, you'll be suspended."

Victoria squirmed uncomfortably. "Suspended? For how long?"

"I don't know, Pleasure. Until Gabrielle says you can come back. Who knows?" Rover softened his voice. "Why risk it? Do you think Jonee would jeopardize her job for you?"

"That's not the point, Rover. My request is not unreasonable; I should be able to leave for an emergency. If something happened to my son, would I be suspended if I had to suddenly leave?"

"But we're not talking about your son. Jonee is a grown woman with too much mouth and too little self-control. Jonee is not this fragile little person you're making her out to be. She's a real wildcat who can take care of herself."

The numerous rules at Pandora's Box were ridiculous. Victoria wondered about the sanity of the mysterious Gabrielle who treated them all like children and controlled their fate without ever stepping foot on the premises.

She weighed her options. With only two hundred dollars in cash, she couldn't afford a suspension, but she took great exception to being told that she couldn't assist Jonee. Being backed into a corner with the threat of suspension didn't sit well with Victoria. With the realization that she couldn't compromise her principles, an image of the thick wad of money that she had cheerfully handed over to a smiling bank representative flashed in her mind. Victoria yearned for the security of it. If worse came to worse, she'd just have to cash in the CD, lose the interest and pay whatever penalties were involved.

"Do what you have to do, Rover. I'm going to take Jonee home." The decision brought Victoria immediate relief.

Rover shook his head and produced a sad smile. Having overhead the entire exchange, Lauren beamed with satisfaction. Catching Lauren's expression, Victoria realized that had Lauren not been within earshot, Rover might have been able to cover.

Lauren did not take her friendship with Gabrielle lightly; she would call Gabrielle and repeat Rover and Victoria's conversation, word-for-word.

Chapter 26

Jonee brooded. The bravado she'd shown earlier was gone. During the silent drive to her apartment, she sat with her head hung low. Searing pain made her keenly aware of every scratch on her face, but despite the discomfort, her fingers were drawn to the angry grooves etched into her skin.

"Should I turn here?" Victoria asked, breaking the silence.

Jonee lifted her head. "No. Turn left at the next stop sign." She spoke in a tone that was cautiously low as if an increase in volume would intensify the pain.

If you could get beyond the false lashes she always wore, Jonee's best feature was her eyes. Dark, wide eyes that twinkled with excitement were now hooded and murky.

Victoria wished that there were something she could say to console Jonee, but no comforting words came to mind.

Throngs of Jonee's neighbors were flocked outside her apartment building enjoying the spring-like weather that had finally arrived. They watched as Victoria struggled to maneuver her car into a tiny parking space in front of the building, with the concentration of spectators at a major sporting event.

"I can stay with you for a while Jonee? Do you want me to come inside?"

Jonee nodded.

There was no way for Jonee to conceal the crimson-colored scratches on her face. Ignoring the curious glances and the nervous chuckles, she and Victoria rushed past the neighbors and went inside the building.

OUT OF ORDER was crudely scrawled on a cardboard sign and propped up against the elevator in the lobby.

"We have to take the stairs," Jonee said in a flat tone.

"To…?" Victoria asked.

"The fourth floor."

Victoria scowled.

Jonee's apartment was an untidy obstacle course. Dirty laundry stuffed in trash bags was lined up at the front door. Victoria had to step over toys, and maneuver around boxes and other obstructive objects that were scattered about in the living room.

Angrily, Jonee flung her workbag across the room, adding to the chaos. She stomped into her bedroom; Victoria followed.

The cramped bedroom that Jonee shared with her son looked like it had been ransacked. Contents streamed from bureau drawers that were too crammed to close.

Jonee examined her wounds in a cloudy bureau mirror and burst into tears. "I'm gonna kill that bitch," she declared, sobbing, then collapsed on the bed and buried her face into a pillow that was already streaked with lipstick and mascara. Strewn onto the unmade bed were two damp bath towels, a child's pair of jeans, a Rugrats tee shirt. Crumpled jeans and a top lay on the floor next to an overflowing wastebasket. Victoria looked around in amazement. Jonee's bedroom—the entire apartment was a pigsty. Victoria wondered what was going on with Jonee. Then, hit with sudden clarity, Victoria felt compassion; she understood that Jonee's environment reflected her inner turmoil. Like Victoria and all the others, some painful event must have driven Jonee to Pandora's. Victoria sat next to Jonee and put her arm around her friend's trembling shoulders. She couldn't recall ever comforting an adult. It was an odd sensation. Despite Rover's words, Jonee appeared forlorn and fragile.

"I feel so embarrassed," Jonee confessed. Loosened by tears, her false eyelashes hung by a thread of glue. Oblivious, Jonee continued, "How could I let that little young bitch fuck up my face like this?"

Trying not to focus on the dangling lashes, Victoria replied, "I guess you didn't expect her to react so viciously. I was shocked. But Jonee, you have to take some responsibility for what happened."

"I didn't touch her stank ass!" Roused by indignation, Jonee sat straight up. "Look at my face! That bitch gouged my face and I'm the one who gets suspended. I don't know what the fuck you're talking about? Why should *I* take responsibility?"

Victoria chose her words carefully. "Rover saw you advance toward Hershey. It looked like she was just defending herself. Even if you and I know that her response was uncalled for, and extremely violent, you have to admit that you created that situation."

"How did I *create* the situation? Was I was supposed to shut up while she pulled all kinds of dirty tricks to get that customer?" Jonee sucked her teeth and finally pulled off the gooey pair of false lashes. "I've seen some rank, crazy shit in my life, but I ain't never seen no shit like that." She held the lashes in her palm and observed them for a moment before tossing them on top of the pile in the wastebasket. "I don't know where that bitch thought she was at, performing like she was at The Source Awards."

"That's how she chose to express herself," Victoria responded. "Why did you let it bother you so much? Don't forget I've seen you in action and I know how much you piss off the other girls when you get greedy for customers. You've been accused of doing some pretty underhanded things yourself, Jonee." Victoria smiled to lessen the severity of her reprimand.

"I do what I have to do when the money's slow. But, I do the normal type shit that all hoes do when it's slow-flashing a little bit...rubbing on my stuff. But that bullshit Hershey did was ridiculous. She made all of us look bad."

"How did her actions make us look bad?" Victoria asked, her brows knitted. "You wanna know what I think?"

Jonee stared back, defiant.

"I think you were so afraid that you wouldn't be able to make any money with Hershey around that you…"

Jonee huffed up and opened her mouth to protest.

"Wait a minute, Jonee. Let me finish. On some level you relinquished your money to her—you sabotaged your efforts when you responded to her…her rap presentation. You gave away your power."

"Please don't start talking that deep shit again, okay? 'Cause I don't wanna hear it. Damn! Can we ever have a normal conversation without you going there? Why do you have to analyze everything, Pleasure? That shit is nerve-racking."

"I analyze things because I'm always searching for answers. I'm as confused as you are," Victoria said sadly.

"Speak for yourself. I'm not confused," Jonee shot back.

Victoria continued. "I really believe that everything we say, do, or even think, creates our reality. It's clear to me that you created that situation with Hershey."

Jonee shook her head. "So since you know so much, why are you whoring at Pandora's? Why ain't you signifyin' at some university? How come you're not writing books and making a bundle like that Eyona woman?"

"Iyanla Vanzant," Victoria pointedly corrected her.

"Yeah, her."

"I'm at the massage parlor because I have no idea what I'm doing or where I'm going. The choices and decisions that I've made have brought me to this point. But my journey certainly doesn't end here. For now, I'm just putting one foot in front of the other—going with the flow. I'm just biding my time and I hope that I can emerge from this unscathed. You know what I mean?"

"No, Pleasure. I don't," Jonee said, sighing.

"It feels like I'm in some sort of limbo existence, but I know that's not possible. I'm creating karma every time I walk through the door of Pandora's." Victoria paused, lost in thought. "I wonder sometimes if prostitution is good or bad? I just don't know."

"You know damn well it's a sin to sell your body," Jonee remarked ruefully. "And you know we're all going to burn in hell." She lit a cigarette and slowly blew out a stream of smoke. "But I'll cross that bridge later," she added, grinning.

"I'm not even sure if I believe in the concept of sin, or good and bad. Before I came to work at the massage parlor, I was in a lot of pain. The pain is still there, but I've managed to mask it-put a Band-Aid on it. Let me try to explain…at times, the very thought of going to work and being touched by all those men makes me crazy." Victoria wrapped her arms around herself. "But then at other times—I really like it. Not the sexual act, per se—the money. I like the money. I like being chosen. I get a physical rush when I'm putting on make-up, choosing outfits, preparing to compete—it's therapeutic."

"Yeah? Well, I can understand how it's therapeutic for the tricks… they're nuts, but how in the hell is it therapeutic for you?"

"It's therapeutic because it lets me forget. I have no idea what would happen if I removed the Band-Aid. And right now I'm not strong enough or brave enough to face my pain."

"Speaking of pain…" Jonee touched her face. "It feels like somebody threw lye on my face. You want to mask your pain? I look like shit and I wish I could put a mask on my *face*," Jonee said, laughing. "Look, let's forget about this shit for a minute. You wanna smoke a joint with me?"

"No, I do not," Victoria said, emphasizing each word. "You know I don't get high."

"How about a drink then? I know you get your drink on 'cause I done seen your ass throwing down some liquor."

"Wine, Jonee. I only drink wine or champagne."

"Yeah, yeah. Tomatoes, tomahtoes," Jonee replied, as she headed for the kitchen.

Trailing Jonee, Victoria got as far as the living room. She decided not to venture into the kitchen. From where she stood, the kitchen looked worse than the other rooms. Trash spilled over, unwashed dishes were piled high, and the kitchen table was cluttered with newspapers and more dirty dishes.

Jonee returned to the living room with two plastic cups filled with White Zinfandel.

"How'd you end up in the business, Jonee?" Victoria asked unexpectedly, sipping the wine.

"Long story," Jonee replied.

"I'm not in a rush. I've got plenty of time. Rover suspended me, too, remember?"

"Why'd he suspend you?" Jonee asked, looking shocked. "You didn't do anything."

"Long story," Victoria said, mimicking Jonee. "It's just for a couple days. I'm not going to worry about it."

"I'm really sorry, Pleasure. I didn't mean to drag you into this mess."

"It was my decision, Jonee. I didn't want you to have to take a bus. And I figured you could use some support."

Jonee's eyes brimmed with tears. "You're all right, girl. In this cutthroat business, a real friend is as rare as finding a hoe who don't wear store bought hair."

Touching her braids, Victoria scowled.

"Okay, I'll tell you how I got in the life. I met this dude. He was Jewish. We met at Community College. Summer classes…"

"You went to Community?"

"Yeah, but I dropped out after the first semester."

"Oh."

"Mark is from a rich family. His people own finance companies—a whole chain. I guess you could call them glorified loan sharks. Mark failed Anatomy and Physiology at Temple and had heard that the classes were easier to pass at Community. He was my lab partner and I guess he got off on helping an ignorant little black girl who didn't know the patella from the mandible. Made him feel superior, I guess."

Victoria nodded hesitantly. She didn't know a patella from a mandible either.

"His dumb ass should have known all that shit since he was repeating the class. But what did I know—I was impressed by his scientific knowledge and flattered by all the attention he was giving me."

"Mark drove a black BMW, always had plenty of cash, took me out to eat in places I had never even thought about entering, and he told me shit like: 'You have an ancient beauty; men have killed for women who look like you.' He told me that he was an artist but his parents insisted that he become a lawyer. We got involved when Mark decided that he had to capture my beauty on canvas. What a joke!" Jonee broke out a bag of weed and started rolling a joint.

"I was from the 'hood and thought I had heard it all," she continued. "But Mark came up with a totally different angle to getting the pussy. During our relationship, I let Mark drag me to museums and art galleries all over Philly and New York. We even went to see an exhibit at the Museum of Contemporary Art in Montreal. Mark would stand around looking at the ugliest, craziest shit for hours. I hated it, but I was in love and love will make you do strange, strange things." Jonee closed her eyes. She inhaled deeply, and then exhaled.

Victoria was not offended by the sweet, pungent smell that permeated the room. It was a hell of a lot more pleasing than the putrid cigarette smoke that Jonee usually blew in her face. Perhaps her inability to conjure an image was affected by the second-hand smoke she was inhaling, but Victoria was having a hard time imagining Jonee standing still and quiet in an art museum.

"He freaked when I got pregnant." Jonee took another puff. "Insisted that I get an abortion. I probably would have if he hadn't acted like my pregnancy was the end of the fucking world. His parents didn't know shit about me, but my mother had welcomed Mark with open arms. She was crazy about him, thought he was the best thing that had ever happened to me. He was my ticket outta the ghetto."

"Mark is Alec's father?" Victoria asked.

"Yeah, he's Alec's biological father. When Mark got scarce during my pregnancy, I think my mother took it harder than I did. She said she should have known better, she should have realized that Mark was only slumming with me.

One day my mother decided that she was gonna get some kind of help for me, so she showed up at his family's main office and demanded to speak to his father. She raised all kinds of hell. She cussed everybody out! The receptionist, secretaries, customers…everybody! And Mark's father wasn't even there. His parents were somewhere in Europe. But the white bastards who worked there had my mother arrested."

"And girl… I flipped when I heard my mom was locked up. She was arrested for disorderly conduct or some trumped up bullshit. I was seven months pregnant, and didn't have no money for her bail. I was so mad; I walked from 29th and Girard to Mark's dorm at Temple. I showed my ass that night. I went off! I totally fucked up his room. His roommate was hysterical, screaming like a little bitch while I was breaking up shit. Mark made some calls and got my mother out.…just like that." Jonee snapped her fingers.

Jonee laughed, but her eyes were sad. "Believe me, Mark Kaplan will think twice before he fucks with another black woman. That was the night he got cured of his jungle fever."

"Did you say Kaplan?" Victoria asked. "Alec is related to the Kaplan Finance people?"

"Yes. But they would never admit it. Mark and his family do not give a shit about my son. They only care about money. My baby is six years old, and to this day, neither Mark nor his family has ever laid eyes on Alec. With the check that I get once a month from his family, I pay Alec's tuition, I buy his clothes…and believe me, I buy Alec nothing but the best. The rest of the money gets put away for his education. Oh! And Alec has some money in a trust fund. He can have that when he turns twenty-five. I would never touch a dime of Alec's money. I want to make sure that he grows up financially secure. I don't want him sweating the Kaplan name or their money. My baby's gonna be a doctor—a fucking surgeon; and he won't need none of their asses. Fuck 'em!"

Victoria felt herself getting angrier, as if Jonee's story was her own. "I know you're doing a lot with the money, Jonee, but that family is filthy rich. What they're giving you is a pittance compared to what you're enti-tled to." Victoria looked around at Jonee's squalid living room. "I *know* Mark's family can afford to put you and Alec in a better environment."

Jonee leaned on an elbow, her knuckles pressed into her good cheek. "Mark don't care about Alec's environment. He works for his family's business; he keeps his income hidden. He claims he only makes X amount of dollars. Alec gets what the Kaplans feel he deserves. No, let me rephrase that. The Kaplans don't think my son deserves shit; they think I should be grateful for the chump change they give him." Jonee's expression was pained.

Jonee wasn't quoting any figures, and Victoria was curious about the exact amount she received in support payments. Victoria didn't get anything from Jordan's father. He was able to beat the system and avoided making child support payments by moving around and jumping from job to job.

"Mark not only hurt me, he hurt my mother and Alec. My son is being raised without a father. Mark is deliberately denying Alec access to a better lifestyle. But that's cool. All Mark would do is fuck up Alec's life anyway."

Victoria gave Jonee a puzzled look.

"He doesn't love Alec, he can't. Guilt is the only thing that would make Mark even attempt to be a father to his half-breed embarrassment from the ghetto. My mom and me shower Alec with love and affection. We try to build up his self-esteem because we know he ain't gonna have no easy time growing up. The kids in our neighborhood call him a sissy, or white boy. My baby don't even know what that shit means. So I put him in private school, where kids won't be picking with him all the time. There ain't that many black kids in his school, and Alec is still the oddball. But I'll tell you one thing, he fits in a hell of a lot better than he would have in one these fucked up neighborhood schools. At least there's no name-calling and the kids don't fight." Jonee looked at Victoria expectantly.

Lost in thought, Victoria was silent. She made good money at Pandora's and it was time to start investing in Jordan. No longer would she squander her money on frivolity. She wouldn't procrastinate any longer. The public school system was not going to destroy her child. She'd begin an immediate search for a good school. Buoyed by her new mission, Victoria was eager to get back to work to start stacking money for Jordan's education fund.

Chapter 27

Victoria was tired. Exhausted. Her suspension was lifted, but she'd been banished to the midnight shift, and working through the night wasn't easy. She hated having to take Jordan to the babysitter late at night and she particularly hated creeping back home exposed by the light of the morning sun. Her compensation, a thick roll of money, was evidence of a hard night's work. Longing for a hot shower and a few hours sleep, she began peeling off clothes. The red flashing light of the answering machine caught her attention. She eyed the machine wearily, knowing the message would be from Jordan, no doubt asking if he could come home. Jordan hadn't adjusted to his mother's new shift or having to stay at Charmaine's until late afternoon.

Delightful surprise gleamed in her eyes when she pushed play and heard Kareem's voice.

"Yo, I got a coupla tickets to Thursday night's show at the Tower Theater. You wanna check it out? Oh yeah, and uh…consider this an apology for last week."

Oh, Kareem, she gushed. *I should be apologizing to you.*

"I hope you can make it," he continued. "Holler when you get in."

He didn't mention who was performing at the Tower. It was most likely some rap group, but Victoria didn't care. After the way she had spoiled their dinner date, she was grateful Kareem had even bothered to ask her out again. Her fingers danced over the buttons as she pushed Kareem's number.

As it turned out, Kareem was a close friend of the Grammy-winning performer, Anasa, a female vocalist from North Philly. Kareem and Victoria sat in front row seats; Victoria was mesmerized by the singer's smooth and sultry vocals. Her unique sound, a jazz vibe mixed with hip hop, was delivered effortlessly.

Though completely enthralled by the performance, every so often Victoria would try to steal a glance at Kareem. But with his eyes shifting constantly from the stage to her face, she was caught each time, and had to look away in embarrassment.

❦

After the show Kareem took Victoria backstage to meet Anasa. Beautiful and earthy, the singer gave Victoria a warm hug like they were long lost friends.

Thirty minutes later Victoria and Kareem were back in his jeep, headed for West Philly.

"The show was fabulous, Kareem! I'm going out to buy her CD first thing tomorrow."

Kareem kept his eyes on the road, but nodded in approval.

"Anasa seems so unaffected by her success. I was surprised at how down to earth she is."

"Yeah, Anasa's keepin' it real. She invited us to the after-party but I had to decline," Kareem announced.

Disappointment flashed across Victoria's face.

"I'm not tryin' to keep you out all night. I know you have to get home and look after your son," he explained.

Jordan was staying over at Charmaine's, but Victoria didn't say anything.

"We can check her out the next time she's in town. We're real tight.

"I could tell," Victoria said, impressed.

"We grew up together. Same street, same block."

The entire evening had been thrilling, but was ending too soon. The ride from Upper Darby to West Philly seemed to take only a few minutes. As they approached her neighborhood, Victoria felt anxious; she wanted to prolong the night. She wanted to tell Kareem how proud she'd felt being with him tonight. She wanted to tell him all about herself, her childhood, being raised by her grandmother, the pain of waiting for her own mother. She wanted to tell him about her own singing career…about Justice Martin, how deeply he'd hurt her. And she wanted to tell him how she'd ended up in the business. She felt vulnerable, but was willing to bear her soul. She was on a self-destructive course. Lost. She wanted him to save her. But a million words unspoken were far too many to speak.

Kareem walked her up the steps to her front door. "Do you want to stop in for a minute?" she asked.

"Naw, I'm cool. And we're cool now, right? Am I back in your good graces?" he asked, tilting her chin teasingly.

"Of course. I don't know what got into me that night. I'm really sorry."

"Sorry enough to hang out with me next week, and listen to some rap? One of my acts, my boy, Indecent, is opening at Club Flow on Delaware Avenue."

Victoria crinkled her nose playfully. "I can't wait to hear the oratorical skills of Indecent."

"Just open up a little; allow yourself to hear the message, I think you'll be pleasantly surprised."

A sudden breeze blew by. Kareem opened his jacket wide, inviting her inside. He closed the jacket around her. She rested against him. The nearness of him was intoxicating. She stood on her toes, offering her lips. Kareem kissed her back, softly. "It's getting chilly baby," he said, pulling away. "We better call it a night. I'll holler at you tomorrow, okay?"

She nodded good-naturedly, but wanted desperately to hold on to the moment. "G'night, baby," he said and kissed her again, this time a quick peck on her cheek.

Victoria went inside and locked the door behind her. She leaned against it before going upstairs to her apartment. She hoped Kareem would have a change of heart and come back and stay awhile. Her hopes were dashed when she heard him start the engine and drive away.

Kareem was being cautious, taking it slowly, she told herself. She knew he was crazy about her, she just couldn't figure out why. Surely, he could have any woman he wanted. Women far less complicated than she. In a flash, Victoria pictured all the glamorous women who'd been back stage, and who no doubt would be at the after-party.

In a moment of self-doubt, she wondered if Kareem had hastily ditched her so that he could be free to mingle at the party.

With a sigh, she decided not to torture herself worrying about what Kareem was doing. He wasn't her man. Not yet, anyway. But just as soon as she got herself together, she was definitely going to claim him.

Chapter 28

D ominique's full-length reflection was cut into jigsaw-like pieces by the mirror panels that decorated the wall. She appraised her image and was pleased that her dark skin glistened from head to toe. Prone to dry, ashen skin, she had tried a myriad of lotions. But no product on the market, no matter how expensive, provided the kind of sheen that a bottle of cheap baby oil could.

Barefoot with jangling ankle bracelets, Dominique looked wild and sexy in a zebra striped push-up bra and matching G-string. The set was one of the many costumes she wore with the combined theme of animal lust and intimidation.

Dominique smoothed more baby oil over her body, and squinted at her image. She saw a lean body and a flat stomach—no flab. But something had changed. Scrutinizing her body, she noticed that she was losing some muscle tone. It was slight, barely perceptible, but a change nonetheless. Still, she had to admit that the years had been kind. Kind enough to allow her to wear the type of bare-all apparel so necessary in her line of work.

Giving herself one long last look, she tried to convince herself not to worry about the double dose of unexpected competition: Reds and that snotty bitch Pleasure. But on second thought, she wondered if maybe she should shed the animal-skin look and put on something that would give her a softer, less threatening look.

She felt off-balance and unsure of herself, but decided to keep on the zebra-striped set. She made a deal with herself-she'd change if she didn't get the first customer.

Sauntering into the lounge, exhibiting cockiness she didn't feel, Dominique flipped through the pages of a magazine that someone from the previous shift had left behind. She was irritated by the glossy images of spaghetti-thin women who were paid a fortune for their smiles. She tossed the magazine aside and attempted to take comfort in the knowledge that the photos had probably all been touched up to perfection.

From the corner of her eye, Dominique watched Reds prancing about in an expensive-looking lavender lace teddy that was cut high with a thong back. As if that wasn't sufficiently annoying, Reds kept flinging her recently permed hair. Reds' thick wild mane was now tamed into silky, luxurious locks. Dominique pursed her lips and took a deep breath. Reds was wearing the second new outfit in a week. The color looked good on her and that, along with the new hair-do made Reds appear brighter, gave her a more youthful appearance. But Dominique refused to comment or compliment her. She couldn't imagine where Reds had gotten the money for these indulgences. Reds' meager earnings at the massage parlor barely covered her liquor bill.

She didn't begrudge Reds her recent purchases; Lord knew the woman was badly in need of some new gear. Dominique was, however, irked by the superior attitude she detected in Reds, the air of nonchalance tinged with impudence. There was definitely a bit of defiance in Reds' refusal to reveal the source of these recent acquisitions.

Just the night before, Reds had offered her a swig of scotch from a new silver flask and Dominique teased her about the upgrade from cheap whiskey to scotch. When she jokingly asked Reds if she had hit the number, Reds smiled slyly but declined to answer.

Reds had been known to divulge far more serious information. A few months back she had told Dominique every incriminating detail of the credit card scam that she and her boyfriend, Sonny D had gotten involved in. So why, Dominique wondered, was Reds acting so petty and mysterious now?

Pleasure's unexpected appearance on the midnight shift had added to Dominique's discontent. After her suspension had been lifted, Pleasure had been placed on the midnight shift—as a punishment of sorts, Dominique imagined. But was it a just punishment? She hardly thought so. Pleasure would probably get the little money that came though. Shit, if Gabrielle wanted to punish the girl, she should have sent her to work with those prissy white bitches on the morning shift. With Reds all dolled up in lace and Pleasure lounging elegantly in a jade kimono that covered a gold corset with·iridescent threads, Dominique's take for the night did not look propitious. Again, she thought about changing her costume and again she changed her mind. Fuck it! She couldn't let those two bitches know that she felt threatened.

Dominique closed her eyes and sat with her arms crossed, ruminating, but the idle chatter between Victoria and Reds disturbed her, gave her an uneasy feeling. It seemed to Dominique that in less than an hour the two had become quite chummy and she imagined the soft murmurs of their voices to be conspiratorial whispers.

When the doorbell sounded, instead of making a beeline to the door as she was inclined to do, Dominique sighed then lazily raised herself from her seat, giving the impression that having to greet a customer was terribly inconvenient.

No sooner had Dominique gotten on her feet when Reds brushed past her saying, "Oh that's probably the delivery guy with my food." She gestured Dominique to sit down.

Dominique rolled her eyes and grumbled as she eased back into her seat. She didn't like Reds telling her what to do.

Reds opened the door for the delivery guy. He was a plump young man with a ready smile and a baby smooth chocolate face. Instead of handing Reds the package, he insisted on carrying the soggy, bulging bag for her. It was a good excuse to get into the lounge to gawk at the women.

"How y'all doing tonight?" he asked, overly-friendly and wearing an excited grin. He took great care in placing the package on a rickety table; it afforded him more time in the forbidden room. It was obviously a thrilling coup for him because on previous deliveries he'd never even gotten past the front door. As if on a spindle, his head turned in every direction, trying to capture all there was to see.

Victoria acknowledged the young man's greeting with an uncomfortable nod and self-consciously clutched her kimono.

Glowering, Dominique looked from Reds to the delivery guy. Reds knew darn well that deliveries were to be handled at the door, not in the lounge.

Reds fumbled around in her purse, then discreetly extracted money from its secret hiding place. As he waited, the cherubic-faced young man cast furtive glances in the direction of the hallway, but was unable to get a clear view. He boldly moved to the doorway and leaned out into the hall, hoping to catch a glimpse of any of the other women who may have been tucked away in one of the rooms. "Anybody else working tonight?"

"Ain't none of your fuckin' bizness," Dominique sputtered, amazed by his audacity.

The twinkle left his eyes. "You better watch yo' mouth, bitch." His face contorted as he spat out the words.

"Get the fuck out!" In a flash, Dominique was out of her chair, ready to shove him out the door.

With an outstretched arm, the delivery guy cautioned Dominique to keep her distance. "You better chill! Cause if you put your hands on me, I'm gonna knock you on your black zebra ass!"

His words brought Dominique to a halt. She was wise enough to heed his warning, and she didn't touch him. Instead, she mouthed off a string of threats and obscenities that included reporting his behavior to his employer *and* the cops.

Reds quickly stuffed a twenty in his hand. "Keep the change," she mumbled.

"Hey baby," he called out to Dominique as he swaggered toward the door. "You can call my boss! Go ahead! Call 'em! He don't give a fuck about a bunch of hoes. Y'all should be glad that we even make deliveries to this fucked up joint. A mothafucka liable to catch somethin' up in here."

"Come on, baby," Reds prodded, taking his arm. "Just leave, okay?"

He jerked away from Reds and pulled a cell phone from the deep pocket of his shirt. "Here, baby!" He taunted Dominique. "While you at it, call the po-lice!"

"Would you please just get the fuck out?" Dominique said in a low, controlled voice, that she hoped still held at least a modicum of menace.

"I didn't think you wanted to call no cops," he sneered. "You know you don't want 5-0 up in this mothafucka." His mouth twisted cruelly, his eyes narrowed into slits. He looked demonic, a cherub gone mad. He left, slamming the door, and leaving behind the echo of his raucous laughter.

For a moment, the three women shared stunned silence.

Then, smiling unhappily, Reds muttered, "He didn't have to go there."

Dominique planted one hand on her hip combatively and gave Reds a look of contempt. "*You* didn't have to go there. You know you're not supposed to let..." But, tired from the delivery guy's verbal assault, Dominique stopped mid-sentence. Her eyes dimmed with resignation as she collapsed into her seat. She picked up the magazine again and listlessly began thumbing through it as she waited for customers to arrive.

Victoria was sick of the constant bickering and fighting at Pandora's. She had hoped that whatever was going on between Dominique and Reds would not erupt into another stupid fight. She couldn't afford any more suspensions and decided that if Dominique and Reds got into it, she would just ignore them; she'd act like they didn't even exist. They could call each other every name in the book, pull hair, rip clothes off, and scratch each other's eyes out; it didn't matter to her; she was not going to get involved.

She wished she could detach herself as easily from the incident that had just transpired. Victoria wrapped her arms around herself as she rocked back and forth on the loveseat. The heat of the young man's words still burned her ears, seared her insides, making her want to throw up. In the den of iniquity called Pandora's Box, Victoria had taken great care in presenting herself with as much dignity as she could muster. She applied very little make-up and never wore outlandish wigs or weaves. She dressed in tasteful outfits and perceived herself as prim and capable of appealing to the romantic side of men while her co-workers flaunted themselves vulgarly, squirming and writhing as if they were in heat. She was a lone flower in the midst of weeds. Or so she had thought. Her inclusion in the delivery guy's hateful tirade had given her a different perspective. When his angry eyes swept the room and settled on her, Victoria had expected to see them soften. But his eyes and words denounced her, too.

Though she tried not to make eye contact, their eyes had locked briefly. Victoria had seen his face before, but couldn't remember where. And she was certain that she saw a flicker of recognition in his eyes also. She sure hoped he wasn't one of the neighborhood thugs who hung out in front of the deli around the corner from her apartment. She hoped he wasn't one of the thugs who uttered uncomplimentary innuendoes whenever she passed by. She wouldn't be able to show her face if any one in the group of rowdies got wind of the fact that she worked at Pandora's Box.

Suddenly, she remembered him! The obnoxious guy who had delivered her coffee on the unforgettable day when she had worked the morning shift without profit. "Hmph," she uttered involuntarily as she recalled how he had lusted openly for the white girls on that shift, white girls who did not conceal their loathing for him, for his blackness.

Victoria covered her face with her hands and continued rocking. Sudden heart palpitations caused her to sit up. She clutched her chest and waited for the erratic heartbeat to subside. Her throat became dry and she struggled to breathe. The sensations were horribly familiar. *Oh no*, she thought, as she gripped the fabric of her kimono. *It can't be happening here!*

She felt an urge to jump up and flee from the stifling environment, but knew there would be severe repercussions if she did. She'd be suspended again, or even worse—fired! But if she was going to die, she certainly didn't want to do it in a whorehouse! She had to get out of there. She had to get home.

"Are you okay?" Reds asked Victoria with a look of earnest concern.

Victoria ignored her. There was no time to appease her curiosity.

"Dominique!" Victoria managed to gasp. "I feel sick. I have to get out of here."

"Go ahead," said Dominique in an unconcerned tone. Her expression said: *Good riddance!*

The second Victoria breathed in the night air all symptoms subsided. Thinking of her empty purse, she briefly considered going back inside the massage parlor. She shook her head and continued walking. She desperately needed to talk to somebody. Kareem! But no, she couldn't call him. He'd made one obligatory phone call since taking her to the show, and he sounded aloof, preoccupied. She hadn't heard from him in weeks, and she felt empty, heartsick—weak. But what did she expect? Disappointment was all she had ever known. She should have known better than to get her hopes up. It was foolish to have believed that someone like Kareem, a young brother with a bright future, would get himself entangled with the likes of her. No, Kareem was out there somewhere, busy carving out his piece of the American dream. She and all her problems were the last things on his mind.

Chapter 29

A few minutes after Victoria left, the first customer of the evening finally arrived. He was a portly middle-aged white man with heavy jowls, protruding eyes and a pouch that hung over his belt.

"Hello!" the man said cheerfully.

"Have you been here before?" Dominique asked, unsmiling.

"A few months ago."

"Who'd you see?"

"I can't recall her name."

The man looked vaguely familiar to Reds, but then all men looked like tricks. She wondered why Dominique was giving him the third degree, and then decided that the altercation with the delivery person—his threats about calling 5-0 had made Dominique paranoid—caused her to suspect that every man who walked through the door was a cop. Reds checked out the customer. Looked him over long and hard. Nah, he was too old and too fat to be a cop.

Frisky as a pup, the man's entire body was excitedly involved as his bulging eyes roamed back and forth from Reds to Dominique. He reminded Reds of a Pekinese.

"My name is Reds," Reds said, without trying to sound sexy. A calm she hadn't felt in years washed over her. She merely smiled as she confidently waited for the man to make-up his mind.

The man pointed a stubby finger at Reds. "I'd like to make your acquaintance." In an old-fashioned gesture, he offered Reds his arm.

Dominique twisted her face in disgust. But the couple, oblivious to her gaze, chatted amicably as they walked up the hall, arm-in-arm.

He introduced himself as Hubert when Reds escorted him into the first session room. Before she had even collected the payment, Hubert began pawing and tugging on the straps of her new teddy.

"Whoa. Slow down, partner," Reds said playfully, though she was slightly annoyed. "Let me take care of the books first."

"I beg your pardon, you must forgive me for the oversight," Hubert said wearing a surprised expression that caused his eyes to bulge even more.

Reds giggled. Hubert looked and sounded comical. He needed to cut that shit out before she lost it, and fell down to the floor, laughing.

Hubert pulled out a thick wad of money held together by a silver money clip and presented Reds with a new, crisp bill. With a wink he put the wad back in his pocket.

At the sight of all that money, Reds quickly pulled herself together. "Make yourself comfortable, Hubert. In other words, STRIP!" she said gaily. "I'll be right back." But before she left the room Reds kicked off the high heels she was wearing. She had his money in her hand and Hubert's wink promised that there was more to come so there was no need to try to heighten her allure by continuing to cramp her poor feet in those miserable heels.

Pleased with the world, Reds padded down the hall in her stocking feet.

Rover always locked the office when his shift ended and never provided Dominique with any cash to make change. This was a terrible inconvenience to the girls on the midnight shift. Customers frequently paid with hundred-dollar bills and the girls usually had to wait until the pizza shop opened the next morning to exchange the money for smaller bills. But when the shop owner was in a foul mood and didn't want to be bothered with making change, someone (usually Reds) had to go out into the morning light and trudge to the bank at the corner. Sleepy and feeling ridiculously out of place with flashy clothing, big hair and smeared-make-up, the unhappy massage parlor employee hated standing in line and mingling with the normal work-a-day people in the bank.

"Here you go," Reds said as she handed Dominique the money. She was startled by Dominique's appearance and gave her a sidelong glance. Dominique, the self-proclaimed dominatrix, had changed her image. She was draped in a pale pink flowing gown and wore a long black wig.

Reds expected Dominique to comment on the image change, but Dominique kept her head buried in the magazine. She extended her palm without a word and avoided looking at Reds. Unfazed by the slight, Reds placed the bill in Dominique's open hand.

"I'll pay you when I get change," Dominique said mechanically.

"Oh! In that case, give it back. I can break it." Reds opened her purse and gave Dominique two twenties and a ten.

Dominique looked surprised, then acted annoyed and put-upon when she returned the money to Reds.

Reds was greeted by Hubert's potbelly when she reentered the room. He was lying on the bed, shamelessly naked as a jaybird. Reds cringed at the unattractive sight. Modest men or those who were polite covered themselves with the towel that was provided at the foot of the cot. It was a common courtesy. Admittedly, her own tummy could use a tuck or two, but she didn't go around flaunting it. Oh well, she'd seen worse.

"I see somebody didn't waste any time getting ready for me," Reds said in song-like tones, as if the sight of his nakedness filled her with extreme pleasure.

Hubert's bulbous eyes flickered with excitement. "Why don't you join me?" He heaved himself up on one elbow and fondled the lace that ruffled around the edges of the lavender nightwear. His fat fingers trailed down to her inner thigh and found its way between her legs.

"You enjoy being touched there, don't you?"

Reds closed her eyes, dreamily. "Hmm," she softly moaned while guiding his stubby finger.

Though it didn't seem possible, Reds noticed with partially-open lids that Hubert's eyes bulged even more when he touched the moist fabric between her legs. He gasped as if he'd just struck gold.

"Ah, yes, darling. Yes, my darling," Hubert rasped. The panting Pekinese hunched over her, frantically working his finger, and breathing like he'd just finished running a marathon.

"Oh, Hubert," Reds cried out dramatically. She joined him on the cot, sidled up to him, purring softly, but her thoughts were focused on the money clip inside his pants pocket. She didn't know how much money he had, but she knew she wanted it all. She deserved it.

"Darling," Hubert said. "You look so delicate and pure. I'd love to taste your sweet pleasure."

Taste her sweet what? Give me a fucking break, Reds thought. This mother fucker had been reading too many romance novels or something. Her acting ability, along with the lubricant she'd used for fake moisture, was working like a charm. She really had old Hubert going!

"Oh honey, I can't let you do that?"

"Why not? You look clean. My dear, you're impeccable."

"It's not that. It's not included in the service and as much as I want it, I'd have to ask you for a tip."

Hubert looked troubled. "Well, can you service me?"

"You want oral sex?" Reds asked.

Hubert nodded. "My wife finds it offensive."

"Well, I don't find it offensive. I enjoy it," Reds said convincingly.

"Why don't you give me another hundred and we'll service each other," Reds suggested. She hated using the word service, but managed to say it in a sultry voice.

Quick as a flash Hubert was off the cot and was bent over fishing around in his pants pocket, mooning Reds with his big, pimpled behind. Reds winced, then shrugged and smiled sweetly. She could endure just about anything for the right price.

This time Hubert paid with two crisp fifty-dollar bills, which Reds graciously accepted. Damn she was good! She wondered if ol' Hubert realized he wasn't going anywhere until she had his very last dollar.

At the end of the shift, Reds started packing up. She was five hundred dollars richer. She usually hung around to help Dominique straighten up the rooms, but she and Dominique were barely speaking so she didn't bother.

As Reds sat waiting for the cab she'd called, she peeked in a compact mirror and scowled at the tired, puffy face that greeted her. The dark circles around her eyes, the sagging cheeks, and droopy eyelids were worn testaments of time that make-up could no longer camouflage. She applied a dab of lipstick, hoping to brighten her image, then threw the mirror and lipstick inside her purse. As soon as she snapped her purse shut, Reds heard the quiet jangle of her new tiny compact-sized cell phone. Reds' heart skipped a beat. The person who'd provided the phone was calling and she never called to simply shoot the breeze. Arianna was strictly business and only called when she had a client for Reds.

"Hello," Reds whispered into the phone. She stood up to leave. She'd wait for the cab outside—away from Dominique's perked up ears.

"I have a twelve o'clock for you."

"Today?" Reds' tone implied that she hoped Arianna meant midnight. She was too tired to work at noon, but she'd gladly call out at Pandora's Box to work for Arianna at midnight.

"Yes, today at noon. Are you available?"

"Uh, I...." Reds faltered. She was exhausted. She had five hundred on her and another two hundred at home. Her cash flow had greatly improved since she'd started working for Arianna on the side, but she was not in a position to start turning money down. "Sure, I can do it. Is it the golden shower guy?" Reds mentally added the easy three hundred she'd make from Arianna's perverted client.

"No, he's a new client."

"Oh," Reds said uneasily.

"This client is paying a lot more than the guy you usually see. He's paying a thousand."

"To do what?" Reds swallowed, then chuckled nervously.

"He's paying for a brown shower," Arianna replied casually.

"Oh, I don't know, Arianna. I don't think I can do that."

"You don't have to do anything. My client is paying to crap on you!"

There was complete silence as Reds struggled to assimilate the words she'd just heard. "What did you say?" she finally asked.

"I said that my client is paying a thousand dollars to shit on you."

And so it had all been a hoax. A cruel cosmic joke. She thought her life had finally turned around; money was starting to pour in just like in the old days. But nothing had changed. In fact, things had gotten worse. Far worse, for never in all the years that she'd been turning tricks, never had anyone requested to shit on her. "You must be outta your mothafuckin' mind?"

"I must say, I'm really shocked at your reaction, Reds. I didn't think you'd mind. Have you taken a look in the mirror lately? You're over the hill, you know. And you've made more with me in a one month than you've made at Pandora's Box in an entire year. How is that possible? Well, it's certainly not because of your flawless features or girlish figure. I made it clear from the start that my clients have a distorted view of the world and you fit the profile of the kind of woman they'd find stimulating. We both know that the customers at Pandora's treat you like shit—so don't try to act as if being shat upon is a new experience. I truly thought you'd be grateful that finally, there's someone in the world who's willing to pay to do it."

Reds had heard enough. She pushed the off button, silencing Arianna.

The cab pulled up in front of the massage parlor. Reds recognized the Middle Eastern driver who had the stone face and abundant curly locks of a stereotypical terrorist. She was seized by the memory of an earlier encounter with him. The cab driver, also struck by a sudden recollection, frowned. A few months earlier, after a particularly bad night, Reds had pitifully tried to exchange sex for the cab fare. Appalled, the cab driver cursed her in his language and demanded his money in English.

"Wait one minute," Reds said, as she pushed the doorbell to Pandora's Box.

"No time for tricks. No games this time," the driver cautioned.

"No games," Reds said. "I just want to see if my friend needs a ride." She'd rather put up with Dominique's bullshit than succumb to Arianna's insane proposition.

Squinting sleepily, Rover opened the door for Reds. Dominique stood in the background with her workbag slung over her shoulder, looking surprised to see Reds.

"Come on and share the cab with me, Dominique," Reds cajoled. Dominique's face tightened. "Come on, it's my treat!" Dominique's face softened a bit. She shrugged, then followed Reds into the cab.

"Forty-first and Brown," Reds directed the cab driver. Dominique looked at Reds quizzically. "Chile, we ain't going home," Reds announced. "We goin' out...and we gonna get fucked up!" She flashed a thick wad of money and Dominique's solemn expression swiftly changed into a sparkling grin.

Chapter 30

An hour after leaving Pandora's, Victoria was back in her apartment. Showered and prepared for bed, but too wound up to sleep, she sat on the sofa pouring over old photographs. She came across a picture of her teenage singing group. She stared at her image and smiled sadly at the baby-faced girl who believed her voice was the key to the happiness and acceptance that had eluded her as a child. Never in her wildest dreams could she have imagined her future-self working as a prostitute. She shook her head in disgust. How could she have allowed herself to sink so low?

I'm quitting! Victoria resolved, standing up. But her tenacity was short-lived. She couldn't quit, not yet. She had to get the money for Jordan's education.

Deflated, she flopped back down on the sofa. She'd have to go back to Pandora's for a little while longer.

Hit with a huge wave of self-pity, tears began to well. She lifted the receiver to call Kareem, but quickly hung up. What did Kareem care? He hadn't even bothered to cancel their concert date; he just left her hanging, waiting for him to call. Besides, Victoria had enough experience with melancholia to know that there was nothing that Kareem or anyone else could say or do that would make her feel better. She'd have to get through it-this profound sorrow—on her own.

❦

Rover recounted the money. Twenty-seven hundred dollars was the combined take from the morning and five o'clock shifts. He stacked the bills into several even piles before returning the money to the safe. Counting money was exhilarating, even if it didn't belong to him. Gabrielle would be pleased with the day's take, and if she was happy, then he was ecstatic.

He eyed the large numbers on his Timex. It was 12:13. Damn that Dominique! Where the hell was she? And for that matter, where was Reds? Thoughtfully, he stroked the stubble on his chin. So far, Miquon was the only girl to show up for the late shift, so Rover had to ask Jonee (who'd already put in her eight hours) to work the midnight shift. Jonee agreed, but he needed more than two girls; he needed Dominique, the so-called night manager, to get her tail in there and handle her shift. Rover let out a long sigh. The skin flick showing at the theater next door was starting in twenty-two minutes and he hated being late.

At the sound of the doorbell, Rover popped out of his seat and reached for his cap, certain that it was Dominique. But when he consulted the monitor, his face fell with disappointment. Instead of Dominique, there was customer standing in the lobby—a nice-looking kid who looked like he'd be more comfortable on a surfboard. Rover had never laid eyes on the young man, and figured he was probably a tourist.

Rover could hear Jonee's clicking high heels rushing to the lobby. He looked up at the monitor and observed her sidle up to the young man with the grace of a cat. Miquon, too big to be graceful, fondled her pendulous breasts and smiled her version of a sultry smile. Given his choices, Rover wasn't surprised to see the lad being led away by Jonee.

A few minutes later Jonee clicked into the office and handed Rover five twenties. With pen poised, she bent down to write her name on the first line of the session log, but suddenly stood up. "I don't know about dude. He's kind of weird."

"They're all weird," Rover said in a flat voice, "but that guy looks really harmless."

"I know, but I don't like the way he looks. You should see his hands... they're huge."

"So the guy has big hands. Since when is that a crime?"

"It's not that... something's up with him. I don't even like the way he was looking at me with his..."

Rover sighed, cutting her off. "You bitched when you didn't make your quota on the last shift, and now you have the good fortune of getting the first session of the night, and you're still griping." Rover looked at Jonee critically. "Some people are never satisfied."

Running acrylic nails decorated with a splash of bright colors through her synthetic blonde hair, Jonee replied, "I know...I know, Rover. But something ain't right. Oh well, fuck it. If you hear me scream, you better come running!" She tried to sound playful, but as she bent down to sign her name, the worried look on her face suggested otherwise. Jonee slid a dollar bill across the desk. "I'm out of condoms."

Rover tore a gold ribbed condom off a roll of Trojans. "Need any gel?"

Jonee shook her head, pulled her polyester robe tightly around her tiny frame and strode purposefully toward the session room.

Rover's thoughts wandered back to Dominique. Irritated beyond belief, he could feel his face flush. The woman had been warned again and again about her tardiness and it didn't do a bit of good. Once and for all, Gabrielle was going to have to seriously address the problem. It was time to get rid of Dominique. Gabrielle needed someone she could count on-someone responsible. Someone who got her ass to work on time so that he could enjoy the few hours of free time that he was entitled to.

He heard a door slam and within seconds Jonee, barefoot and naked beneath her robe, burst into the office. "I'm not doing that mothafucka! Let him have his money back 'cause he's asking for some crazy shit that I'm not into."

"What does he want you to do?" Rover asked with a weary chuckle.

"He took his belt off, and started talking some shit about how he's gonna teach me a lesson. He tried to sway me with some extra dough—tossed five big ones on the bed, but I told 'em the mint don't print enough money for me to let a mothafucka whip my ass." Jonee shook her head in disbelief. "I told you, Rover… That mothafucka is whacked!

"All right, I'll handle it. You go wait in the lounge."

Jonee gave a slight shudder and hastily retreated to the lounge.

Rover opened the desk drawer and took out the five twenties that Jonee had given him. He folded the bills in half and carefully placed one of Arianna's pink business cards in the crease. With a cheerful whistle he strolled out of the office and tapped on the door of the session room.

Chapter 31

U sing a different voice for each character, Victoria put a lot of effort into the bedtime reading of *The Little Engine That Could*. She had run out of steam by the end of the tale, and was relieved when Jordan, mercifully, didn't request a repeat. Admitting defeat, he yawned, rubbed his eyes, and wiggled into a comfortable position.

Victoria kissed her son goodnight, tiptoed over to the light switch, and waited. Within seconds, Jordan was fast asleep. Victoria clicked off the light.

Still recovering from the drama with the delivery guy, Victoria hadn't been to Pandora's for two days. The thought of going back turned her stomach inside out, but she'd have to go back if she expected to get enough money to enroll Jordan in private school by September.

Victoria curled up on the sofa with the letter from the admissions office of a private elementary school near Penn's campus. The letter informed her that the deadline for the scholarship program for kindergarten had passed. There was, however, limited financial assistance for the $18,500 annual tuition. To be eligible for this assistance, she'd have to schedule an appointment with the school's Financial Director. A copy of Victoria's personal financial statement, a letter from her employer, pay stubs, and a signed copy of her IRS 1040 statement would be required prior to the meeting.

Worried, she bit her bottom lip. She'd paid taxes the previous year, but had no current pay stubs, and she doubted if a hand-penned note from Rover would qualify as a letter from her employer. She pushed the papers away. Without proof of employment, she couldn't even set up a payment plan. Between now and September, she'd have to come up with the full amount. She decided to put the certificate of deposit she'd recently purchased toward the tuition, but she'd have to really hustle to get the rest of the money.

When Jordan was safely enrolled, with tuition paid in full, she'd quit Pandora's, get a real job, and apply for a scholarship for the next year.

As she sat pondering Jordan's education, the doorbell rang. She glanced at the kitchen clock as she pressed the intercom button. "Who is it?" she asked.

"Kareem."

Victoria felt her heart might stop. She did a quick scan of the living room. Papers were strewn about on the coffee table, but the room was otherwise in order. She checked out her image in the wall mirror, tightened the sash of her chenille robe, smoothed out the disorder of her hair, and buzzed Kareem in.

She was silent as her eyes swept the length of his body. Kareem was wearing a red Sixer's jersey with the number 3 emblazoned across his chest, baggy denim shorts, and unlaced Timberlands. He looked good, handsomely urban, as if he stepped from the pages of *Vibe* magazine. Tingling all over, she controlled the urge to collapse into his arms and cover him with kisses. But he didn't deserve her kisses. Not yet. Not until she heard what he had to say for himself.

"Hi," she said, in an icy tone that didn't match the warmth in her heart.

"I know I'm wrong for not calling you, Victoria. But, uh, I had some issues to deal with. I couldn't talk to you until I sorted through some things." Kareem's voice was low and serious, his expression grave. "We need to talk. Can we sit down?"

Victoria's face fell. "Sure," she answered in a voice barely above a whisper as she led him to the sofa. Her stomach tightened into a knot. Not knowing what to expect, she was braced to hear dreadful news. Genital herpes-type news, or gonorrhea, or worse. *Oh, Jesus!* Then she realized she was allowing her imagination to run wild. A memory of their one-time encounter, informed her that no communicable disease could have gotten past the latex barrier between them. Victoria relaxed, suddenly able to handle whatever was on Kareem's mind. She looked into his eyes, expectantly.

"I know I promised to take you to see my act, but, uh…the show got cancelled, and I lost a lot of money. I know I should have called you, but the way I was feeling at the time…I just didn't want to talk to anybody.

"Oh, Kareem. I'm so sorry. I know how much…"

"Can I finish?" he asked. Victoria nodded obediently.

"But that's not the only reason I stopped calling."

Victoria sat up, erect.

"I think your job…uh, the kind of work you do, is standing between us. It's the reason we can't get this relationship off the ground.

Anger flashed in Victoria's eyes. "Don't go there, Kareem," she warned.

"I have to. We've been tiptoeing around the issue; it's a taboo subject. Look, it's time to bring it out in the open."

"Oh really? Well, I think it's time for you to leave." Victoria stood up. Her right leg began to shake, and her mouth twitched in indignation. "Who the hell do you think you are, coming over here, uninvited I might add, with your self-righteous attitude? Who are you to pass judgment on me?"

"Calm down, Victoria. Just listen to me."

"Don't tell me what to do. You're in my goddamn house. She gestured wildly, and did a neck twist that would have done Miquon proud." *Oh my God, what was she saying, and why was she acting so ghetto?* She felt like she was outside herself, observing herself, and what she saw was a snarling half-crazed woman.

"Do you think you're better than me, Kareem? Is that what this is about?" She knew she sounded irrational, but couldn't stop herself. "Don't forget, we met at my *taboo subject*. You *paid* to be with me." She paused, enjoying the pained expression on Kareem's face. "Now, it's out in the open. Satisfied? And since it's been established that I'm a whore, tell me, Kareem, what does that make you?"

Kareem recoiled. "I never called you that."

"You implied it. Now as I was saying," she taunted. "What does that make you, Kareem? I'll tell you. You're a trick! You're nothing but a trick."

"Don't say that, Victoria. You know we're more than that." Kareem spoke softly, and reached for her hand. But Victoria didn't like his placating tone, and jerked her hand away. Kareem looked pained, but continued. "I only went to your job once. The night I met you. My boah and I were driving past the place and he told me that there was a bunch of freaky jawns up in there that would do anything you wanted for a buck. I didn't believe him and just went in to check it out. And I saw you…"

"That's bullshit, Kareem. You saw me and what? You had to have me? What kind of freaky thing have you been waiting for me to do, huh Kareem? Just get out!" she screamed, pointing to the door.

But instead of leaving, Kareem pulled Victoria down to the sofa and onto his lap.

"Let me go!" she yelled, but his muscular arms enclosed her from behind. Victoria struggled, but Kareem refused to let her go. She stamped his Timberland-protected feet, wishing she had on steel-toed boots instead of the flimsy, ineffective bedroom slippers she wore. Kareem didn't flinch; he tightened his hold on her. She spit and sputtered, scratched and kicked, but Kareem held on.

"You're hurting me, Kareem," she said through clenched teeth as she thrashed about, trying to break his steel-like grip. "Jordan!" she screamed. "Jordan, Call 911!" But Jordan didn't stir, and Kareem didn't let go.

Tears of frustration rolled down Victoria's face and onto Kareem's arms.

Kareem held her tighter, brushing the side of her face with his lips, rocking her as she twisted and squirmed. She felt herself growing limp, her sobs becoming softer. He held on firmly, waiting patiently to feel her body relax in surrender. Kareem kissed the top of her head, and whispered into her hair, "I'm sorry, Victoria. My words came out all wrong. I didn't mean to say anything to hurt you."

Finally, she was still. Barely loosening his grip, Kareem turned Victoria toward him. She fell onto his chest, crying quietly. He smoothed her hair, murmured soft soothing sounds. She continued crying until finally, exhausted, she fell asleep encircled in his arms.

Chapter 32

It was a recurring dream.

Victoria is sitting at a dressing table, gazing into a brightly-lit vanity mirror. She's in the dressing room of a huge amphitheater. It's her dressing room! Champagne, flowers, and baskets of fruit surround her. She expected to feel tense and on edge, but she's quite calm as she prepares to give the first performance of her cross-county tour. Then without warning, as she puts on the final touches of her make-up, she hears the intro of her opening song. Panic-stricken, she looks at her watch; it's show time! Inexplicably, she has dawdled, and lost track of time. How could this have happened? Her manager should not have allowed this to happen. Such negligence was unacceptable. She'd have a few choice words for him. She scurries to the door, but stops suddenly, realizing that she's wearing only a bra and a G-string. Where were her clothes? Where the hell was her wardrobe person? Oh screw it; there simply wasn't enough time to locate her clothes. In just a few more bars, the band would be playing her cue.

Bolting out the door, she prays that the audience doesn't notice that she's undressed.

She zips through a maze of darkened corridors, her breathing is harsh and labored. She can't find her way to the stage. She hears her assembled musicians playing the intro over and over, while the audience, apparently worked into a frenzy of anticipation, chants her name. "Victoria, Victoria!" While still trapped in the maze, Victoria surprisingly hears a thunderous applause as her voice booms from the amphitheater's sound system. Frantically she wonders: How can this be?

An hour after drifting off, Victoria awakened to the sound of her music. She sprang from the sofa to the stereo system across the room, and with the click of a switch, silenced her vocals.

Kareem smiled uncomfortably. "I was checking out your music selection while you were sleep, and I ran across your CD. I heard the first two tracks, and they sounded tight. How come you never told me about your music career?"

"Because it's nonexistent. There's nothing to tell."

"Then explain that voice I just heard."

"I can't. Not right now."

Kareem sat down next to her; he patted her arm. "Okay, I'm not gonna push you. We'll talk when you're ready."

Victoria gazed kindly at Kareem. "I'm pretty confused about a lot of things, but I'm trying to put my troubles aside for awhile. I have to concentrate on raising my son. I'm looking for a private school for Jordan; that's my priority right now."

Kareem nodded, and Victoria felt encouraged.

"I read an article about the public school system," she continued. "Public schools aren't working, Kareem. Black kids start off okay, but then bad grades and acting out begin. They lose the desire to learn by the time they reach the fourth grade. I just can't let that happen to Jordan."

"I know you're a good mother," Kareem said, putting his arm around her. "But how do you expect to give Jordan your best if you don't take care of yourself?"

"What are you talking about? I *do* take care of myself," she protested.

"Then what's wrong? Why are your eyes so sad?"

Victoria dropped her gaze and sighed.

Kareem reached out and stroked her hair. "You know I care about you, and if I didn't think you felt the same, I wouldn't be here."

She took a deep breath, but couldn't deny the deep feelings she had for Kareem.

"I want to be a part of your life—your son's life."

On that note, Victoria allowed her lips to curve slightly into a smile.

"And I'm going to do whatever it takes to keep you smiling," he whispered, and squeezed her against him.

"I do want you in my life, Kareem. But how is it possible with…with the work I do? I want to get out of the business, but I can't. Not yet."

Kareem spoke softly; his brown eyes were warm and sincere. "I can help you, Victoria. You don't have to carry this burden alone."

"Yes I do. I have to get out of this on my own. You can help me by being patient."

"I'll be whatever you need me to be. Patient, gentle, strong. Whatever," he said. Their lips touched lightly. She turned her lips to his. Victoria and Kareem stood up. Their bodies molded together, still kissing, he swooped her into his arms and carried her to her room.

Kareem and Victoria lay together on her bed in the near darkness, his fingers working quickly to untie her robe. Startled, then smiling, that this sensual woman's nightclothes were covered with Disney characters. Then he eased off her nightshirt, his lips swept over her shoulders, his hands moved to her breasts.

Clutching his tee shirt, Victoria trembled and, then slipped her hands beneath the fabric. Slowly, her hands traveled from his flat tight stomach, to his hard, hairy chest. Kareem's hardening nipples aroused her. Overwhelmed by the desire to touch every part of him, her hands quickly left that area to explore his broad shoulders and his back.

"Kareem," she cried out.

Kareem moaned a response, and then spoke with his face buried in her hair. "You know I want you, you know I need you. But there's a problem."

"What's wrong?" Victoria asked, alarmed.

Kareem smiled slyly, and placed Victoria's hand in the center of his chest. "I've got a sensitive heart and I don't want you to break it. Feel me?"

Victoria touched him all over. "I feel you," she replied.

Chapter 33

Shards of sunlight sliced through the slightly parted blinds, forcing Victoria into consciousness at dawn. She blinked irritably, but was instantly comforted by an awareness that Kareem lay next to her. But that feeling was brief; it was replaced by a pang of apprehension. Morning-after uneasiness. Last night, she believed she had a firm grip on Kareem's heart, but in the glare of the morning light she was not so certain. She hoped she hadn't deluded herself.

Victoria lay still. She could feel the rise and fall of his breathing and longed to be close to him. She wanted to feel his breath on her back. She wanted to feel *him* on her back. Not wanting to wake him, and not wanting to break the spell, but needing to be a part of him again, Victoria held her breath and began to ever so slowly slide her body backwards into his curve. As she got closer she could feel his wiry, masculine body hair tickling her back, and the back of her thighs. She was almost there. Then, as if on cue, a strong arm enveloped her waist, and in one swift motion, Kareem pulled her the rest of the way. Nuzzling her neck, he whispered in her ear, "G'morning, baby."

It was just a simple greeting, yet his words soothed her like a declaration of love. His response to her tentative advance reassured her. She need not proceed with caution. She was safe in his arms.

Victoria couldn't resist kissing the arm that so lovingly held her, while Kareem used his free hand to fondle her back, her shoulder, her neck. And as he began to stroke her belly and her breasts, Victoria reached behind, stretching out her hand to caress his thick, muscular thigh. The moment she touched him, she felt his throbbing hardness begin to move against her, pulsating and seeking something warm, something dark, something moist, and something equally hungry. Her fingers, winding up the length of his thigh paused to rake through the tangled mass of thick pubic hair, then using just a fingertip, she traveled the length of his desire. As she gently massaged, Kareem groaned. Victoria was struck by a tightening in the pit of her stomach that swiftly cascaded down to her loins.

With no will of her own, she allowed determined hands to shift her position, and pull her on top. Kareem gripped her shoulders and lowered her mouth to his. With her eyes shut tight, Victoria grimaced as she struggled to control the urge to simply devour him.

"Open your eyes," Kareem instructed.

Victoria's lids fluttered open.

"I love you," he said, holding her in his gaze.

Limp with raw passion, and too weak to keep her head up, she collapsed onto his chest, murmuring, "I love you, too, Kareem."

Victoria rolled off Kareem; she wanted her man on top. Lying on her back, she drew up her knees and parted them slowly. Kareem gave a low, throaty sound as he moved into the space her open thighs had created. Victoria reached out to guide him, but Kareem brushed her hand away. Burying his face between her legs, he parted her wet, sensitive lips, kissing and sucking before using his tongue to taste the nectar deep within. Victoria's body arched and fell; her knees locked Kareem in. A sound, not quite human, building up inside fought for release, and Victoria could feel herself losing the battle to control it. And just as she was about to fall into the abyss, Kareem stopped abruptly.

"No, baby, not yet. Wait for me," he urged, as he lifted his moist mouth and began to journey upward, kissing and licking his way to her lips.

"Hurry, Kareem," Victoria pleaded, writhing and reaching, and pulling him toward her, but Kareem refused to be rushed. She bit down on her bottom lip in a struggle for self-control.

Kareem entered her, filling her slowly. He didn't thrust wildly or deeply, it was a slow rhythmic ride. But Victoria, crazed by the unbearable sweet pain, clutched and clawed, and pulled him in deeper, thrusting her body, demanding immediate release.

"Okay, baby. All right," Kareem said hoarsely, giving in to her demands. Quickening his pace, he met her thrust for thrust until they both collapsed.

Smiling with her eyes closed, Victoria lay flat on her back. Kareem, propped up by an elbow stared down at her, wiping perspiration from her face with his fingertips.

Her eyes opened. "Jordan's gonna be up soon," she said with a long sigh.

"Yeah, I figured that. I guess I better get myself together and slip out quietly."

"Aw, Kareem," she whined. "I don't want you to leave, but Jordan…" She stopped abruptly, recalling her muffled cries. She wondered how loud she'd been?

"Oh God, I have to check on Jordan. I hope he didn't hear us."

Victoria and Kareem sat up, their eyes scanned the room until they landed on the trail of clothing scattered about on the floor. Kareem got up and tossed Victoria her nightshirt and began quickly picking up his own clothes. She pulled the nightshirt over her head and rushed to her son's room.

Jordan was curled up fast asleep. Victoria breathed a sigh of relief. Jordan wasn't used to having a man around, but Kareem was in her life now, and she'd figure out a way to inform Jordan in the least threatening way.

"He's still asleep," she said softly when she returned to her bedroom.

Completely dressed, Kareem sat on the side of the bed, adjusting the tongue of his Timberlands. The sight saddened her; she really didn't want him to go. But it was best that he leave before Jordan woke up.

"So when am I gonna meet the little guy?" Kareem smiled brightly. "After you introduce us properly and everything, Jordan and I are gonna have a little talk…man-to-man," Kareem feigned a serious expression.

Victoria couldn't help smiling as she experienced a double delight: the sight of Kareem's devilishly-handsome face and the thought of him interacting with her son. A male influence was so badly needed in her little boy's life. Did she dare hope for that?

"Do you want me to come back later on? Say around two or three.... late afternoon?"

"Yes, Jordan and I would be *delighted*." She emphasized the last word.

"What does Jordan like to do?"

"Oh, Jordan's not hard to please. A trip to McDonald's will win him over."

"Does he like amusement parks?"

"He sure does," she said, smiling.

"Then, let's take a ride to Great Adventure. We can pick up a Happy Meal on the way." Kareem winked.

Be still my heart, she thought, imagining the three of them together. Happy. A family.

Chapter 34

Arianna eased her newly-leased Lexus up to the curb on Naudain Street, glanced at the clock on the brilliantly lit dashboard, and sighed. It was one in the morning; she should have been home in bed. But alas, money called. The street was so quiet, she wouldn't have been surprised if the soft hum of the engine roused her sleeping neighbors, causing porch lights to flicker on, and curtains to part.

Arianna chortled, imagining her neighbors' reactions if they were to discover the bawdy activities going on right under their smug noses? Most likely, they'd try to create problems for her, accuse her of violating city-zoning laws. The big fuss, however, would end in a whimper—her cozy relationship with the city's Licenses and Inspections enforcement chief ensured her of that.

Before turning off the ignition she gripped the steering wheel, bracing herself for the ordeal of tracking down one of her girls. It was late, and by now their pathetic asses had probably retreated to the dark shadowy places where narcotics dulled their senses.

Three hours earlier she had locked up the house, and had gone to her apartment on the Parkway, mentally-exhausted, but satisfied with the day's profit. Now she was back.

Motivated by images of Versace's fall line, she had agreed to reopen when Rover called her at home with the news that he had a potential client who was willing to pay up to a thousand dollars for a spur-of-the-moment, hour-long session with a female submissive. The last customer of the night had been some big guy Rover had sent over. The guy wanted to take a strap to Ming, Arianna's in-house dominatrix. He was quickly introduced to the pleasures of bondage and discipline. At the end of the session his back and buttocks were covered with red welts. He thanked Ming profusely and promised to come back in a week.

Ming would never agree to switch roles and play a submissive. Not for any amount of money, so there was no point in summoning her. That role required the services of Reds or Bethany, and it absolutely galled Arianna that she was unable to locate either of the two women.

Before leaving her apartment she had called Reds repeatedly on the cellular phone that she had given her, only to get an incessant ring. Hadn't she told the dim-witted woman to keep the phone turned on at all times? Arianna was incensed; it didn't matter that she had furiously dismissed Reds less than twenty-four hours ago. She still expected Reds to check in with her and was bewildered by her impudence.

When she called Bethany's most recent pager number she got a recorded message informing her that the number was no longer in service. Only a low-life of the worst kind would fail to pay a ten-dollar a month pager bill.

The client, who called himself John, of course, was scheduled to arrive at two a.m. With only an hour to locate a submissive, Arianna sighed heavily and stepped out of the car. It had been warm out when she locked up, but now it was chilly. Wearing a short-sleeved floral dress, she wrapped her arms around herself and dashed inside the house.

Arianna remembered that Sheena, who had gotten word of Reds' and Bethany's sudden windfall, had expressed an interest in working for her and had given her several telephone numbers: a neighborhood bar, and the home of a friend. Arianna assumed that the latter was a place where Sheena got high. She quickly tried the number at the bar.

"Is Sheena there?" Arianna inquired.

"Sheena? Sheena who?" an irritated woman asked.

Arianna exhaled audibly. "Tall, thin, Sheena."

"Anybody here named Sheena?" the woman bellowed over loud bar music. Arianna grimaced and held the phone away from her ear.

"No. Don't nobody know no Sheena."

"Would you mind asking if anybody there...?" Instantly, Arianna was listening to a dial tone.

With the end of a pen, she angrily punched the numbers to the presumed crack house and felt heartened when the man who answered the phone sounded alert and oriented enough to assure her that Sheena was expected soon. Great! She thanked the man and told him she'd call back in a few minutes, surprising herself with the sincerity in her voice.

Arianna cupped her chin in one hand, and with the painted nails of the other hand, tapped the desk impatiently. She frowned down at her Movado; it was 1:15.

Feeling frantic, she called Reds' cell phone again. Still no answer. She slammed down the phone in disgust. How could such useless women—such poor excuses for human beings—put her in such a desperate situation? One thing was for sure: she was not going to blow the money that was being offered. She'd find someone to do the session. If worse-came-to-worse, she'd drive around and pick up a girl off the street.

Fifteen minutes later, in search of a hooker, Arianna cruised along the downtown streets in her Lexus. She was prepared to offer as much as three hundred fifty for an hour-long session. But the pickings on the streets were slim—there were a few hideous transvestites as well as some of the homeless, mixed in with ordinary pedestrians who poured from the bars and clubs in the area. It was the mayor's fault! In an effort to attract the affluent back to Center City, the mayor had launched a campaign to clean up the city. Heightened police pressure had driven prostitutes away from Center City, forcing them to relocate to the working-class neighborhoods. The Kensington section of the city had become a haven for prostitutes. Arianna knew she'd have her pick from the dozens of girls who hustled under the El on Kensington Avenue, but there really wasn't enough time to drive all the way there and back. She narrowed her search to the few streets in Center City where hookers were still known to frequent: 12th and 13th and Arch up to Walnut and parts of Broad Street.

Arianna turned up her nose at the unlikely prospects and steered the Lexus back to Naudain Street.

She made a few more unsuccessful attempts to locate Sheena, Bethany, or Reds before giving up. It was sadly apparent that if she wanted to collect the thousand-dollar fee, she'd have to do the session herself, and the very thought of dealing with a client made her shudder. This John guy would have to up the price to two grand if he wanted to have a session with her.

Tanned and startlingly handsome, John arrived wearing faded jeans and a sky blue sweatshirt with "Nantucket" embroidered in letters across the front. He looked more like a college jock than the typical paying client. He was definitely a novice—most likely some rich kid who attended the nearby Ivy League University. Arianna presumed that this John guy had grown tired of jerking off to S&M videos and now wanted to experience the real thing.

In a no nonsense tone, Arianna told him that the agreed upon fee had increased—being that the session was so last minute and all. Without batting an eye, the young man pulled out a wad, and eagerly forked over the cash—two thousand in large bills.

Excited by the sight of so much money, Arianna felt a rush, then collected herself and went on to explain that nothing rough would be tolerated. Light paddling was okay, as was verbal abuse, but restraints were not allowed.

"Yeah, sure," he said, simultaneously nodding his agreement. "But, uh is it okay to play water sports?" he inquired uncomfortably, his face red with embarrassment.

Arianna arched a brow. "You want to pee on me?"

"Sort of," John said with a nervous grin that displayed perfectly-even, white teeth.

"Sort of!" she replied sharply.

Unable to meet her gaze, John mumbled, "I mean, uh yeah."

"Well I don't think so, and I'd like for you to leave now. You can have your money back." Arianna pushed the stack of bills toward him, and stood up for emphasis.

John looked panic-stricken. "I'm sorry. Please...keep the money." He pushed the money back toward Arianna. "I don't want to leave. I just thought..."

"Thought what? Do I look like someone to be pissed upon?"

"No. Not at all." John's eyes swept the floor in contrition. "I'm really sorry. I'm new at this. I've never done anything like this before."

"I didn't think so." She sat down, and leaned back in her chair confidently.

"I was hoping you wouldn't see through me, but I guess you did." John chuckled.

"I feel exposed and thoroughly ridiculous—but I really want to go through with this. Ya think you could kind of show me the ropes? Uh, no pun intended," he added, laughing.

The calculator in Arianna's brain was working overtime. In spite of his very casual attire, she sensed that John had money—real money. Well, perhaps not John personally, he was too young, but his background was one of wealth. His easy access to cash and the Rolex that peeked beneath his sleeve attested to that, as did his demeanor and tone of voice, now that he was feeling more at ease. Arianna softened. The young man had been sufficiently chastised, and appeared to be appropriately remorseful.

"I can certainly teach you the fundamentals of being dominated, but of course you realize that before you can become a proficient master, you'll have to experience what it feels like to be a slave."

"Of course," John said, looking at Arianna with pure adoration.

"After a few sessions of obedience training, you'll be ready to practice on a submissive. And when I think you're ready, you can advance to spanking, water sports...and believe it or not, some of my girls enjoy being tortured. How does that sound?" Acknowledging the bulge in John's pants, Arianna knew this session would be a piece of cake.

She led him to the peach-colored bedroom. She wasn't going anywhere near the dungeon, no point in getting his hopes up. She left the physical stuff to Ming. Arianna got off on the psychological aspects of dominating another human being.

She'd strip him of his will, make him totally dependent upon her. Her beautiful and adoring slave would also become a continuous source of cash—lots of cash!

Chapter 35

Arianna reclined on the chaise lounge in the Victorian bedroom. "Get undressed," she ordered.

Anxious to oblige, John shed his sweatshirt. Grinning, he tossed it onto the shiny hardwood floor.

"Pick that up. How dare you litter the floor?"

"Sorry." Still grinning, John grabbed the shirt. "What do you want me to do with it?" he asked, looking around the lavishly-furnished, frilly room. A crystal chandelier cast soft shadows upon the airy lace curtains at the windows. Freshly-cut tulips arranged in an antique porcelain pitcher sat atop a cherry wood bureau. A canopy of silk was suspended above a four-poster bed that dominated the room. The bed was adorned with a matching silk bedcover and ruffled lace throw pillows.

"First of all, you're going to have to learn to address me properly."

"Oops! Sorry. Should I call you madam?" he asked with a sly grin and a wink.

Arianna bolted upright from her reclining position. "Do you find me amusing, John?"

"No, I just..."

"Then wipe that ridiculous grin off your face."

The smile vanished.

"I won't tolerate disrespect or impudence."

"What did I do?" John asked, holding up both hands.

"Please address me as Mistress."

"What did I do, uh... Mistress?"

"That's better," she said, ignoring his question. "Now continue undressing, then fold your clothing and make a neat pile on the floor beside the bed."

John hurriedly did as he was told, but kept on his boxers.

Arianna shook her head in disapproval. "I want you to stand before me. I want you completely naked. Is that clear?

"Yes, Mistress," he said in a cracked voice that did not endear him to her. His pained expression indicated that he was no longer enjoying himself; he looked appropriately humiliated and seemed to finally understand that she was not to be taken lightly. Before the session was over, Arianna resolved to have this spoiled, rich brat crawling on all fours.

John kicked off his boxers. Arianna pursed her lips in displeasure. Then remembering her rules about tidiness, he scampered to pick them up. It occurred to Arianna that John wasn't nearly as handsome as she'd thought. In fact, he looked like an idiot, falling apart before her eyes. Breaking the spirit of this tall, apparently well-bred, young man was delicious fun. She felt her nipples harden; her abhorrence of John was definitely an aphrodisiac.

John attempted to cover an ever-growing erection with his hands, as he dutifully stood naked before Arianna.

"Remove your hands!" she commanded.

Slowly, bashfully, John allowed his hands to fall to his sides, revealing a now fully-developed erection.

"What do you think you're doing?" Her fiery gaze was fixed on John. "I didn't give you permission to do that!"

"To do what, Mistress?" There was a combination of fear and frustration in his voice, yet remarkably, his member remained at attention.

"You offend me with this...this vile display of lechery."

"I didn't mean to..."

"Get that thing out of my face this instant, you filthy degenerate!"

Hunched over, John scampered to his pile of clothing and used his boxers to cover his manhood.

Suddenly rising from the chaise lounge, Arianna stood up and pointed at John. "Get in the corner. NOW! You revolting creature!" She pointed to the far right corner of the room, where a magnificent Boston fern in a ceramic pot stood on a wicker plant stand.

Facing Arianna, John squeezed in beside the fern.

"Don't look at me," she barked. "Turn around, face the wall!"

John spun around to face the wall with his arms crossed behind his back, he modestly concealed his buttocks with the boxers, which dangled, from his hands.

"Now take care of your filthy business out of my sight."

"What do you mean, Mistress?" John asked, looking over his shoulder. He was visibly-shaken, near tears. Arianna found his discomfort invigorating.

"Get rid of the erection, it's disgusting. I don't care how you accomplish it—use your hands if you must. I can't train you properly if you're in that condition. Now turn around—face me when I'm addressing you!"

John turned around again; a perplexed frown wrinkled his brow. "But you said…"

Arianna held up a silencing hand. "Do as you're told!"

Arianna arose from the chaise lounge. "I'll give you ten minutes to take care of your filthy urges." She gave John a lingering look. He fidgeted uncomfortably, his hands wringing the boxer shorts. Feeling charitable, she patted his arm and said, "I'm going to change into something more comfortable." She watched John's eyes flicker with hope, then added, "I'm going to go downstairs to find a dog collar and leash for you, then we can begin your training. Do you have a color preference?"

John gaped at her.

Arianna smiled when she detected panic in his eyes. Satisfied, she whirled out of the room.

❦

Exactly ten minutes later, Arianna returned. She was nude beneath a silk chiffon robe with crystal beading. In her hands, she proudly held a black studded dog collar and a linked chain leash.

John stood in the corner, unmoving, with his back to her.

In an uncharacteristically gay tone, Arianna said, "You may turn around." John made a nervous glance over his shoulder.

Arianna held out her arms, and shook the leash and collar at John, inviting him to come forward for a fitting.

John made a tentative turn, and then turned around completely, revealing his still rock-hard organ. It was aimed like a missile at Arianna.

Shocked and rendered speechless by his obstinacy, Arianna just stared at him for a moment, and before she could find the words to express her fury, John shot across the room, and tackled her onto the bed. Arianna emitted a stunned yelp. The collar and leash flew from her hands, landing in a loud clatter on the nightstand.

"What the hell is wrong with you?" she demanded. "Stop it, get back to your corner this instant!" Arianna was frightened, but tried to maintain an authoritative tone.

"Shut up, bitch!" John spat, as he pinned her down and tore open her robe.

She winced when she felt a rip in the delicate fabric, then shrieked when she heard the sound of the crystal beads, one-by-one, hitting the floor. But even as she struggled with her attacker, Arianna couldn't help wondering how she could successfully defend herself and still salvage her beautiful robe and exquisite beads.

"Get off me, you bastard," she screamed, clawing uselessly at his chest. She was amazed at the ineffectiveness of her squared-off acrylic nails.

"Help me! Somebody, please help…" But her words were cut off, muffled by the boxer shorts that John now held over her face.

She thrashed and kicked soundlessly. With eyes, wide and wild, she tried to tell him that she couldn't breathe, that her air was being cut off—that he was smothering her with his fucking boxer shorts! Calm down, she told herself. Stop struggling, maybe he was just temporarily out of control but capable of coming to his senses if she stopped fighting. Arianna went limp, but became immediately aware that the only purpose lying motionless served was to allow John easier access as he forcefully separated her legs with his knee.

Angrily, he thrust himself inside her, and while seemingly in the throes of ecstasy, he pulled the underwear away from Arianna's face and flung them aside.

Panting and gasping for breath, she began to wriggle beneath his weight, trying to topple him over, but couldn't.

Stopping mid-stroke, John looked down at her, his expression puzzled. "Relax." he said, "Don't you want to enjoy this?"

"Relax? How can I relax when you're acting like a raving lunatic?"

John's face hardened, and Arianna realized that he didn't appreciate being called a lunatic. Her lips spread into a smile of apology. "Stop, please. Don't do this, okay? Your money's locked in the middle desk drawer. You can have it back...all of it! Take the money and just leave, okay?"

"No!" he said. "Not until I make you cum." John feigned a look of worry. "But, I heard whores don't cum, that true?"

Arianna was silent, taken aback from being called a whore. She was a whore when she worked for peanuts at Pandora's Box, but now with the rates she charged, she considered herself a businesswoman, a fucking entrepreneur. Her silence was prolonged because she didn't know how to respond. John was obviously quite crazy, and the wrong answer could prolong his stay and escalate the potential for violence. She chided herself for not carefully scrutinizing him before agreeing to a session. But, she reminded herself, other than the fact that he was far too young to have so much cash to throw around, there was nothing particularly unusual about him.

"Speak up, whore. Cat got your tongue?" John taunted.

"I'm capable of multiple orgasms," she blurted, finally. "Especially with a good-looking guy like you." She tried to smile seductively, but felt completely ridiculous considering how frightened she was.

John smiled broadly. "Great, that's good to know because I'm gonna give you the best orgasm of your life. The hell with multiples, one big one is all you'll need."

Arianna nodded, the strained smile plastered on her face.

John's pumping resumed, accompanied by grunts.

On cue, Arianna began to moan softly, determined to give the performance of her life. She hoped that her active participation in this sexual misadventure would buy more time to plan an escape.

Her eyes darted around the room in search of a weapon. She thought about the gun that she kept locked in the desk drawer. Damn! If only she had a gun tucked under the mattress, she'd gleefully shoot this sick motherfucker right between the eyes.

John increased the tempo, and Arianna matched his speed, moaning louder.

"This is going to increase your pleasure," John said in a tone that implied Arianna was in for a real treat. With one hand, he suddenly gripped her by the neck. In response to Arianna's wide-eyed panic, John said reassuringly, "Don't worry, this is completely safe. I've done a lot of research on sexual asphyxia." John paused for a moment, as if expecting Arianna to smile and nod in agreement. "Now, all I'm going to do," he explained patiently, "is decrease your oxygen—just a little." John then wrapped both hands around Arianna's neck and began to gently squeeze.

Arianna gawked at him in disbelief. Did this maniac think she was going to cooperate and lie still while he choked the life out of her? She desperately tried to tear his hands away from her neck, but managed only to briefly lift a finger or two.

Aroused, apparently, by her resistance, John applied more and more pressure without changing the rhythm or tempo of his macabre sexual dance. He gave little notice to Arianna's flailing arms, bulging eyes, or even the tongue that protruded from her slackened mouth as he proceeded to fuck the life out of her.

Chapter 36

The wheeled travel case snapped shut easily. The vinyl duffle, however, bulged with decadent paraphernalia, would zip only halfway. Victoria rearranged a few items in the bag, pulled and tugged until finally the zipper closed. Instead of the two or three outfit changes she normally carried to work, the two pieces of luggage were stuffed with practically every article of lingerie and every sex gadget she owned. Nothing would be left to chance; she'd have the right look, the right attire, and the right equipment for any situation that could possibly arise during her final week at Pandora's.

No formal announcement had been made. She hadn't even told Kareem. The idea came during their day trip with Jordan. Kareem told her he had to take care of some unexpected business in Los Angeles; he'd be gone for a week. The thought of not seeing Kareem for seven long days did not thrill her, but his spur-of-the-moment departure, she reasoned, would give her the time and freedom to put a plan in motion. She'd work doubles, even triples if Rover allowed her. If necessary, she'd camp out at Pandora's for the entire week. She'd do whatever it took to get Jordan's tuition, and hopefully a little extra to tide her over until she got on her feet. And then, she would start her new life with Kareem, unsullied, untainted. A normal person in love, being loved.

After hustling Jordan off to Charmaine's in his pajamas, Victoria drove to work in silence. Lacking spirit, she wondered how she'd summon the strength to get through the night. With her mind on Pandora's, she clenched her teeth and fought the nausea that accompanied the thought of being touched by a stranger. No music played from the radio or tape player; she needed absolute quiet to get her thoughts in order. An uneasy feeling crept over her as she approached Pandora's Box, but she quelled the urge to turn around and go back home. *Come on, you can do it,* she told herself. *Just one more week, and this madness will be over.*

The girls from the five o'clock shift were still milling about.

"Hey, Pleasure!" Jonee yelled. "You should have been here earlier; it was black girl's night up in this joint! Girl, we got paid! Every time the doorbell rang, it was like… ca-*ching*—more money for one of us. Even Miquon made money!" Lowering her voice, Jonee added, "The white girls didn't make shit! None of 'em. Not Lauren, Kelly, or Sydney."

"Kelly worked tonight?" Victoria asked.

"Yeah, but she rolled around nine o'clock. That junkie figured she'd have a better chance trickin' on Broad Street instead of sitting around here doing nothing."

Victoria shook her head at the shame of it, as she pictured Kelly out in public with her now pink-tinted hair, wearing a G-string or something that revealed as much of her tattooed butt as the law allowed.

"You know they can't stand to see us make money—and with all the money they be making, you'd think they wouldn't mind if we get a piece of the action every once in awhile. But nooo, we s'pose to just sit around looking sad while they stuff their pockets."

Victoria nodded, but didn't really care since she didn't benefit from the windfall.

Grinning impishly, Jonee sipped beer from a can that was badly camouflaged by a brown paper bag. She sat on the arm of Victoria's chair.

"Look!" Jonee whispered, elbowing Victoria. "Look at Lauren. Her face is tight!" Jonee covered her mouth to muffle her giggles. "Now that's one mad ass hoe. I know you been kinda chummy with Lauren, but believe me, she's just like the rest of 'em when it comes to money—she can't stand to see a black girl making more than her."

Victoria cut her eyes at Lauren, and sure enough, Lauren's face was a crimson, angry mask. "Hmm," Victoria muttered without elaborating as she began to pull out items from the travel case.

Jonee eyed the luggage. "Damn, girl, you movin' in?"

"Could be," she replied mysteriously.

"I guess you heard Dominique and Reds been MIA for two days."

"No, I haven't heard anything." Victoria looked around and was surprised that the two women were not present. "I thought those two were permanent fixtures on this shift. I hope they're all right."

"Ain't nothing happened to them hoes. They out getting they high on, spending up all Reds' money.

Victoria's eyebrows rose in question. "Reds' money? What money?"

"Where you been, girl? You ain't heard?"

Victoria shook her head, but had already lost interest. She was calculating how much she could possibly make if she had six or seven customers per shift, each tipping fifty dollars, at least.

"Reds' been on the down low, working for Arianna during the day."

"I thought that was just a rumor. Arianna really has her own place?" Victoria screeched with renewed interest.

"Uh huh. Miss High Siddity done opened up a little hideaway and I heard she got it hooked up nice. She's specializing in S&M and all types of freaky stuff—nothing normal. But hey, to each his own."

"You're kidding," Victoria said in a voice that urged Jonee to continue.

"I ain't lying. I don't like that snotty little bitch, but I gotta give credit where it's due, cause Miss Thang is gittin' paid! And she's been spreading the wealth with desperate bitches like Reds and Bethany. Sheena, too." Jonee paused, then added,"But, I heard she can't rely on Sheena."

"I didn't know Reds was into dominance. I thought that was Dominique's specialty."

"The way I hear it, Reds ain't doing the dominating."

"What!" Victoria was fascinated.

"Yeah, girl! Reds is over there gittin' her ass whipped by tricks! They be tyin' her up, smacking her around, spittin' on her—shit like that."

"I find that hard to believe, Jonee. Why would anyone…?"

"Fuck if I know. Look, Pleasure, some bitches will do anything for a dollar. Hmph! All I know is… it wouldn't be me. Hell no! 'Cause I ain't the one. Just let a mothafuckin' trick try some bondage bullshit with me…" Jonee paused with one eye narrowed threateningly. "Girl, I'd kick his ass up and down Market Street and then I'd turn around and fuck Arianna up for getting me involved in the first place." Jonee tilted her head, turned the beer can up to her lips and drained it.

Victoria tried to shake away the mental image of poor Reds being tied up and flogged by some sadistic, demented customer. Too bad Reds didn't have the foresight to sock away some of the millions she claimed to have earned in her youth. Victoria sighed heavily, and then turned her thoughts to her own plight. Although she was anxious to get her night started, the first customer would be the most difficult. A sudden thought of Kareem made her heart sink. She forced his image from her mind.

Victoria's eyes swept the room; she wondered who was staying over from the previous shift. She didn't feel like putting up with Miquon and was relieved to see that she, along with Lauren, and Sydney were packing up to leave. Jonee, she noticed, hadn't made a move.

"Who's working tonight?" Victoria asked Jonee.

"Just me, you and Chelsea."

"You're staying? Why? I thought you got *paid* already. Why do you need more?"

"Girl, my money ain't been right since that suspension. I'm trying to play catch-up."

Victoria rolled her eyes to the ceiling.

"Oh, I forgot," Jonee said, nodding knowingly at the luggage. "I guess your money got fucked up, too."

Victoria sized up her competition. Jonee was looking a little rough tonight. All the activity from the previous shift appeared to have taken its toll. Jonee's bare lips were outlined in a deep maroon. The lipstick she had worn now decorated the rim of the beer can she'd tossed in the waste can, and her wig, a long honey blonde pageboy was slightly askew. Still, Victoria knew that Jonee's disheveled appearance wouldn't matter at all to any of the lustful men who came out after midnight. Jonee was a tireless worker whose persistence and stamina could often pull even the most reluctant customer. Jonee would be a formidable opponent.

Tall and pretty Chelsea, on the other hand, just didn't seem to appeal to the customers, and Victoria had never been able to figure out why. Well, one thing was for sure, she wasn't about to start racking her brain over it tonight. Tonight she was extremely grateful that Chelsea lacked some hidden ingredient that had the potential to stand in the way of Jordan's education fund.

A few minutes later, at the sound of the bell, the three women scuffled to get to the door, but instead of a customer, there stood Sheena, looking gaunt and haggard as usual. Jonee scowled at Sheena, then marched back into the lounge.

"How many working tonight?" Sheena asked.

Regarding Sheena with disinterest, Victoria shrugged and looked at her watch.

Sheena put on a wrinkled thong teddy, slipped her feet into a pair of once-white skuzzy slippers, and began to pace nervously back and forth. Victoria tried to avert her gaze each time Sheena walked past. But it became increasingly difficult for her to keep her eyes from zooming in on Sheena's skinny, ashy, sagging butt.

"Wanna wear this, Sheena?" Victoria gently unfolded a glittering Lycra bodystocking, and presented it with its price tag dangling. Grinning and nodding, Sheena snatched the delicate bodystocking.

"Aw shit now, check you out Sheena," Jonee teased. "We ain't gonna be able to make a dime with you prancing around in Pleasure's fancy gear."

The grin on Sheena's face widened.

"That's gorgeous," Chelsea said. "I can't believe you're letting Sheena wear it."

Victoria shrugged, and turned to Sheena. "You can have it Sheena, it's too small for me.

"Damn, Pleasure, why didn't you let me try it on?" Jonee asked. "I ain't skinny like Sheena, but I probably could have squeezed into it. I would have paid you for it, too. I hope you realize Sheena ain't gonna take care of it—you ain't even gonna recognize your shit the next time she comes dragging through."

"How you know what I'm gonna do?" Sheena asked in weak protest.

"It's obvious. Look at that wrinkled up mess you wearing right now."

"Leave her alone, Jonee. She can do what she wants with it—it belongs to her now." Victoria turned to Sheena. "Try it on."

Sheena pulled off the teddy, and modestly covered her frail body with a towel as she slipped into the bodystocking. It was a little baggy, but Sheena didn't seem to mind.

Victoria smiled, satisfied. Giving Sheena the bodystocking was a small price to pay. Now that she was appropriately covered, Victoria wouldn't be forced to behold Sheena's ashy little behind and sickly looking body all night.

Chapter 37

2:30 a.m. Victoria was antsy. She'd switched outfits, changing into a stretch lace micro chemise, which revealed her bare cheeks and the string of her thong. She'd polished her nails, read a few articles in *Essence*, watched something stupid on TV, chatted with Rover, and still no customers.

Curled up on the loveseat next to Chelsea, Jonee drifted in and out of sleep, asking repeatedly if any customers had arrived.

Sheena, apparently worn out from pacing, finally passed out on the sofa with her arms and legs flailed every which way, her open mouth emitting an unattractive wheezing sound.

Chelsea was wide-awake and talkative. "Do you have a man, Pleasure?" she inquired somewhat anxiously.

Victoria gave her a puzzled look, and then shook her head. She refused to disclose personal information to Chelsea or anyone else at Pandora's. Jonee, of course, knew more than most, but only what Victoria wanted her to know. She'd deliberately provided only sketchy details of her relationship with Jordan's dad, and had only hinted that she didn't get along with her mother. She hadn't spoken a word about her relationship with Kareem or her music.

Chelsea's eyes gleamed with excitement. "Well, I'd like to introduce you to my man. His name is Jay. He can help you."

"Help me? How?"

"You know, manage your money, invest it for you. Pay your bills." Chelsea mistook Victoria's brow, furrowed in confusion, as a look of interest, and continued enthusiastically. "See, I chose this life so I could have my own business," Chelsea patiently explained. "Jay is my business partner. He's the thinker; I'm the doer."

Victoria nodded dumbly.

"Most working girls don't have a man," Chelsea continued. "And you see how they end up—strung out, their lives in disarray. They need someone to guide them. Look at Reds. Now that's a classic example of a woman who needed guidance. All that money wasted," Chelsea said, shaking her head regretfully. "I've been with Jay for five years, and he's going to retire me in a couple of years. After I retire, his younger girls will continue working until they've earned enough to retire, too. See, our business is more like a corporation. With everybody's input, we've been able to buy beachfront property in Wildwood; we have a Jaguar, and we've recently invested in a prizefighter from Puerto Rico

What was all this talk of *we*? Victoria didn't see any evidence of Chelsea owning anything other than her clothing and her work attire. Granted, she didn't have to ride SEPTA back and forth to work like some of the girls; she traveled by taxi. But who, Victoria wondered, was driving the Jaguar? And the younger girls she referred to, had to be earning the lion's share of the *corporation*, for certainly Chelsea's contribution was no more than a pittance.

"Chelsea, are you talking about a pimp?"

"I don't refer to him in that way," Chelsea said, looking offended.

"Forgive me for being politically incorrect, but I'm just shocked that you're into something like that." Victoria paused to study the air, then leaned forward and asked in a whispery voice, "Do all of you live together—with him?"

"No, he lives by himself, and so do I. I have a very nice apartment in Powelton Village."

Victoria tried not to scowl; Powelton Village was very close to her own neighborhood. She didn't like the possibility of their worlds colliding once she left the business.

"The newer girls share a house out in the suburbs; no one has to worry about paying bills or anything…Jay takes care of everything."

"I see," Victoria said, lips pursed in disapproval. She'd worked with Chelsea for seven months and hadn't an inkling that the woman was deranged? The revelation just confirmed Victoria's belief that Pandora's Box was a magnet, attracting misfits and lunatics. Thank God she was getting out before she lost her tenuous grip on sanity.

Victoria rose from the chair, indicating the conversation was over. A visit with Rover had to be better than listening to this nonsense.

"So, what do you think, would you like to meet him?" Chelsea pressed. "Jay can explain the arrangement much better than I can."

"Chelsea," Victoria said in the most condescending tone she could manage. "How would it benefit me to have a pimp? And, why would I want to start denying my son and myself so I can help make payments on someone else's luxury car? I'm so insulted that you would think…"

"Pleasure," Chelsea cut in. But instead of the wounded look Victoria had aimed for, Chelsea's expression was superior, as if having a pimp, and being a part of a stable was something to be envied. "A while ago, I overheard you talking to Jonee about private school for your son. You sounded worried about his tuition. You make a lot of money, Pleasure, but it's obviously mismanaged. I was just trying to be helpful."

Stung, Victoria appeared to recover fast. "Touché," she replied as she sat back down, trying to look unruffled. Her heart thumped in anger as she rifled through her duffle bag, her fingers frantically searching until she located her CD Player. Needing to hear something soothing, she inserted a New Age CD, *Healing Harmony*.

The doorbell's sound gave Victoria a pleasant jolt. Smiling with relief, she and Chelsea stood up simultaneously. Jonee sprang up next, finger-combed her wig, and hustled past Victoria and Chelsea. In acknowledgement of the bell, Sheena began to stir, but then settled into a different position.

Jonee gleefully yanked the door open. She exhaled noisily. "It's for you, Chelsea!" she yelled. Jonee spun around, annoyed. She bumped into Victoria. "You might as well sit down; that's Chelsea's man."

"Her pimp?" Victoria asked in a whisper.

Jonee nodded with undisguised disgust.

"How come you never mentioned that hot topic?"

Jonee shrugged, an irritated one-shoulder movement.

An image of the vintage *Superfly* appeared in Victoria's mind. With a hand over her mouth, Victoria covered up a ripple of laughter. She continued toward the door, curious to see this modern day pimp.

But Victoria almost choked on her laughter as she gasped in shock. She wanted to run back to the lounge but couldn't move; her legs were rubbery, useless. Holding onto the doorknob for support, her eyes flicked up and down in disbelief. *Justice Martin!* The devil himself stood right there in the lobby, as handsome, as well-dressed, and as well-coiffed as ever. The long locks were gone; he'd started them anew. His head was adorned with short, shiny, coils that had an incongruous majestic effect. Other than a quick double take, and a tightening of the muscles around his mouth, there was no noticeable indication that he recognized Victoria.

"I'm not a customer, baby. I just wanted to have a word with Chelsea." He laughed out each word in superior amusement.

Chelsea nervously joined in the laughter, and mouthed to Victoria with tremendous pride, "This is Jay."

Along with the life that returned to her legs, came a burning humiliation and an awareness of her exposed behind, which prevented Victoria from making a graceful exit. Under the scrutiny of Justice's mocking eyes, and feeling close to hysteria, Victoria backed out of the lobby.

"What the hell's wrong with you?" Jonee asked when Victoria returned to the lounge.

"I know Chelsea's pimp," she muttered to herself as much as to Jonee. "Oh God!" she whimpered, wringing her hands.

"You used to work for him or something?"

"No!" Victoria screamed, which made Jonee flinch. "I just know him, that's all."

There was a chorus of laughter from the lobby. Victoria burst into tears.

"Damn, Pleasure. What the fuck is wrong with you? *What?* You got a thing for him or something? Girl, he don't mess with no black women. Only Chelsea, and she ain't even all black. All his bitches are white. Young and white. From places like Sweden and England and shit."

Oh, God! Victoria moaned, as she recalled Justice's British receptionist.

"He don't allow his white girls to work here. Oh, hell no! They can only work in high-class places, escort services, shit like that. They keep his pockets fat and carry Chelsea's dead-ass weight. Nobody can figure out why he puts up with Chelsea."

"Well, why did you wait until now to tell me?" Victoria shouted irrationally, wiping away tears.

Jonee gave her a perplexed look. "It slipped my mind, I guess. But, girl you gotta tell me something. Whassup? What are you crying for?"

They heard the door close. Victoria quickly dried her eyes.

Beaming, Chelsea reentered the lounge. "Jay's so sweet. I told him we were having a horrible night. And look what he gave me for luck." Chelsea proudly held out a hundred dollar bill.

"I bet you better not think about spending it, 'cause you know when the night's over, Big Daddy's gonna want his good luck to come right back," Jonee taunted.

"Pleasure," Chelsea said, ignoring Jonee. "Jay told me to tell you, good luck!"

Victoria groaned and told herself that Justice's appearance was a bad omen. The night wouldn't get any better. She should quit. She should march back to the office right now and quit. But then again, the night couldn't get any worse. To hell with Justice Martin, the pimp! The way he'd worked her, she should have known what he was. Well, she wouldn't let him chase her out. Hell, he was the person responsible for her being there. And he knew it, and apparently found that fact hilarious.

The pain—the shame of it all was unbearable. But she was determined to get through the night. And if she could get through the night, she'd make it through the week. This experience would be tucked away with all the other sad and tragic memories that were stored inside her patched-up, pieced together heart.

Chapter 38

Jostled from sleep at 4 a.m, Victoria, Jonee, and Chelsea dragged themselves to answer the bell. Two young black guys stood in the lobby. Looking refreshed and energetic, they smirked at the sluggish women. Victoria immediately recognized the horrid delivery guy. His buddy—a tall, gangling, thuggish type, accompanied him. Out of uniform, the delivery guy wore baggy black shorts and a black tee shirt. His sidekick was dressed almost identically, except his tee shirt bore the faded image of some forgotten rap artist.

Victoria promptly whirled around, shaking her head. She knew she should have followed her instincts and gone home.

"Wassup wit that bitch?" the sidekick asked.

"Man, fuck that hoe, she probably ain't getting enough dick!" Both men broke out in raucous laughter.

"Do y'all wanna see one of us or what?" Jonee asked irritably.

"Yeah baby, give us a minute," the delivery guy shot back. "Y'all the only ones workin'? Where all the white girls?"

Jonee sucked her teeth. "Damn, Bro', what's your problem? Why you tryin' to see a white girl?"

"I ain't got no problem, baby, and I ain't tryin' to be smart, but if I'm gonna pay for it—then you know…I wanna try something different."

"Y'all ain't even got no Ricans?" the sidekick piped in. "Now, that's whassup. They some stone cold freaks!"

"No, we aint' got no Puerto Ricans!" Jonee snapped. "Whatchu see? Black girls only, right? Now, what y'all gonna do?"

"I guess I'll take her, she close enough." The delivery guy pointed to light-skinned Chelsea.

Chelsea offered as much of a smile as she could muster, and led the delivery guy to a session room.

"And what about you?" Jonee asked the sidekick.

"I ain't doin' nothing tonight. I'm just gonna wait for my man. But check it out—can I wait in there with y'all?" He pointed to the lounge.

"Hell no. You ain't allowed in there. You gotta wait in the lobby. And it might be a long wait 'cause dude look like he gonna be awhile. You know what I'm saying? He don't look like the type for no quickie!" Jonee laughed. "So why don't you come on with me?"

"Naw baby, I'm cool. Like I said, I'll check y'all out when you got a bigger selection."

Jonee gave up with a groan and retreated to the lounge. "Fuck it," she grumbled to Victoria. "As tired as I am, I'm not about to beg no ignorant black mothafucka to spend his money on me." She lit a cigarette and angrily blew smoke in Victoria's direction, then apologized and quickly fanned it away. "I already made six hundred dollars," she bragged. "I can afford to lay my ass back down and wait for the next customer. These niggahs ain't trying to look out for us. They jealous of us anyway."

Victoria looked at Jonee quizzically. "That's right," Jonee continued. "They don't want to see us doing better than them. They jealous 'cause we can get money just like that!" she said, snapping her fingers. "And if they ain't selling drugs, then they gotta take bullshit jobs cleaning toilets or delivering pizza!"

"Not all black men sell drugs or work at menial jobs, Jonee," Victoria interrupted "You're being stereotypical and…"

"Why you taking up for those two niggahs? They damn sure don't feel no loyalty toward you." Jonee took a long drag on the cigarette, coughed and then smashed it out in the ashtray.

Victoria scolded herself for trying to reason with Jonee.

"And the young bucks that come in here, don't even know the meaning of the word *tip*!" Jonee continued raging. "When the cheap bastards break down and give a sistah a session, they try their damnedest to fuck you half to death. And don't let 'em fuck up and cum too quick. Oh no, they think 'cause the hour ain't up yet, you s'pose to be nice and let 'em go again. And they *still* don't wanna tip a dime extra." Jonee tsked and rolled her eyes. Then, in anticipation of a long wait for the next customer, she yanked off her wig, balled it up and pitched it into her open workbag. She spread two towels over the cushions of the loveseat and curled on top of them before snuggling under a polyester robe that was left behind by one of the girls from the previous shift. Within seconds, Jonee was snoring.

❦

Victoria settled into the flower print chair, and closed her eyes. Despite being haunted by an image of Justice's cruel face, somehow in the quiet of the night, the familiar sounds that indicated the conclusion of Chelsea's session (the low murmur of voices, the opening and closing of doors, water running in the bathroom) were oddly comforting, and lulled her into a light, but peaceful sleep. But that sleep was quickly interrupted by loud angry male voices, followed by an ominous popping sound, and then Chelsea's piercing scream.

The delivery guy raced down the hall. There was a gun in one hand, and he was strong-arming Chelsea with the other. The sidekick who had been waiting in the lobby burst through the door. "What the fuck happened, man? You get the money?"

"No! I had to pop that stupid mothafucka. He wouldn't open the fuckin' safe," the delivery guy shouted back.

"You popped 'em for nothin'?" the sidekick blurted out, incredulously. "Man, that's fucked up! Did you waste 'em?"

"How the fuck do I know? Man, I wasn't checkin' to see if the motha-fucka was still breathing!"

"Come on, man, let's roll. Let that bitch go!" the sidekick screamed in a firm voice.

"Fuck that! I'm not leaving 'til I get some paper!" With the gun at Chelsea's side, the delivery guy dragged her toward the lounge.

"Aw, shit. This is fucked up!" the sidekick complained, then followed.

Aroused by the commotion, Jonee sprang to her feet and leaped across the room to huddle in the chair with Victoria.

"Oh my God, what's going on?" she wailed.

At the sight of the delivery guy marching Chelsea into the lounge at gunpoint, Sheena, awake but groggy, let out a fearful groan.

The delivery guy pointed the gun at Sheena. "Make another sound, bitch, and your stank ass gonna be leaving here in a body bag."

Jonee began to shake violently. Victoria hugged her tight, while fighting to control her own chattering teeth and make some sense of the situation.

"All right, you bitches better start making ends meet. I ain't got time to be fucking around, so start handing over the paper."

"But I already told you, I gave Rover all my money," Chelsea whined, terrified.

"You got money, bitch. I know damn well my dick ain't the only one you sucked tonight. Now get my fuckin' money!" He shoved Chelsea onto the sofa with Sheena.

Seized by panic, the women gaped at the delivery guy.

"Come on, bitches," he demanded, waving the gun. "Start digging in your pocketbooks—bras, panties...whatever! I don't give a fuck—just give me mine, so I can be out!"

Victoria quickly produced a twenty-dollar bill.

"Bitch, you know you gotta do better than that," he cautioned, poking Victoria in the chest with the gun. She could feel the icy-cold barrel of the gun through her flimsy lingerie, but fearing that her heart would stop, she dared not look at it. She kept her eyes fixed on the delivery guy, willing him to be reasonable, compassionate. *Please Lord, let this nightmare end!*

"I...I didn't get a session," she stammered. "You were the first customer on our shift."

"Fuck that…"

"Here, here!" Jonee screamed and threw a wad of bills, bound by a rubber band.

"Count that shit, man." He pitched the money to the sidekick.

"Okay, now I'm gonna ask you again—where's your fuckin' money?" He glowered at Victoria.

"I…I…" Her throat was extremely dry, her body shook violently, and Victoria could not finish the sentence. She prayed the delivery guy would understand that she was simply incapable of uttering a coherent word.

"Don't get scared now, mothafucka," he taunted. "I ain't forgot your ass. You wasn't scared when you slammed that door in my face!"

Victoria's face contorted in confusion. *What door?* Then clarity hit like a body shot.

"That's right, bitch. Think about it! You ordered coffee one morning, a coupla months ago, and I was nice enough to bring it to you. And all I did was ask you some questions about the white joints you was working with and you went off on me! Started acting all annoyed and prissy and shit, like I had did something to you personally." The delivery guy paused briefly, then leaned in close. "But you fucked up when you slammed the door in my face!"

She didn't see it coming—the flash of metal that slammed into the side of her face. She lost consciousness immediately and was spared the pain of being hit repeatedly—of being pistol whipped by the furious delivery guy.

Jonee and Chelsea screamed in horror. Sheena covered her face, and cried into her hands.

"Come on, man, stop!" The sidekick grabbed the delivery guy's arm. "Stop before you kill that hoe. We made six hunnert—let's roll!"

"Wait, man. I ain't collect from the other two bitches." The delivery guy pointed the gun at Sheena. "Whassup crackhead? How much you got?"

"Oh Jesus," Sheena sobbed. "I ain't got no money; I swear to God. I just got here, and we ain't had no customers. Oh God, they gonna kill us all!" Sheena's racking sobs were turning to convulsions. Tears and snot covered her face.

"She ain't lying," Jonee offered bravely, while cradling Victoria, whose bloody face was swelling rapidly.

Down the hall, Rover came to, awakened by the women's screams and the searing pain in his left shoulder. His white tee shirt was covered with blood. His blood! He remembered the gunman and his eyes darted to the safe. It was still closed.

And with great relief, he grabbed the phone and punched 911. Gabrielle would be so proud of him.

Chapter 39

V ictoria's face was not permanently damaged. Her doctor
assured her that the swelling would go down in a few of weeks,
but that was little consolation as she stood gaping at her
reflection in the bathroom mirror. Her head seemed twice its normal
size. Her battered, misshapen face looked permanently disfigured.
Unable to stomach her image for another second, she popped a painkiller,
turned away from the mirror, and padded into the kitchen.

Victoria opened the cabinet and reached for a bag of Mocha Java.
Spooning dark mounds into the coffeemaker, her thoughts drifted to
Jordan. Victoria winced as she imagined her son's reaction to her appearance.

But Jordan had spent the night at Charmaine's and wasn't expected
home for few hours. That gave Victoria time to fabricate a story. She
could say that she'd been in a car accident, or that she tripped and fell,
or bumped into something. There was no way she could tell her child
that his Mommy had been pistol-whipped. That was entirely too much
information for a five-year-old to handle. She replayed the events of the
previous night, fast-forwarding past the encounter with Justice, the sound
of the gunshot and her own horrific encounter with the gunman. She
didn't want to relive any of that.

After the two robbers were handcuffed and led away, Victoria and

Rover were transported by ambulance to Graduate Hospital's emergency room. Jonee and the others, having no visible injuries, didn't require immediate attention, and were spirited off to a different hospital. Rover was treated for a bullet wound to his arm. The bullet, it turned out, had gone straight through, doing no real damage, but he was kept overnight for observation.

Victoria sat down at the kitchen table, with the morning newspaper and a steaming mug of coffee that she hoped would soothe her. She quickly discovered that trying to sip hot coffee with badly-swollen lips was a painful endeavor, but she so needed her Java jolt that she suffered through the discomfort.

As she turned the pages of *The Philadelphia Daily News*, she was braced for a bold headline reporting the robbery and murder attempt at Pandora's Box. It dawned on her that when the police officer had taken her statement, she had groggily given her real name. An article mentioning her name would provide proof—a printed testament to the sordid lifestyle she'd been leading. She'd be disgraced. Her neighbors would point fingers and click their tongues.

And what about Kareem? How would he react when he found out about last night's mishap? How would he feel knowing that her profession was no longer just their dirty little secret, but was now public knowledge?

With brows knitted in agitation, Victoria continued searching through the newspaper, but amazingly, there wasn't even a blurb.

Gabrielle, she figured, must have greased some powerful palms and managed to quash the story. For that intervention, Victoria would be forever grateful.

Still perusing the paper, Victoria came across a two-paragraph article about the strangulation murder of a twenty-one-year-old prostitute. The young woman ran an illegal establishment on Naudain Street, the article stated.

Victoria gripped the newspaper. In fear of what she was about to read, she squeezed her eyes shut, then opened them as if that action would rearrange the words, change the story. She held the newspaper close to her face and brought the words into focus. Her hands trembled as she read: *the residents on Naudain Street confirmed that the white Lexus parked in front of the house belonged to the woman, whose nude body was discovered by a cleaning woman. The victim's identity is being withheld pending notification of her family. There are no suspects.*

Victoria gasped; her mouth went dry. The dead woman was Arianna! She barely noticed she had dropped the newspaper. She slumped in her chair, motionless. Victoria grimaced at the pictures that flooded her mind. She saw Arianna lying lifeless on the floor; her neck was twisted at a grotesque angle. Unable to shake the awful image, she lowered her head and said a prayer for Arianna's soul. Admittedly, she had disliked Arianna, but God knew she would have never wished her any harm.

After a long night of tears and soul searching Victoria thought she was all cried out, but the terrible news of Arianna's death brought raw emotions back to the surface. With the sleeve of her robe, Victoria wiped away burning tears. She wept softly at first, a low mournful sound that escalated into a full-fledged wail when she admitted to herself that it was reckless...and yes—selfish—of her to jeopardize her safety, and the well-being of her child, by working in a seedy, dangerous place like Pandora's Box. Had she not survived last night's attack, Jordan would have ended up a motherless ward of the state, raised in foster homes...or with Zeline. A sharp sensation shot through her heart at the thought of poor Jordan growing up as she had—convinced that he was defective and unlovable.

Then a blazing anger began to dull the pain. It was unconscionable for a mother to allow a child grow to up as she had, believing that her birth, her very existence, was wrong.

Zeline, oblivious to Victoria's pain, had no idea how badly scarred and messed up her daughter was. She didn't know that as a child, Victoria had been crushed to overhear her telling one of her friends, in a hushed, martyr tone, that Victoria's birth was a tragic mistake, the result of an inept abortionist.

Well Victoria had had it. She was tired of skulking through life as a culprit, the walking wounded. It was time to end the self-punishment.

"Nana," she whispered, crying. "Please forgive me. I'm sorry for losing the money you left me. I'm sorry for what I've done to myself, and I'm sorry for any harm I may have caused my son. I'm in a lot of pain, Nana, and my wounds are not going to heal easily. I know I need help. Professional help. And I'm going to get it. Then, when the pain and the anger subside, when I'm feeling stronger, I'll reach out to her. I'll offer my love again and again. I won't give up on her. I love her so much—my mother, your daughter, Zeline."

Epilogue

"Hey, Victoria," Kareem yelled. "Slow down. I thought this was supposed to be a nature hike."

Victoria looked over her shoulder and smiled. "This *is* a nature hike," she said, without breaking her stride. "Look at all this nature," she said pointing to the trees, the rock formations, and running streams.

"I know, I know," he said, panting. "But shouldn't we be walking at a leisurely pace, taking in the scenery?"

"You're the picture of health, beautifully-buffed, but you need to work on your endurance," she teased. "Come on slow-poke, at least try to keep up."

Victoria smiled to herself as she continued to race-walk, and then broke into a jog along the rugged terrain of the orange trail in Fairmount Park's Valley Green. Kareem lagged far behind.

It was the beginning of spring, and all of God's creations were in their full glory. She could hear the sound of the running stream as she approached it, and was overcome with joy. She loved this particular spot in the park, and thought it her sacred place.

At her therapist's suggestion, she'd begun to keep a journal. She pulled it out of her backpack, and sat on a huge rock beside the stream. Pen in hand, Victoria quickly conveyed her appreciation for the beauty of nature and especially for the new life she called her own. She held out her left hand admiringly. The diamond Kareem had put on her finger glimmered beautifully in the sunlight. Jordan was attending the Charter School in Wynnefield, and doing very well. Victoria thought it important to be home when her son arrived from school. Fortunately, she could restrict her club dates to weekends. She spent her days guiding Jordan toward becoming a well-adjusted productive man, who could appreciate the strength of a black woman without fear, without threat.

A smile crossed her face. The man she wanted Jordan to become sounded a lot like Kareem. Kareem had played such an important role in her healing. Through his production company, he found her gigs in intimate jazz clubs that were becoming so popular in the area. He was also using his connections to shop her demo.

And where was Kareem? Victoria stuffed the journal into the backpack and stood. He should have caught up with her by now. She should be hearing his footsteps crunching twigs and pebbles along the path. She trotted back in search of Kareem.

In the distance, she spotted him. He was bent at the waist, palms pressed against his thighs.

Victoria ran to him. "Kareem St. Claire, you know that's a shame. You really gotta get in shape if you wanna keep up with me."

"I guess I'm gonna have to hold you down if I expect to have a conversation with you," Kareem countered. Then very softly, he asked, "You feel like traveling, baby?"

"Yeah, I guess," she said, not knowing where the conversation was leading.

"And when does Jordan get out for spring break?"

"Two weeks."

"Perfect. Start packing. We're going to L.A. We can spend a day or two at Disneyland. Let Jordan have some fun before we get down to business. I gotta talk with the folks at Interscope Records. They can't wait to meet their next big artist." Kareem paused. "That's you, Victoria, the lady with the voice of an angel."

In that rare experience when one recognizes she's been blessed, Victoria closed her eyes and savored the moment. Then her joyful screech echoed through the trees of Valley Green. Her dream of a recording career was finally coming true.

"But baby, the picture's not complete."

Victoria looked at him questioningly.

"We can't go all the way to California and not stop by and see your mom."

Victoria was quiet for a moment. "You're right, Kareem. When we get there, I'm going to drive to Pasadena to have a talk with her—alone. I have to tell my mother that I love her, and that with the help of therapy I'm able to understand how hard it was for her to accept an unwanted pregnancy at sixteen. She wasn't ready for me, and I forgive her. If she can handle that, and if she wants to be a part of my life—of our lives, then I'd be honored to introduce you to your future mother-in-law, Kareem."

"Whatever way it goes, baby, you still got me. I'm in for the long haul. You feel me?"

"I feel you."

Kareem put his arm around her, and pulled her close as they made their way together down the long winding path.

ABOUT THE AUTHOR

Allison Hobbs resides in Philadelphia, PA. She is a former singer, songwriter, and studio background singer who toured with major R&B acts. During the era of the Philly Sound, she was part of a female trio called Brown Sugar who were signed with Philadelphia International Records and later recorded with Capitol Records. Allison is a self-taught artist whose prolific body of work portrays scenes of black Americana. She received a Bachelor of Science degree from Temple University.

You can visit her on the web at http://www.allisonhobbs.com.